D0994004

LANTY HANLON

LANTY HANLON

A COMEDY OF
IRISH LIFE

BY

PATRICK
MACGILL

CALIBAN BOOKS

Published 1983 by Caliban Books,
25 Nassington Road, LONDON, N.W.3
Published in the United States by
Caliban Books, 51 Washington Street,
Dover, New Hampshire 03820, U.S.A.

ISBN 0 904 57380 X

Library of Congress Information:
Author: Patrick MacGill
Title: Lanty Hanlon
Library of Congress No.: 837811
C.I.P. Data applied for

Printed and bound in Great Britain by A. Wheaton & Co. Ltd.

CONTENTS

LANTY HANLON

CHAPTER I

THE PROUD PARISH

Thirst and Thrift are never fellows.
—*A Ballykeeran Proverb.*

I

LIKE a beggar's garb, a poor habitation is envied by none. But Ballykeeran, the place of my young days and the place of my age, once occupied the proud position of being the most envied parish in the land.

There was no place to rival it. Ballyroon, that elbowed it, had pretensions, pretensions without proof, colour or substance. But Ballykeeran, with its worth open to the world, never bragged nor boasted. Ballyroon was as nothing in its eyes. We peeled our potatoes with knives when Ballyroon used its fingers, used forks years before Ballyroon used spoons, and had paraffin lamps when Ballyroon had only rush-lights.

In the parish of Ballykeeran in those days, the days of my youth, when there was a drop duty free to sweeten all discourse, no good man was ever dull and no woman old before her time. Of money we knew very little, and paid in kind for most commodities. Four pounds of butter were given for a scythe, eighteen eggs for a teapot, and a hank of home-knitted yarn for so much tea and sugar. The miller was paid in grain, the grocer in butter, the tailor in wool, and thus without the clatter of a penny we fed and clothed ourselves.

But how about the widow woman, whose substance was no more than that of the poor beggar on the road? you may ask. She had neither the hands for the hard work nor the straw for the thatching. But for all that the house was thatched well from eave to rigging, for the Ballykeeran man always saw his neighbour with kindly eyes.

Yes, surely it was a parish to know in those days!

Even at the hour of his birth a Ballykeeran man is conscious of the honour that has been granted him. He does not come crying into the world, as is done in other parishes. When he knows where he has come to, he realises the luck of getting to such a place and perks up immediately and laughs in his mother's face. Yes, he knows he has come to the great parish of Ballykeeran.

Strong in stock and store were its houses; butts of butter in the pantries, every season the season of cream heavy milk, hens laying summer and winter, a fat goose to board any day of the week! A place of abundance and generosity was Ballykeeran of the large heart and lavish hand. Its doors were shut against nothing save the wind and the rain. To the lone beggar on the dark road a Ballykeeran light meant hospitality —a supper, a bed, and the blessing of God.

Not alone was the parish rich in its own substance, but it was also rich in women, girls of grace who were the pride of the country-side.

The young men of Ballykeeran never married outside the mearing of their own parish. And why should they, when the prizes within were so winsome and worthy? In womenkind no other parish can equal it. Ballyroon is proud of its women, and I do not blame it for that. But this is what our young men say at the season when they can afford a bed for two, the ranting season when the bed is cold for one and it is no sin to marry:

"Better a Ballykeeran girl with a hen than a Ballyroon woman with a horse!"

But not alone in the grace of its girls does Ballykeeran occupy a premier position. In muscle and mettle my own parish stands high.

What about the famous tug-of-war between Ballykeeran and Ballyroon, the Bishop of the diocese, the wrinkles of threescore and ten on his saintly brow, one of the onlookers?

Strong on the strain, steady in purchase; a contest between giants! Bodies like tree-trunks and muscles like knobs on an oak. Bulls, no, rocks! Look straight ahead but don't follow your eyes! The will to win and brawn to back it! Ballykeeran for ever!

"Who are these men?" asked the Bishop, when cheers rose for the winners.

"The Ballykeeran men," he was told.

"I might have known it," said the Bishop.

This was the Ballykeeran to which I came on that never-to-be-forgotten summer day, the Ballykeeran which now holds my home with its wide acres, the Ballykeeran which has been made famous by Lanty Hanlon, G.H., he whose story I tell.

II

Without doubt this man was the best of Ballykeeran breeding. Whatever he did, he did better than anybody else. In that was his success and his failure. Some strange fate seemed to watch over him even from the very beginning, even from his christening, which in itself was not like the christening of an ordinary child.

Who could drink like him, let down a bottle of porter without moving his Adam's apple? Who had strength like his, the power to hold a live salmon by the tail between finger and thumb? Who had courage like his, the pluck to combat the MacMonagles bare-footed and in a red petticoat? Who had pride equal to the pride of the man who sat beside Lord Kingarrow on the banks of the River Garrow and cast his fly on the waters.

"Who gave you permission to fish here, my man?" asked Lord Kingarrow.

"Who gave you permission to ask that question?" the man enquired.

"I am Lord Kingarrow," was the answer. "I own all this country as far as my eye can reach."

"I'm Lord as far as my fist can reach," was the remark of the man, swinging his fist round so that it caught Lord Kingarrow's face and knocked him into the river. Need I say that the man was Lanty Hanlon, G.H. A prophet without honour in his own country! Away! Ballykeeran knew otherwise.

Hereunder, without preamble or preface, I shall give a short account of the life of Lanty Hanlon, G.H., as he lived it before I met him. This in part is from what he told me himself, part from what I heard from the scholars in the National School.

Lanty Hanlon was the son of a man whose name was the same, a poor farmer whose farm in hill was barren, in holm below flood-level, which in short means that it was a mean holding, unable to father its rental. The elder Lanty was a poor man who drank spring water when his one cow was near note and fed on Indian meal in seed-time. But despite his poverty in worldly goods, humility, simplicity and honesty were his parts and he stood high in the favour of all men.

His neighbours that were, when speaking of him after his death, would cast up their eyes and say:

"Oh, aye! Old Lanty, God rest him! A good, decent man in his time."

Young Lanty was born on St. John's Eve, Bonfire Night, when every brae had its blaze and every field its fire, when the sounds of merry-making, fiddling, dancing and singing were loud in the hills and glens of Ireland. On that night Lanty was born and on the same night his mother died. A strong woman too, but a great birth will have its penalties.

A fortnight later the youngster was baptised, his baptism one of the most interesting events in the annals of the parish. Instead of water and salt, whisky was used in the ceremony, and this the way of it.

At that time the parish priest was an old man, burdened with all the frailties and shortcomings of years, his hearing impaired, his sight feeble, the sense of smell and taste diminished.

Andy Bawn was beadle and rang the bell for Angelus morning and evening, swept the floor of the church after service and did the hundred and one other jobs compatible to his calling, lit candles, arranged the flowers round the altar, hung and dusted the pictures, filled the holy water stoups and the baptismal font.

These things were within his legalised and sacred profession, but outside and beyond them he had other callings, amongst which illicit distillation played a prominent part. On this he made profit, and on this he got drunk at frequent intervals.

On the evening preceding Lanty Hanlon's baptism the old beadle was well in his cups, and coming back from his work at the worm he carried the newly distilled potheen in a capacious bucket, the same being used to carry water for benediction to the chapel.

The hour was nine in the morning. The old man suddenly remembered that this was the day and this the hour on which a man child was to be christened. He went into the chapel, leaving the bucket under a piece of sacking in the porch.

Raising the lid of the baptismal font, to his horror he found that there was no water there. No christening had taken place for a fortnight. The weather had been very hot. The font was dry!

Andy rushed to the door, saw the christening party approach, and at the same moment heard the creak of the priest's key in the sacristy door. The nearest well was some two hundred yards off, the only available bucket was full. The beadle was not at a loss. Lifting the bucket, he emptied its contents in the baptismal font.

Filling a little tin mug with the christening water, he went out to meet the party, which consisted of the two sponsors and the little squealing atom who was known in the days that followed as Lanty Hanlon, G.H.

"Is he waiting for us?" asked the male sponsor, Peter Ruddagh.

"We're not late, God help us, are we?" asked the woman, Oonah, Peter's wife.

"Too soon. Too soon!" said old Andy. "His reverence is not up yet at all. Just a sup, a wee sup to warm you, before you come in."

"What is it at all?" asked the woman, looking at the proffered pannikin.

"Something good, something good," said the beadle with a sly wink. "Just a drop for the two of you."

"But I've the pledge," said the woman.

"It's more than I have," said Peter, a glutton as he reached for the tin. "Yum! you can make it better than any of them, Andy!"

"And you'll have a drop of it too," said Andy,

looking at Oonah. "Just a wee drop, the weest drop!"

"But I've the pledge on me, Andy," said the woman.

"But what is a pledge anyway at all," said the old man. "It's only for them that don't know when to stop when they begin."

"And it's a good sup," said Peter.

"The best in the world," said Andy.

"But I've no liking for it at all," said Oonah. "And when I did take it, and that was not often, it was always the heartburn that it gave me."

"Just one sup," pleaded Andy. "It's only to be thrown into the gutter if I can't get rid of it. And I got it ready for the two of you."

"Well, a drop, and no more," sighed the woman. "God forgive me, but seeing it's going to loss and all."

She put it to her lips, kissed it, and distaste showed itself in wrinkles on the corners of her lips and eyes.

"G'on!" urged Peter. "It doesn't bite!"

A second time she essayed with greater success and even drank two sups. Then she shook her head deprecatingly, but still held the pannikin.

"A wren could do better than that," said Andy slightingly. "Try again."

A third time she tried, tried and fell. The pannikin was returned empty. A pledge was broken.

Within the church! Stood round the font did the sponsors with the child. The old Father, good easy man, whose cassock was streaked with snuff, droned the Latin through his nose. A delicate aroma of hops, barm and peatwater filled the air, and for some reason gave a more reckless note to the song that the robin sang above the sanctuary lamp. The priest could not smell. And the others? Well, it was one another's breath they were smelling, surely!

The name of the child? Lanty.

When the christening water was put on him, a great smile came over his face. It seemed that even at that early age the boy realised that a meet honour had been done him.

III

Born as he was to little or no fortune of his own, he grew up just like the other bare-footed boys of Ballykeeran; played pitch and toss, ball, marbles, stole apples, gave black eyes to other boys, got black eyes, wore the bottom of his trousers sliding down green braes on his hams, a nuisance to everybody as all hearty youngsters, God bless them! should be.

At night he slept without his shirt. This was in obedience to his father, who had but a poor opinion of anyone who needed a shirt for his dreams. "A man who wants a shirt in bed will want a fire in the spade-field," said the old man.

From the very start, however, Lanty showed not love for the spade. "My father spent all his years cutting worms, and what has he to show for it this day?" he once said, and his age at that time was only thirteen. This showed that he was more than a cut above the ordinary.

At the National School he beat everybody in

learning, even the master. When Lanty left school at fourteen, the master spoke to the boy's father. " This young rascal of yours has taken all that I can give him in learning and is on the look-out for more. All that you can do now is to throw him into college and make a priest of him ! "

Great the admission, good the advice !

Lanty had great conceit in himself. Never would he allow anybody to get the better of him in an argument. He could prove black was white and by a twist of the tongue make a man twice his years his fool. Nothing was too big for him and there was nothing that he had not the heart to attempt. He never went back on his word. When he said a certain thing, that thing was gospel to himself, for he backed it even when he knew it to be false. Even a false gospel has its adherents.

Once when he was a youngster he had a watch, one that he won as a prize at school. It was the best watch in Ballykeeran, he vowed ; the only watch that kept time correctly. All other watches were generally wrong by half an hour, but not Lanty Hanlon's. The neighbours thought otherwise.

" We know we're right," they said.

" You think you're right," was his word.

Behold there was an eclipse of the sun. Half-past eleven of a summer morning its hour.

" Now we'll prove whose watch is wrong ! " said the neighbours, and gathered together. Lanty Hanlon was one of the party. His watch was half an hour ahead of the others.

Eleven o'clock by Hanlon's watch. No eclipse!

Eleven o'clock by the other watches. Darkness settled on the world. Oonah Ruddagh could be seen in the half-light praying. The end of the world, surely!

"Now, is your watch right?" asked the neighbours, looking at Lanty Hanlon.

"Of course it's right," was Lanty's reply. "The eclipse is late."

Many another story is to be heard concerning Lanty Hanlon as a boy, and all these stories testify to his ability and cleverness. Hereunder a little incident to show you the boy, manwise at the age of fourteen.

The month was June, with the corn in blade, the apple in blossom and the nesting birds loud in the ivy of Ballykeeran parish church. Father Dan, the successor of the good man who had christened Lanty Hanlon, was telling his beads by the sacristy door. The Angelus bell was ringing and a heavenly calm had settled on the whole country-side. The blessing of God was on the world!

Father Dan had finished his prayer, kissed the cross, and taken a pinch of snuff when he became conscious of someone by his side, a bare-footed boy whose head hardly reached the priest's elbow.

"Ah! my little boy, what is your name?"

"Lanty Hanlon, your reverence!"

"The son of a decent man," said the priest. "And what can I do for you now?"

"It's trouble between my father and Peter Ruddagh," said Lanty, the boy. "And it's to the law they're going about it!"

" The law is never a poor man's friend," said Father Dan. " It's like the briar that shelters sheep in a storm, and keeps their wool as payment. Now what is the trouble ? "

" Last Candlemas my father's two cows calved, and one cow had twins," said Lanty. " That means three calves to the two cows——"

" That's true. What a cute boy you are ! "

" Well, Peter Ruddagh bought the three calves at so much, and not having the fodder for them, he asked my father to keep them till June, promising to pay him the money then, with so much for the feeding. The bargain was struck, the money to be paid over when the calves change hands."

" That's fair and above board," said Father Dan. " What is there to go to law about ? "

" The price of stock has gone up," Lanty explained. " The calves are now worth three times the money agreed on. My father wanted money and he sold the calves, sold them the day before yesterday. There is nothing wrong in that ! "

" It's all wrong, my boy," said the priest. " Once the bargain was struck the calves were no longer your father's property."

" And if they go to law, my father and Peter Ruddagh, Peter will win, will he ? " asked Lanty.

" Win ! Of course he will win," said Father Dan. " I'm ashamed that one of my flock should go to law over such a case. And Lanty Hanlon too ! A decent man ever and always ! "

" And Peter Ruddagh will win the case ? "

asked the youngster. He wanted to be certain on this point.

"Of course he will win!"

"But my father thinks the law is on his side," said Lanty.

"The law is not on his side," said Father Dan. "The bargain was made, and from the day on which it was made your father was nothing more than the keeper of another man's property."

"So he will lose?" asked Lanty.

"Of course he will lose. If he wanted to find out whether he would lose or not, why did he not go to the lawyer instead of his old parish priest?"

"But the law costs too much," said my cute Lanty. "And anyway it wasn't Peter Ruddagh that bought the stock from my father. It was my father who bought the calves from him, and Peter sold them yesterday!"

"Well, I never met a cuter little rascal than you in all my life," gasped the priest. "What is the world coming to at all!"

But the world was just the same. The only difference was that a great man had come into it!

When his days of schooling came to an end the boy was apprenticed to a village grocer, one Mick Flaherty, long dead, God be his comforting! Flaherty was licensed of course, like every other decent village grocer in Ireland.

Hard-working, zealous and prompt, Lanty became an adept in the art of wrapping sugar in paper horns, in cutting thick plug, weighing snuff and pouring out porter. Fairness and honesty were two outstanding traits in Lanty's favour. The soul of decency, he never incurred his master's censure nor a customer's reproach. That the tobacco he cut was a little damp was now and again noticed by those who bought, but still what could be expected in a shop whose floors were flooded in wet weather; that from a roll of tobacco weighing eight pounds Lanty got requisite return in butter, eggs and wool, was noticed by the grocer. Perhaps he made a little for himself from the extra weight which water gave to a roll, but that was nobody's business. He was a decent boy, esteemed by all, one who would go out of his way to oblige his fellows.

On Sundays, when the public-houses were shut against drouthy customers, the obliging Lanty brought a few bottles of whisky to chapel and sold these after the service to the worshippers at a little above the ordinary price, six eggs or twelve, according to the buyer.

Shortly after Lanty took up his duties a strange thing was noticed in the drinking-bar. Several grooves cut by a knife were to be seen in the counter, shallow towards the outside but deeper towards the spot occupied by the bar-tender. In this manner the porter spilled by the customers flowed inwards towards the swill-tub. On the day following this beer was re-sold, probably to those who had bought it on the previous evening. Lanty made money on the drippings.

Five years he spent in the grocer's shop, always hard at work and never biting his nails when his head and hand could be better employed. He wanted to make money, not for its own sake, but for what it could attain.

"But how will it all end?" the people asked

one another. " There will be a downfall one of these days."

But why should there be a downfall ? one might ask. And people did ask. The answers were many and were given with the dropping of one eyelid or the uplift of two eyebrows. A word simple in itself will gain much by the action that is fellow to it.

In Ballykeeran I have seen a lass go into a wood where a young man cut bushes. A week later the girl looked ill at ease. " What has upset her ? " I ask.

" Cutting bushes is a funny job," I was told, and the one who spoke dropped an eyelid and put a finger on his lip. That is all, but I know that a girl's reputation is ruined.

In the same manner did the wise ones make answer to those who questioned the prophecies relating to Lanty Hanlon's future.

" Whisky for his christening ! " said one with a doleful shake of the head.

" His father and his grandfather and his great-grandfather always went hungry in the lean days of May and June," said another. This really did not want any by-play. Poor was Lanty's stock ; what did *he* expect to be ? Surely there would be a downfall.

The downfall did come, and at the early age of twenty-one. One evening, wintry it was and cold, and the young man stood behind the counter biting his finger-nails. No customers ! No trade in porter drippings and wet tobacco ! In hand he had thirty pounds, which he had counted three times that day.

A good sum surely in hard, bright gold. He put the gold pieces on the counter and spread them out with his big hand in a slow, caressing touch. A fortune! His heart filled with pride and joy. How he had worked to gather it together in grooves, drippings and wet tobacco!

At that instant he would have liked to show the money to somebody. What young man had as much in pocket as he? None. Thirty pounds! Why not celebrate it in some way! Poor boy! The Devil was at his elbow tempting him!

He reached for a bottle, poured a slight modicum of whisky into a glass, raised it to his lips, smelt it and put it down again. He had never drunk before, but now with thirty pounds in his keeping why should he not make himself merry? Only a little drop, of course. Just wet his lips. He drank!

Oonah Ruddagh, seven eggs in her checked apron, came in half an hour later. Darkness had fallen, the paraffin lamp was not lit, the shop was deserted.

"Lanty Hanlon, I want a quarter pound of tea and half a pound of sugar!" Oonah called. There was no answer.

"Well, this is a nice fix for a widow woman!" Oonah wailed. Her man had just died. "As if I couldn't pay for what I want!"

"What is it now that's wrong with you?" asked Mick Flaherty, coming from the back room where he had been eating his supper. "Where's the lamp? Where's Lanty? Where's everything?"

"It's nothing to me where anything is!" said

Oonah Ruddagh, and her voice was that of a woman who bore a great wrong. "What I want is a quarter pound of tea and half a pound of sugar."

"Just a minute, please, Oonah Ruddagh, till I light a candle," said Mick Flaherty, a civil man always. "But saints of glory! what is that at all?"

What had startled the man was a queer sound, half whistle and half hiccough, which came from the darkness. It filled the shop, was heard in the kitchen, rolled out into the rain-spattered street, attracted the attention of lone passers-by. A crowd formed at the door. What was it at all?

"It must be something in the shop," was the wise remark of Flaherty, as he tried to strike a match with trembling fingers. He had a weak heart, the poor man!

"It must be in the shop, surely," said Oonah Ruddagh, who had no doubt about the matter.

Mick Flaherty lit a candle and with cautious steps surveyed the dark space under the overhanging lip of the counter. Something white was to be seen, something that lived! The position was precarious. Mick Flaherty drew back a step. A cautious man, he remembered that with his weak heart a sudden shock would be fatal. Doctor's orders. Better withdraw!

The withdrawal was effected with such precipitancy that even now it is classified as one of the wonders of Ballykeeran. Mick Flaherty vaulted the counter with the agility of a harried hare, and coming in contact with Oonah Ruddagh, knocked the poor woman down.

"And me a widow woman too!" she groaned. "What's coming over you at all, at all?"

There was no reply. Mick Flaherty was already at the police barracks telling the sergeant in charge that there was something wrong in his shop, that a man, mother-naked, was under his counter. This man's throat was cut. He was dead, surely!

Accompanied by four policemen armed to the teeth he returned. Oonah Ruddagh was there still. A quarter pound of tea and half a pound of sugar she wanted, and she was not going away till she got it. And her a widow woman too! The sound, half whistle and half hiccough, was louder.

"It's somebody with the sleep on him," said the sergeant. "And for a man with his throat cut it's a loud snore he has!"

They looked at the back of the counter and there lay Lanty Hanlon asleep, Lanty Hanlon, who true to his father's instructions had removed the apparel of the day, and not having any for the night, spread himself out on the damp floor as naked and unashamed as the innocent cherubs over the sacristy door in Ballykeeran parish church.

Drunk was the unfortunate boy, absolutely drunk, filled throat-high and an empty bottle beside him. Nothing could be done with him in that state, so the stalwart police threw a few rags round him and carried him to bed. Twenty-eight sovereigns were discovered on the counter. Where were the other two? Who knew? But Oonah Ruddagh (who never wasted her time) paid in gold for a shawl three weeks later.

Next day Lanty was sermonised by the priest, the schoolmaster, the grocer, the police-sergeant. But not Lanty to hang his head!

"If no one committed sin you would have no job," he told the priest.

"I'm not at school now," he told the schoolmaster. "It has nothing to do with you," to the grocer; and "I never take advice from a policeman" were his words to the sergeant.

IV

Nothing could cure him until the twenty-eight pounds were spent. Then he steadied himself. He was now in a woeful plight. Not a penny had he to his name; the little holding stuck against the side of the hills like the hind-leg of a dog was all that his father had left him. Not a farm for a go-ahead man! What was he to do?

One day he heard Oonah Ruddagh speak. The poor woman was not feeling well.

"You are a decent boy, Lanty Hanlon," she said. "And the learning that is in your head! Maybe with it all you would know a cure for the fever that has hold of me and many another one in the parish."

Lanty cocked up his ears. Fever had gripped the people and people who were ill wanted a cure. Why should he not cure them?

No sooner said than done. The juice of a few onions, a mashed turnip and nettles, a little senna for crispness, sugar for flavour, and behold the mixture was complete. Her fever was at its height when Oonah took it. Oonah was cured.

Far and wide the fame of the medicine spread. People came for the medicine that cured Oonah Ruddagh. Lanty was not slow to profit by the occasion. A shilling a bottle! Cure guaranteed! Lanty Hanlon hired a donkey and cart, went round the country with an assortment of bottles, *Hanlon's Travelling Pharmacopœia*, sold his mixture and cured the afflicted. Three deaths only in Ballykeeran. Ballyroon had seventeen. Lanty went to Ballyroon, sold and conquered. Who wanted a doctor when Lanty Hanlon was near? The happiness he brought, the money he made! Onions, turnips and nettles turned to gold under his hand.

But one day he fell, and for a week, more than a week, a fortnight, he kept seeing bottles to the bottom. Nothing could stay him. His complaint was beyond the scope of medicine. He saved others; himself he could not save.

How many jobs did the man try before I met him! Tea selling was one, and for a year his vans ran through the country, carrying tea to the most out-of-the-way places. In this he succeeded as he succeeded in everything. When he dealt in fish there were sovereigns instead of scales on the fish which he handled. At one time his knitting stores were a godsend to the people of Ballykeeran, Ballyroon and many another broad parish. When he sold second-hand clothing in country fairs, Hanlon's stalls were a feature of every market-place.

His last venture before I met him was in wool dyeing. To wool, the weaving, spinning and dyeing thereof, he devoted more attention than to anything else. By assiduous research in lichen he formulated certain theories on dyeing which earned him the title of Guild's Honoursman. The world near and far knew Lanty Hanlon, G.H. He was proud of this; Ballykeeran was proud of this. Nothing like G.H. in Ballyroon!

Ballykeeran was too narrow for his fame. It spread outwards and afar. Towns and big cities came to know his name. One day came a letter registered, offering Lanty Hanlon an appointment as manager of a large woollen factory.

Ballykeeran heard the news. The whole parish sorted itself round one central point, the brave Lanty Hanlon, G.H.

"Will he go?" the people asked one another.

"And why shouldn't he go?" was the answer. "Who would stay in a place like this if there was a chance of leaving it? Nobody!"

Ballykeeran gave the answer, you must remember. Suppose Ballyroon gave it!!!

"Will you go, Mr. Hanlon?" asked Genevieve Flaherty, the fair daughter of Mick Flaherty, a quality wisp who could speak French and who never knew the bare road without shoeleather.

"I go," said Lanty Hanlon, G.H.

"I hope you'll not forget your old friends," said the fair Genevieve. "We'll all be dying to hear from you. You must write me a letter now and again, you know."

"I'll write," said Lanty Hanlon. He was very excited and ready to promise anything at that moment.

"And you'll be goin' and leavin' us, Lanty Hanlon?" asked Maldy Ruddagh, daughter of Oonah, a winsome slip of a wench, bare-footed because the weather was warm and her portion slight. For all that she could not talk French, and had little of quality in her, Lanty Hanlon gave more ear to her words than he did to those of Genevieve Flaherty.

"I am going," Lanty made answer. "And there's one that I'll be sorry to leave!"

"Genevieve Flaherty?" enquired Maldy, who, like every woman in matters of soft talk, was quick on the uptake.

They spoke to one another at the gable end of Oonah's house. The roses were out and the birds were in song. Lanty plucked a rose.

"This is for her whom I grieve to leave," was his word, and he handed the rose to Maldy. Then, as if frightened at what he had done, he strode away and took the road to his home. Where was the courage of the man who had in after-years braved the wrath of the MacMonagles.

Next day he hied away, dressed in high attire, a gold pin in his tie, a rose in his buttonhole, a coach and pair his equipage. The railway was not laid at the time. Ballykeeran with its band, fife and drum, followed him.

Steeling his heart for the occasion, indifferent to the agony which the excitement would cause him later, Mick Flaherty strode behind the carriage. With him was his daughter, dressed in her proud finery. Came also Oonah Ruddagh and Maldy, Oonah's boots round her neck because of her corns, bad scrawn to them! Maldy wearing a red rose, a thing which was noted by all, for the girl seldom wore flowers. There also was Eamon Larrimore and Paddy Cosdhu, men who in after days were to play a grand part in the history of the parish.

At the Ballykeeran-Ballyroon cross-roads the carriage came to a halt. Afar to the eastward stretched the road which was to be followed by Lanty Hanlon, G.H.

" A speech ! A speech ! "

Lanty Hanlon stood upright, his thumbs in the sleeves of his waistcoat.

" I'm sorry to leave you, good men and good women," were his words, short and to the point. " A great honour has been done me by the way you have come out to bid me good-bye. It is grand to see all the faces which I have known from childhood. Oonah Ruddagh——"

" Poor me with the corns and the heat," sighed Oonah.

" Mick Flaherty, Paddy Cosdhu, Eamon Larrimore, all decent men. To these, to the hearty youngsters of the fife-and-drum band, to the fair girls who are more beautiful than the roses they wear " (only one wore roses. Did Lanty not see the others ?), " I can only say : Prosperity be yours, and God be your comforting until I come back again. I go away a Ballykeeran man and native of no mean parish, and when abroad I'll do what Ballykeeran expects her absent sons to do, the right thing, to keep the name of Ballykeeran from the gutter. One day I'll come back, and then I'm going to do something that will surprise you. What this will be I'll not tell you now, but when it comes it will be something of which you all will be proud and which will make Ballykeeran the first parish in the land. That's all I have to say. And my last words are Ballykeeran for ever!"

The carriage rolled away. The band struck up. Lanty Hanlon, at the end of a mile (Irish), looked back and saw his people still at the cross-roads, a motley assemblage of red and white, woollen clouds and quilted petticoats. The band was still playing! Slan leath!

V

A year went by and Lanty did not return. The mill of which he became manager was some six-score miles away from Ballykeeran. But though Lanty did not appear in flesh, rumour made up for the lack of first-hand information. The Guild's Honoursman was making great headway. The lords and ladies of the land bowed to him. He had a house with a window to every day of the year, and one room in this great house was filled with gold. He would return one day—remember the promise he made!

The good people waited, and some, on the strength of Lanty's promise, went easy in the fields, putting more faith in an Honoursman's word than the trustworthy spade.

Genevieve Flaherty, dressed in her best, waited three hundred and sixty-five mail-coaches, and to no purpose. But did she expect that one who went in a carriage would return in a coach? Maldy Ruddagh's hopes, which lived longer than her rose, died at last, and she left Ballykeeran and went out to push her fortune in America.

Then one day at the end of a year and three months a man came to Ballykeeran, travelling neither by carriage, coach, nor cart, but by the oldest form of movement known to man, Shank's Mare. Who was the man ?

Everybody saw the homecoming : Eamon Larrimore, whose white chin-whiskers fell an inch at the sight ; Paddy Cosdhu, who dropped his coloured clay pipe, a prime smoker, in surprise, and broke it ; Oonah Ruddagh, who afterwards embellished the story as much as occasion permitted, and added more than truth should allow. The hour was that preceding the one on which the stage-coach would come, and Genevieve Flaherty, decorating herself in proud array, looked from her casement window and saw Lanty Hanlon, G.H., passing by—bare-footed !

For a week afterwards the driver of the mail-coach did not see the daughter of Flaherty. Genevieve was slightly indisposed.

The Honoursman hied to his house, followed by the rag-tag and bobtail of the parish, went in, shut the door behind him, and a week's daylight afterwards did not see him walking in the ways of men.

One day Oonah Ruddagh brought a letter from the post office, and went to the door of Lanty Hanlon's house.

" Lanty, asthor ! are you in there at all ? " she called through the keyhole.

" I'm here," said Lanty Hanlon, opening the door. The look of his face was hard, his clothes were in tatters. "What do you want, Oonah Ruddagh?"

"It's a letter that I have for you," said Oonah. "Three days the postman rapped at your door, and three days you didn't answer. So the post office told *me* to try you, seeing that I was with your mother when you came, and my two hands were the ones that took the caul from your head. And if a caul has no luck, nothing has, but by the way you've turned out, there wasn't much luck in you having it. But it was the christening that you had, Lanty!"

"Give me the letter," said Lanty Hanlon, and the sparkle of friendship was not in his eyes.

He took the letter, read it, and whistled through his teeth. A second time he read it, and a smile was on his face; a third time he read it, and danced a step on the stone floor.

"And once I could do a step like that—barefooted," sighed Oonah Ruddagh. "But not now and the corns that I have between the toes and on the soles of my feet!" With knuckles on hips, and toes turned in, she faced Lanty. "And what will be in that letter?" she asked.

"All is not lost, Oonah," said Lanty. "I had a job that was more than a job and I lost it——"

"But why, Lanty, asthor?"

"The ancient curse, Oonah, the ancient curse—whisky," said Lanty Hanlon. "But now I'm going to be cured. The big firm which is going to ruin because I am not there, want me to go to a house where I will get cured—an inebriates' home. I'll stay there for two months, then I'll come out and I'll never taste whisky again."

"Then my prayer will follow you, Lanty, asthor," was the hearty word of Oonah. "But for all that I have my doubts. Whisky for christening-water, you know—" Ballykeeranwise, one eyelid rested flush on her cheek. "The House of Correction is little good put against God's will. That's what I told Maldy and the days she waited for you coming back!"

"Has Maldy gone?" asked Lanty Hanlon.

"Off and away to America," Oonah told him. "'Waiting?' I asked her. She shook her head, but that shake had everything in it but the truth. 'He's a weak crutch to lean on,' I said. 'A man that's half dead with the drooth, God help him!' And she went away, the youngest of my stock and the last."

The two sighed in unison. But why sigh? Life was sent for laughter, and Lanty Hanlon realised that an hour of sorrow is an hour wasted.

"All will be well, Oonah, if you wait long enough," he said. "The merrier the heart, the longer the life, and the devil fly away with the one that grumbles!"

That night he went off again. Six weeks he spent in the inebriates' home, and left it, his heart and system steeled against temptation. On the way to the job he met a friend. Well, what would you expect! A drop for friendship's sake, a drop to sweeten discourse, a drop to the memory of old friends, and, belly full, Lanty reported to his masters.

No hope! A waste of money! He was given his fare home and told to be gone. Next morning he reeled back to the mill; his fare had been spent in strong waters. They took him to the railway station, bought his ticket and put him in a carriage. The train went to Ballyroon. From there he could walk home, damn him !

When his guardians had gone he came from the train, sold his ticket and next day again reported to the mill.

The police took the matter in hand and drove him from the district. Forty leagues north-west lay Ballykeeran, and with eyes to the north-west Lanty Hanlon, G.H., padded the hoof homewards.

His adventures of the road ! Who is to tell them ? Three things are known concerning the journey. A Ballyroon farmer gave him a pair of boots, the parish priest of Ballybarra gave him a coat, and Manus Glynn, the half-witted son of Widow Glynn, who lived on the outer mearns of Ballykeeran, put him up for one night. When he went to bed, he hung his trousers over the half-wall which partitioned the byre from the sleeping-room. A cow ate the trousers, and Lanty Hanlon, Guild's Honoursman, not being able to find a second pair, went out on his journey the next morning in a red petticoat, the gift of Widow Glynn.

CHAPTER II

THE RED PETTICOAT

Better a good retreat than a bad stand, but neither are worth much.

—A Ballykeeran Proverb.

I

MY own name is Neddy MacMonagle, and I come into this story because, in the first place, I am the teller, and in the second place, I was henchman of Lanty Hanlon, G.H., in the heyday of his great career, at the period when by the power of his mind he raised Ballykeeran to a place of grand prominence in the world. I was with him then, I, Neddy MacMonagle, who was once a tinker's brat on the high-roads of Ireland, but am now a man of property and position, in the parish which gave birth to a man, the greatest of his place and period.

Truly it is my place to speak to the world and tell the history of my beloved master, and this history will now be taken up on a long-gone summer day in a tinker's encampment which stood in a hazel-decked glen near the village of Ballykeeran.

At that time I did not know my years. Were they twelve, thirteen or fourteen? This I remember and this all. On the previous day I had met a girl on the road, a young girl with golden hair, a strange calling look on her face; legs white as bog-blossom, and naked to the knees. She walked on a dusty highway and her very toes were white, such little toes! To think of it! Taking notice of a girl's toes and never heeding them before.

And I was ashamed, because I was in rags with my knees out through my trousers and maybe the tail of my shirt showing. . . . I may have been fourteen, but nothing more. The open air, the hard life, the bed by the wayside, makes for age, and one is old before the feet stop growing.

It was in the early days of June with a raw spring past and the promise of summer in the land. A good day for the road, for the weather was fine; a fitting day, because it was time to move on. The twelve straight policemen of Ballykeeran had ordered us to go; the country folk had all their pots and kettles mended, and were well stocked in milk-strainers, tin dishes, pans and graters. It was time to be off and away, surely.

I got up from my bed, which was the green earth, yawned and stretched myself. It was now six o'clock in the morning, the sun high over the hills, the dew drying from the grasses.

I rose, dressed for the day, dressed as I had gone to bed, in my little woollen jacket (stolen by my mother two years back and fifty miles away), my cordoran breeches, once part of my father's trousers (previous owner unknown), and a buttonless shirt fashioned by my mother from a charity apron. My clothing began at the neck and finished at the knee.

With the exception of a donkey and myself all the party were asleep. They lay in the wood by the roadway, nineteen in all, felled scarecrows, loud in their healthy snoring. A rowan shade was sanctuary for one, a tussock pillow for another, the well of our donkey-cart that bedded three women was roofing for five children who lay on the ground. This was our resting-place, with its rolling stock, a donkey-cart and barrow, its live folk, nineteen human beings, a donkey and a dog.

All looked very peaceful, even my father, MacMonagle, the great MacMonagle known far and near, up hill and down brae in many a barony. Far-famous and feared, a fighter of note, he now lay at his ease in the shade of the hazel where the mists of the morning rose like the breath of a steaming midden.

Even as I write I can still see him, his shoulders mighty as a half-door, his teeth tusks, his hair heather. The rays of the sun streaming through the trees lit up the dewdrops on his beard, causing them to sparkle like polished pin-heads. I thought that the balm of morning which rested on his face had penetrated his being, making my father in his sleep what he had never been in his waking moments, a man of peace.

I made my way through the undergrowth towards the river, taking care to pick my path, for the slightest touch on one of the saplings brought a sparkling shower of dew on my head.

The wet grasses drenched my legs to the knees and the close, cool lane of hazel and rowan was filled with the fresh scents of morning. Startled birds, thrushes, sparrows and robins, hopped from twig to twig, making great noise as if they were cursing me.

I cleared myself from the wood and came out on the bank of the river. An open space lying hand-smooth sloped down to the water. On it the sun shone proudly and the dew was already gone. Here the trout were rising to the flies, shooting up so quickly that their rise and fall was just like a spurt of quicksilver. Circles of light caught by the sun rolled outwards to the banks, cutting and crossing one another at every move, and breasting the whole shiny sheet was a party of ducks enjoying their morning bath.

II

How happy they looked that morning, especially their leader, a proud-bosomed drake with a holly-green head and dear little yellow legs that walked in the water as if he were lord of the river, fowl, fish and everything thereon and therein. Now and again he strode abreast a charming duck, paid her compliments and a little attention, as was natural. Then he heaved off, quacking to himself and proud of his position. A dozen wives to his name and boss of them all. Well, well!

I lay down on the brough, placed my elbows on the ground, put the heels of both hands together as a rest for my chin and got ready for mischief at once. Wasn't I a MacMonagle in those days!

"Wheet, wheet! Wheet-a-wheet!" I called, quiet if you like, but with a coax in my tongue and loud enough for the ducks to hear. At once there was a little commotion amongst the feathered folk; they came together, nodded one to the other, brim-full of suspicion, and spoke deep down in their throats. They knew the call of their feeding-time, but its hour was not as yet and its place was otherwhere.

"Wheet, wheet! Wheet-a-wheet!" I put from me again, and the green-headed one stood off from the others, nodded his head, tilted it sideways and set his eyes on the bank where I rested. He was taking it all in. Presently he would come into the brough, followed by his wives, and we would have a good breakfast, surely.

"Wheet, wheet!" I called again.

"Louder than that, ye whelp!" came a deep voice from the bushes behind. I turned on my belly like a cart-wheel on its hub, ready to take to my heels. My father was speaking!

He came out into the open. Clumsy enough he was to look at, bodied like a bullock, his mighty beard, red and stiff as rusty wire, falling over his naked chest, his shoulders a half-door, his legs a stallion's. He wore a red flannel shirt turned down at the neck, corduroy trousers, patched on knee and bottom and held up by a hempen rope girt round the waist. He wore boots differing one from the other in colour (one was black, the other brown), in size (one was a number eight, the other a number eleven) and in shape (one being square-toed and the other pointed), but even these ill-assorted boots had one saving grace: they had been obtained cheaply. They had been stolen.

"Don't slack off!" urged my father, coming nearer. "Don't slack off or I'll skin yer backside!"

"Wheet, wheet! Wheet-a-wheet!" I went on, one eye on the ducks, one on my father, a hasty man, quick to land out with his fist or foot on the least possible pretext. But all was well! The feathered folk were gliding towards me.

"Wheet! wheet! wheet!"

The voice was not mine. It came from the other side of the river, from amidst the bushes that grew there. The birds stopped, turned and looked back. Evidently they recognised the call.

"Cripes! I'll skin ye!" roared my father, rushing at me. By a quick movement I sidled round and shot off like a swallow, my father hard on my heels, hurling imprecations on my head, my eyes, my voice, my feet, my legs, my guts. Curses came from him like sparks from a lime-kiln.

Finding he was not able to break the tangle of undergrowth through which I, being smaller, was able to scoot like a rabbit, he stooped, picked up half a dozen stones and flung them at me.

One whizzed by my ears like a shuttle; a second sung through the undergrowth, swishing the dry twigs round my legs. That my father saw where these stones fell was not to my liking. I had known him in such a mood before and had often tempered his rage in my own way.

When a dozen stones had been thrown I took shelter in a clump of ferns. Waiting there, I listened to others dropping. One came very close, and I sent up a piteous howl as if I had been stricken. On hearing this cry of agony my father ceased his handiwork. Vengeance being satisfied, he molested me no further.

No breakfast! Well, well! It had often been like that before! So having nothing else to do I went back to the river, limping a little, of course. The stone had hit me on the leg (any leg) above the knee where my trousers hid the bruise. The ducks were gone. Trout, finning one another in air, rose to the flies in the slack water. On the brough was my father, drying himself after his morning's wash.

Every morning, summer and winter, my father washed, and this the manner of his ablutions. In the first place, we always settled down at night by a brook or river, so that we could have water near at hand for cooking. In the morning my father got up, his hour of rising depending on his fighting or drinking of the night before. A sober night gave him a bad temper, a drunken night a worse.

Going to the stream, he lay down on his hands and knees, stuck his head down into the water until his eyes, ears, mouth and beard were hidden from sight. Taking his head out, he stood upright, shook his hair in the wind, puffed like a wind-broken horse, and in this manner he shook himself until he was dry. He never used such luxuries as soap and towel. These were unknown amongst our people, for few of us ever washed from one year's end till the other.

"No ducks for our breakfast this morning, Neddy!" said my father with a twist of pleasure on his lips, for in addition to the good-humour which his wash generally gave him, he had noticed my limp. Even if I did not limp it would have surprised me if anyone (even my father) could be in a surly mood that morning.

"Just another minute and I would have one of them by the neck," I said.

"Always too slow, ye devil's brat!" said my father in gentle scorn. "Ye'll never make a MacMonagle!"

"Wait till I grow up!" I said, with the cock-sureness of a boy. "Then ye'll see!"

"See hell!" exclaimed my father, spitting over his beard. "It takes three things to make a MacMonagle: a stout heart, a good belly, and a light finger. And ye've neither o' them!"

The first was needed in a fight, the second in a tavern, and the third in a theft, and in these three arts, fighting, thieving and drinking, my father was master. But that was to be expected. He was a MacMonagle.

But here at the start I must explain all about it, who we were, what we were, and our place (if I may say so) in the social order and the scheme of things.

My father was the MacMonagle, the sole and only head of the MacMonagle clan, the gang of roving tinkers, whom every corner of Ireland knew and whom every corner dreaded. One day we were here, another there, Cork or Donegal, Ballymote or Ballinasloe, ransacking a widow's henhouse, thieving in the market-place, pinching sheep from the hills, sleeping in a black-hole or a ditch, thieving, fighting, drinking, drinking, fighting and thieving, until we were known and feared in the seven corners of the land.

In the ordinary sense of the word we had no learning. I have, but my education came afterwards, and if you read the story you'll hear all about it.

Now when I speak of " we " I mean my father. To my thinking then, we were brought simply into the world to please him, we, his two brothers, his uncle, his wife, the wives of his brothers and uncle, and the children begotten of these unions, twenty-nine in all. And for our own peace of mind we had to do as he ordered, work and spy and steal, back him in an argument and cheer him in a fight.

I mean in a fight with an outsider, of course, but when he fought a man or woman within the clan it was purely a personal affair, the business of two, and in the hands of two the decision.

Fights amongst ourselves were common, especially amongst the women, and these brawls, disputes and arguments were carried on with the most bitter animosity, with tearing of hair, clothes and faces. A fight amongst men left bruises and black eyes, amongst women, tears and scratches. The closed fist is never a woman's weapon.

The men mostly fought with sticks, now and again for prefection in the practise of the art, sometimes because they disagreed on a matter, and oftener when drunk than sober. Then the women joined in, and after that the children.

Ah! the days that were! Even now when my eyes look out on the long mearing that holds fat acres, hill and holm and all my own, I sometimes sigh for the happy far-off days, the days when I was young.

"And ye've neither of them!" said my father after a long silence and pulling his fingers through his beard, which crackled like dry straw.

As he spoke he looked round, taking stock of the place. His eyes were alert, ready for anything. What might not happen now, seeing that the twelve straight policemen had warned us the day before. The weather was too good for the black-hole, and my father wore a red shirt. He never bought a shirt, and that which he now wore was not in his keeping on the previous day. It was time to be on the road, surely.

"They're sleepin' like pigs!" he grunted angrily, and from the distance we could hear the healthy snoring of the sleepers.

III

As we listened a snore louder than any with which we were familiar came from the near distance. In this snore, half hiccough and half whistle, loud as a wind between hills, there was something strange. The snore of a giant! My father put up a silencing hand, took a step or two to the left and looked into the thick undergrowth beneath the hazels. For a minute he stood thus, then pulled the branches gently aside and looked at something therein.

I stole quietly up behind him and looked through the parting at a man lying asleep on the ground, naked to the sky, save for some reddish garment that served the purpose of loin-cloth. On the ground beside the man lay his clothes and boots, arranged in a snug little pile.

Quick on an opportunity was the spadework of my father's hard-hammered philosophy. As rapidly as possible and in keeping with the situation he thrust the branches aside until a clear way lay between himself and the sleeper's clothes. Quickly and quietly as a hawk on its prey he darted on the bundle of clothing, snatched it up, and shot like a shuttle through the undergrowth back to our people. I followed.

Then things happened. The first sleeper in his path lay under a rowan tree, a youngster of twelve or so, and this youngster was raised upright by the ear, given a cuff to bring him to his senses and a kick to put him out of the way. Then my father lifted a pail half-filled with cold water, emptied part on the sleepers in the cart, part on those lying beneath the vehicle, and the remainder on the sleepers under the trees. They arose spluttering and swearing.

" Hook it at once ! " roared my father. " Harness the cuddy and slide. The polis are after us ! "

The police ! What more was needed ! The men, with the cold water running down their bodies, harnessed the donkey to the cart, threw all the stock of our trade—tacks and tins, soap and solder—into the well of the vehicle. The boy, legs to the neck, whom my father had cuffed, ran off trundling a barrow.

The dog, recipient of many a kick in the excitement, feeling that its place was not here, hurried after the long-legged boy. Other children followed, terrified. The women picked up their belongings and went off at an easy pace. They afraid of the police! No fear!

Holding the reins, my father gave the donkey a kick and off they went, the donkey, the man, hard on the heels of the others. I followed behind.

The peace of the world lay over the highland glen through which we went. The road in front lay like a white crooked ribbon, winding through holt and holm, losing itself here, coming into sight there, and always rising to the higher hills that showed on the lip of the sky.

The roadway was without a soul; the rural people were busy with their work, for now was the time for the turf on the spread-fields. Up on the braes, where the brown heather fringed the fields like the hem of a great shawl, the limewashed houses showed like resting gulls; cows lowed from the pastures, geese gaggled in the gutters and hens cackled over their newly-laid eggs. The great summer and the young blood! Why do we grow old?

A mile of the journey was done, maybe two. My father took a black, short-stemmed clay pipe from his pocket and lit it. The journey was now very slow; the donkey, head down, was straining to a rise. The sun shone; the pipe bubbled; the tinker vanguard was out of sight.

I followed, a little distance to rear, within hail but out of hold, as the saying has it, my eye now on my father, walking cumbrously, then on the gravel-polished wheel going round and round, rising and rising, fringed with powdered grit, which it threw away in filmy whorls as a mill-wheel sheds water. In the same way are the hours of life shed, like a wind through the whins, leaving neither sign nor surety of their stay.

But did I think in this way then? No, I fear not. I was young—and a tinker. Neither had my father such thoughts, for he, above any man I have ever met, was akin to the four-legged creatures in simplicity. He was, if I may say so, a hard man without soul or heart. Age and circumstance, hardship and hazard had not the least effect on him. He rose as briskly from a drunken sleep in a ditch as from a sober sleep in a hayrick. Whole and healthy, he would go on living to the end of time. Death! Well, he had heard of it, but what matter. A MacMonagle die in a bed, who had never slept in one!

He turned round, spat in his pipe, pressing the tobacco with his finger, put the pipe in his pocket and looked down the road which he had travelled. A startled look showed in his eyes.

"There's somebody on the run after us!" he exclaimed.

I looked round. Something showed on the highway a quarter of mile to rear, something that might have been a human being, a man, but dressed as no man ever dressed to show himself on a public road.

"Who can it be at all?" I asked, and my voice was not the voice of a bold MacMonagle.

"Him!" said my father, a world of meaning in his voice and giving the poor donkey a kick. "Gee up, Neddy!"

Holding the reins, using his voice as an incentive, his toe as an urge, he raced the donkey along the road. Behind, two furlongs away a moment before, but not so far now, came the figure of vengeance, its transition in space that of a swallow, its movements shuttle sure.

"Like greased lightning!" grunted my father. "That means more toe for Neddy!"

The toe was administered. I ran.

Looking back over my shoulder, but still running, I could see that the pursuer, clothed meagrely in a red petticoat, was making headway. What could be seen in my hurried glance was a pair of legs, knee-naked, a spread of red cloth, a white arm beckoning, and a great furzy head. Staggering a little, like a cow running on a field of ice, he was breaking ground with the distance between himself and the cart appreciably lessening.

In a dim semi-conscious manner I was still aware that the peace of the world was yet over the land. Cows lowed, hens cackled, and dogs barked lazily. Calmly and sublimely the hills rise in the air, aloof, apart, austere, their age-old calm unsubdued. Of man and his little doings they knew nothing, cared nothing. Absolutely indifferent, they looked down the dip of the coombe where beneath their hush raced a donkey and cart, a tinker and his son, followed by a mighty-muscled man, mother-naked, save for a red petticoat.

"And wait till I get my hands on you," he roared when he came within ear-distance.

But my father showed no desire to wait. With the free ends of the reins he lashed the buttocks of the donkey and, leaning a little off the perpendicular, swung a foot round and hit the beast on the belly. The animal, passive and obedient up till then, seemed to resent this. Standing on its hind-legs, it shook with temper, then swerved to the left and tumbled into the roadway ditch. The cart followed the donkey, jerking the clothes which had been looted that morning into the hedgerow.

Fearfully I ran, losing ground and sweat, my heart going like a frightened sheep's. The naked terror followed, and I, the barefooted, slack-gutted rearguard of the MacMonagle clan, timed out a slow measure on the dusty roadway. Like a Hallowmass wind, the man in the red petticoat came closer, a hand seemed to press down on my shoulders, my spine gave way, and staggering sideways, I rolled into the roadside ditch.

Sure of its mission, the Terror whistled by, on to the cart like a hawk on a sparrow.

But could such a run be without its jump? No fear! He came to the scene of the calamity, hopped on the road-verge as if he were a rubber ball, bounded into air again, over the cart and swooped into the hedge, his red petticoat spreading over the white blooms like a great red blossom. With a quick movement he pulled on a coat, then crawled out of the spiked thorns, and bare-footed and undismayed he faced my father.

IV

" I'm Lanty Hanlon, G.H.," he said with an air of dignity. " What you are or who you are doesn't matter a damn ! I want satisfaction, and I'm ready to settle the business, anyhow or anywhere ! "

" What business ? " my father enquired lamely, looking at the man in the red petticoat. He seemed a little frightened, more with the novelty, perhaps, than the danger.

" Name your weapons ! " ordered Lanty Hanlon.

" Weapons ! "

" Knives ! " Lanty Hanlon suggested.

" Knives ! What knives ? "

" Pen-knives, if you like ! " said Lanty Hanlon with an air of exquisite disdain. " But let us get it over ! "

" We'll soon get it over," said my father, grabbing a stick from the roadside and assuming a warlike pose. " Clear out, or you'll get this shoved down your dirty gullet ! "

" So you want something to happen ? " asked Lanty Hanlon. His voice was low, his face benignant.

" More than anything in a petticoat will be able to give me," said my father, giving Hanlon a tip on the jaw with the stick.

Then something did happen. The man in

the red petticoat stroked a bleeding jaw with one hand while the other, shot out, came in contact with the stick, on which it closed. The stick was snapped in two like a spale thrust between the spokes of a moving express. Then, while their owner wore an air that was almost impersonal, two arms tightened round my father in an embrace which might have been of love if not so tight. He lost purchase of earth, went quietly upwards until he rested in air just at the point where the arms of the man in the red petticoat came to an end. These arms bent ditchward ever so slightly, and from a great height my father fell like a sack into the hedgerow.

Without strain or stress was the feat performed. On the roads of the world I never before or since saw anything like it. Having done this deed, worthy of a giant, the man stood straight as a rush, a god in a red petticoat. And he spoke.

"You have fallen into the pismires, MacMonagle," were his words. "Come out. I would speak to you."

My father stood upright in the ditch, and as the ditch was deep the tip of his head was merely flush with the road. Blood ran in wriggly lines down his face, from the tip of his nose, the lobes of his ears. Bruised and bleeding, he now tried to look as if it did not really matter when the cows came home. With one eye on Lanty Hanlon, he pulled himself out to the roadway.

"You'll do me a favour if you take off your trousers and give them to me!" said the one in the petticoat.

"I'm damned if I do," said my father, but as

he saw the fist of Hanlon close, he muttered: "All right! You can have them, ye devil's spawn!"

And there he sat down and took off his trousers, and the man with the red petticoat put on the trousers—the patched, fringed, tattered trousers which my father should have handed to his descendants long ago.

"And what am I to put on if I'm not to walk all day mother-naked on the roads of the world?" asked my father.

"The petticoat, for that is what becomes you," said Lanty Hanlon.

Having spoken, he went to the hedgerow and began picking his appointments from the flowering thorn. He put on a semmet, creasing down its sleeves and buttoning it with care and concern, a dickie streaked with dried mud, a gum collar and a made-up tie. Putting on his coat and waistcoat, he brought from the pocket of the former a pair of stick-on cuffs which he shoved under the sleeves of his coat.

On seeing him garbed in this high attire, my estimation of the man had fallen. The starched cuffs had detracted from his manliness. In these there was something weak, unseemly. Cuffs and collars had, to my thinking, shorn the man of all that was heroic, brave and manly.

V

Attired, Lanty Hanlon, G.H., bowed to my father, who was already in the petticoat, and strode away, master of all circumstance, with his jaw high in air. He came towards me, not because I was there, but because his road lay in my direction. Immediately I walked off, timing my pace to that of the man, my jaw on the lip of my shoulder so that I could see the road behind.

I led, Lanty Hanlon followed, and in this manner we did a full mile of the road, meeting nobody, for the thrifty rural folk were busy with their labours on hill and holm. On each side of the highway the bushes stood in a quiet calm, their leaves covered with a fine coating of dry dust. The soft odour of the green herbage pervaded the atmosphere and a languid quiet lay over the shady roadway. On the holms rested the fat cattle, in the bushes the birds twittered over their nesting, and from somewhere in the distance came the sound of a mountain brook that sang to its fall.

Another quarter of an hour passed. I was still as far from him as at the start, but I was getting rather weary. We might go on like that till the end of time. I decided to wait for the man. So I came to a stop, stood by the roadside, but alert and ready to hop into the fields on the least sign of danger. He came near, nearer, and head high amidst the drooping branches, passed by unseeing. I followed and passed him in turn, but he took no notice. I did not belong to the same world as Lanty Hanlon, G.H. Again I stood.

He advanced looking into great distances, as if he had the weight of the world on his soul. Saw me! No more than a barrow could see me!

He was passing, and lurched towards me, blindly as it seemed. But his blindness hid an eye that could see, there was method in his staggering, for as he passed his arm shot out, his hand came in contact with my shoulder, on which it closed. He drew me round with a great quiet strength, until I found myself fronting him.

"H'm!" he grunted. "What name have they given you?"

He spoke over my head, as if I were nothing more than the button on his shirt. My eyes were on the ground.

"What name have they given you, my boy?" he repeated, and I could feel his eyes on my head.

"Neddy," I said with a gulp.

"Do you know who made you and placed you in the world, Neddy?" he enquired.

"I don't know," I said. But what a funny question, I thought.

"And, Neddy, do you know the first letter of the alphabet?" was his next question.

"No, indeed, I don't."

"Were you ever at school?"

"No, indeed, I wasn't."

"Or at church?"

"Once I was in, and I saw an old man dressed like a woman, and him talking to himself, and then when he was quiet the others began talking, and wee boys with white shirts outside——"

"You Pagan!" said Lanty Hanlon and released his grip on my shoulders.

Immediately I took to my heels and ran. Getting to a safe distance, I stopped and looked back. Lanty Hanlon was standing where I had left him, his hands in his trousers pockets, his eye fixed on the road. He was deep in thought.

Suddenly he raised his head, looked for me, then at me, when he discovered my place.

" Neddy ! " he called.

" What ? "

" Come here ! "

His voice was friendly. I approached, came near, but not too near. My aching shoulders still bore testimony to his mighty grip.

" Nearer ! " he called.

" I'll not then," I made answer, ready to take to my heels again.

" As you like, Neddy," said the man. " Now stay where you are and answer my questions. What age are you ? "

" I don't know at all."

" What do you want to be when you are man big ? "

" Nothing," said I. Up till then I wanted merely to grow up and be as strong as my father, who to my thinking was the strongest man in the world. Apart from that I gave very little mind to the days to be. Now, however, on that day, I was shown that what had hitherto appeared to be true was not true. A man had come, stronger than my father, and that man was Lanty Hanlon, G.H.

" But you want to be a tinker, don't you," asked the man, looking at me, " with a donkey and cart going round the country, breaking people's heads with an ash-plant, getting tight and locked up, and thieving from the poor widow women of Ireland ? "

" I don't want to be like that at all, then," I said, though even at that early age I had attained a certain proficiency in the last-named misdemeanour.

" It's not to be allowed," said the man, closing his mouth until it was a string-purse with the string tightened. I stepped back in a hurry, for the look was not one that I liked. " It's not to be allowed. From now till the day I die or you die, you're to be my servant, my henchman ! Follow me ! "

As he said this he felt in his pocket and took therefrom something which my father had not time to find and keep. This he threw towards me and it dropped with a ring on the road at my feet. I bent and picked the thing up, a crown piece, as big and white as the bottom of a new tin mug.

Lanty Hanlon heaved towards me, his boots grating the dried road-grit. I jumped the ditch into an adjacent field, and being a MacMonagle, retained the crown piece in my hand.

He went by, his eyes on the roadway, his hands in his pockets, paying not the slightest attention to me. I was not in this world at all. After a while, however, he stopped and looked back.

" Follow me, Neddy ! " he called. " Follow me. There's a good meal and a future waiting you. Follow me ! "

And as in a trance, bare-headed and barefooted, I, a renegade MacMonagle, threw aside a future of tinkerdom, fighting men, quarrelling women and dirty children, roving, thieving and vagabondage, and followed Lanty Hanlon, G.H., down the rocky road to the barony of Ballykeeran, which to-day shows broad acres and strong house and housing all my own.

CHAPTER III

THE LETTER

Sweet as a letter over the deep water.
—*A Ballykeeran Saying.*

I

THE house of Oonah Ruddagh stood the spit of a bearded man away from the road, a thatched house and a poor house, the house of a widow whose children were out and away in the world.

"We are going in here for a drink," said Lanty Hanlon when we came opposite the dwelling. "Follow me!"

He went in, stooping a little, for the door was a small one and Lanty was a tall man. I came close on his heels, to find an old woman sitting on a hassock by the fire, her heels in the ashes, although the month was June. The woman was Oonah Ruddagh.

"Under God, the day and the night, is it Lanty Hanlon that I see?" The old woman rose to her feet and caught Hanlon's hand. "You've been away long, and are you cured?"

"I'm not cured, Oonah Ruddagh," was the answer of Lanty Hanlon, as he sat himself down.

"My own words," said the woman. "When

you went away from here, dressed in your high attire, to get cured of the drunkenness, I said, 'What God will not do for a drouth the House of Correction will not be able to do.' My own words, Lanty, and I'm never far wrong. Never!"

"Oonah, for God's sake hold your tongue," said Lanty Hanlon, and his voice was hard. "Your old tongue would drive more men to hell than all the whisky in the world!"

"But, Lanty, asthor, it breaks my heart to see what the drouth has done to you," said the woman. "Lands you had and houses you had, stock you had and store you had, and where has it all gone?"

"Into my belly," said Lanty Hanlon.

"Oh," sighed Oonah, with a down-droop of her lips, "into your belly, and the miracle is how can it hold it? And all the people hereabouts said when you went away three months ago in your high attire to get cured of the drouth in the House of Correction, 'He'll come back cured!' and this is how you come back"—she looked at the man's trousers—"rags and patches like a scarecrow at Christmas."

"Oonah, talk of something else, for the love of the saints!" roared Lanty Hanlon, rising to his feet. "Talk of your neighbours, of your cows, of the weather—of anything!"

"Well, it's the grand weather that's in it, anyway," said Oonah Ruddagh, giving voice to something that could not be discountenanced.

"It's all that," said Lanty, wiping the sweat from his forehead.

"And you'll be tired on it too, maybe?" queried the woman.

"Tired's not the word," said Lanty.

"And you as well?" the woman enquired, looking at me.

"No," I said.

"Not the weest bit?" she asked.

"A wee bit, maybe," I said diplomatically.

"Just like all young vagabones," said Oonah Ruddagh with a laugh. "All up to mischief and wearing out yer arms and legs in devilment. And hungry too, I bate."

"No," I said.

"He could ate a bull if I know anything about him," said my master. "He's a MacMonagle."

"One of them, indeed?" enquired the woman. She drew up her eyebrows until they sank beneath her hair and fixed a questioning look on me.

"But an honest boy for all that," said Lanty. "And a scholar. Metaphysics, trigonometry and algebraic equations."

"Does he know all that?" asked the woman.

"That and more," replied Lanty Hanlon. "Philosophy and geography——"

"And him so young!"

"Euclid as well."

"But it can't be good, too much learning like that," said Oonah Ruddagh. "There was one boy that I knew, as I should, for he was the only child of a half-sister of mine. And he knew that much, and him only twelve, that the schoolmaster couldn't stand up to him in an argyment. And that boy died of the decline, and him coming on thirteen. Four years back, it was, but with the larning that was in his head, what could you expect ? I said as much often and often. Now," she asked, looking at me, " have you a cough on you at all ? "

" No," I said.

" And do you ate too much or too little ? " she enquired. " One's as bad as the other, you know."

" He can ate till he bursts," said my master. " He's a MacMonagle, and now he's my servant ! "

" I know the MacMonagles, the divils that they are," said Oonah Ruddagh, " and the way that they had when they were round here the winter afore last, with two hens of my own took away one night, and me here in the house lyin' on the bed of sickness with the rain fallin' heavens hard and a downdrop from the roof on the floor. I put a curse on them and their divilment, and I trust from my heart that it fell on their heads. And you "—she put an angry eye on me—" and you were with them, I bet."

" Indeed and I wasn't," I lied. " This is the first time I ever was in this part of the world."

" It'd break my heart to think of you with them, and them up to all sorts of divilment, and you no more than the height of two turf," said the old woman with a sigh. " And yourself wasn't at the robbery of the poor at all ? "

" No," I lied.

" And the sickness that was on me at the time was that terrible," she continued, shivering as if a spasm of pain seized her.

"But you're well on it now, Oonah, good woman?" Lanty asked.

"Just middling," she said. "But it's the pains that I be having, and them up and down my legs and in my back."

"Just so," said my master, assuming a wise look, and, blending wisdom with compassion in his face, he stretched out his hand towards her.

"Your pulse!" he said solemnly.

She raised her hand, thin-veined and thin-skinned, and gave it into Lanty's keeping. He felt her pulse, his head to one side and his lips moving as if counting the beats.

"Yes," he said, with becoming gravity. "It is a bit quick, but it will pass, good woman, it will pass."

"That's what the doctor said. And the hard money that he took for saying that. And it didn't pass."

"Of course it didn't," said Lanty, with the air of one who understood. "A doctor's out to make money and that's all. And if the people had sense and took turnips and onions boiled and mixed together, with a nettle or two added, they'd be as well as jumping horses. This mixture is to be taken, one teaspoonful with water three times a day, and it was used by St. Patrick in the days long gone, and he cured a Queen in Tara of her ills, and though this woman (her days are long past)——"

"God rest her," said Oonah.

"And though she had been confined to her bed for long and many a day, she got up from her bed when St. Patrick gave her the mixture, and she went about the house leaping like a hare for the rest of her life."

"My a my!" said Oonah. "But I'm not as bad on it as all that."

"And this mixture, stamped and licensed, was sold from the Hanlon Travelling Pharmacopœia at two-and-six a bottle ten years ago. That was before I retired from that business," said Lanty Hanlon.

"Before you went to the dogs," said the old woman, with a wheezy sigh. "Before you went to the dogs for the third time. And the money you made at that job!"

"I can make money at any job," said my master, hiding his thumbs behind the sleeves of his waistcoat.

"But it's great sorrow that must be on you, Lanty, asthor, when you think of all the gold you've let slip through your hands."

"Lanty Hanlon, G.H., regrets nothing," said my master.

"Not even *her*, now, Lanty?" asked the old woman, pointing a lean finger at a smoke-grimed picture of a young girl which hung on the chimney-brace. At that time I thought the picture was very beautiful, but what should a boy of fourteen know about women? Oonah took the photograph down, dusted it with her checked apron, and held it up to my master.

"It doesn't do her justice," was all that he said, but from the look in the man's eyes I could tell that all his thoughts were in the spoken word.

"Well, Lanty, asthor," said the old woman,

again seating herself on the hassock, putting her hacked feet to the fire, blowing her nose into the corner of her apron, and taking a snuff-box from her bosom. "Lanty, asthor, will you put a letter on one of them for me?"

"That I will," said my master. "And what one of them will it be, now?"

"Her," said Oonah with a knowing nod.

"Maldy, or Norah, or Oonah?"

"It may be Norah, but it isn't, and if I said it was Oonah I would be tellin' a lie," said the old woman. At that moment I noticed that she had a very cunning eye, which from time to time was stealing a furtive look at me. I say an eye, although she had two, but her habit was to shut one when using its fellow. "And not bein' one or other of these two it must be the one that's left. And if ye don't know that, Lanty, I don't know who is to know, for were ye not as good as bespoke to her afore ye went to the dogs, God help ye."

"There's more than one way of going to the dogs, Oonah," said my master with an innocent smile. "And maybe it was the easiest way I took."

"Manin'?" asked Oonah, holding her snuff-box between her two dry-veined fingers, just as a cock on a dunghill holds an encumbrance on its claw before shaking it off.

"Nothing, Oonah, nothing at all." His voice was as innocent and free from guile as that of a child. "So if you give me pen, ink and paper, I'll write your letter."

"Not my letter," said Oonah, to whom, in all

seeming, certainty was a strong perquisite. " It'll be Maldy's letter, if ye'll be good enough to write it."

" Very well ! Get me what I've to write on, then ! "

From a hole in the chimney-brace Oonah produced a pen, so thickly encrusted with cobwebby soot that it looked as big as a cow-stake. With a few rubs of the woman's apron the cow-stake diminished in size until it became what it really was, a penholder fashioned from a hazel twig.

" And these are the nibs." Taking a little packet from her breast, she produced therefrom three nibs. " And the size they are ! "

" Well, what the devil d'you want ? " asked my master with amused tolerance. " Not shovels, surely ? "

" Well, say what ye will, Lanty," Oonah protested. " But do they look worth their cost ? Two eggs I gave away for them, these wee things ! "

" And ink ? " my master enquired, taking no heed of Oonah's say.

" Aye," said the old woman with a knowing nod. " Mick Flaherty didn't get me over the ink. 'How much will ye be asking for one o' them bottles, now ? ' I put to him, and him standin' behind the counter of his shop, lookin' over his big, high collar like a donkey over a white-washed wall. And I mind him well with his bottom out through a pair of second-hand britches. 'Three eggs, Oonah,' says he. 'Three eggs,' I says, and my face said what my tongue didn't, and out from the shop I walked like this!"

She walked towards the window (one pane whole, three squares of cloth where the other panes should have been), her chin high, infinite disdain in the eye that was open.

"Just like that," she said, coming back and standing in front of my master.

"So you have no ink," he enquired.

"Haven't I, indeed?" Oonah retorted. "The ink that the girls used many a time, made of black soot and spring water."

"Home industry," said my master, laughing down his throat. "Well, get it for me!"

From the corner of the room the old woman brought a pint bottle filled with a muddy liquid that might have been lifted from a bog-hole and placed it on the table in front of Lanty Hanlon.

"And this the paper," she said, bringing him a musty tea-wrapper from the bole in the chimney-brace. The paper, once white, now, after long confinement in the dry recess, was yellow and crinkled, so that at the present moment it had shade and texture similar to that of the woman's skin.

II

"Now ye can begin," she spoke as Lanty creased the paper to some sort of orderliness under the leaf of his hand. "Like this: 'Dear Maldy, I am sendin' ye these few lines hoping they will find you in good health, my dear Maldy, as they

—no—as this leaves me at present.' Have you that down ? "

" —Me—at—present. Aye, Oonah, it's down."

" I had three weeks that I thought I was goin' to die," Oonah soliloquised. " But don't speak anything about that, Lanty. It's neither here nor there, for all that I had the Holy Oil put over me by Father Dan. But I'm an old woman, surely, and the old must go if it's only to make room for them that's growing up."

" As this leaves me at present," said my master, looking at his pen while he waited for the old woman's mind to settle on the matter in hand.

" The pratees were put in early, tell her," Oonah continued. " Seed from the last year's crop and that a good one, maybe two tons and maybe more—say more, Lanty—four tons if a pratee ! Have ye that down ? And good feeding for the Winter and fine seedin' for the Spring. Bad cess to the frost that struck them down. But not a word about that, Lanty, asthor, but go on and tell how God, that keeps His eye on the widow, has given me a fine head of corn on the brae, and the two cows, Branny and Sprikkle, gave milk the best in the barony. Don't say that they're givin' milk now, for that wouldn't be altogether the truth, since poor old Branny died. But don't let on about that, Lanty ! "

" I'll be as close as the grave," said my master.

" I'll give ye credit for that, and you are not in the drink, Lanty," said Oonah, her voice taking a melancholy turn. " It's hundred pities the way ye've gone astray ! "

" The—best—in—the—barony," said Lanty,

as if he had not heard the latter remarks of the woman. "Now, will we tell her about the planting of the potatoes ?"

"Aye, Lanty, and the neighbours that came and helped—Eamon Larrimore, Paddy Cosdhu, Murtagh Neddy, Owen Gahey, Manus Glynn—and they worked as hard as if they were on their own land. And mind, put down the ones as well, them that wouldn't help the widow woman"—she pursed her lips in righteous indignation—"Dennis Freely, Barney Daly, and Kevin Roe. And these ones"—Oonah's lips slackened a trifle—"tell her that God won't be hard on her even if she forgets them in her prayers. That's what ye can tell her, Lanty," the old woman wandered on, a quiet smile of bliss showing on her face as she thought of her effective revenge.

"Them—in—her—prayers," said my master, his pen poised.

"Tell her that I pray for her every night, and my sleep is troubled with thinking of her as well as the others. That's all the news at present, your loving mother."

"But that's no letter," said my master, looking at the old woman. "You haven't told her anything. A girl away in America doesn't want to know about crops and cows, but about the ones getting married, the ones that may be married, and the ones that are married, and——"

He struck his fist on the table, a fist as heavy as a hatchet. The bottle of soot and water danced a hornpipe and Oonah uttered a shriek as if the fist had stricken her shoulders.

"But what would I be tellin' them things like

that for ? " asked Oonah, recovering, and giving a shrug of disapproval. "The marriages that are in it nowadays, what are they ? Nothin'. Paddy Cosdhu, that can carry his holdin' under his finger-nails, to Eileen Doherty, that looks as if she'd been all her life on sunburnt pratees ; and Norah Friel—Slanty-bottom we used to call her father ; God rest him for all that—to Micky Shemus, that cannot do a decent day's work in any field. It would be a waste of good paper to speak about them ! "

" Well, tell lies about them and make the girl laugh," my master advised. " She'll want a laugh after steamin' away her soul and body all day down in some filthy cellar, cooking belly-fodder for big-gutted pigs who don't care a damn whether the girl lives or dies. Tell her lies, tell her anything. Say Peggy Roe gave birth to twins——"

" Peggy Roe, and her past sixty and not married on a man ! "

" Well, that's the reason you should tell it ! " Lanty declaimed, getting to his feet. " That lie would keep her laughing for a week. And it would do no harm to Peggy. Tell her that Micky Wor kicked the roof-beam in a dance——"

" God between us an' harm, and him bed-rid for close on seven years ! "

" And that Paddy Cosdhu murdered his wife——"

" It's what he might do, for to have *her* lookin' in his face every mornin' when he wakes up ! "

" Well, whatever you like, Oonah," said my master, sitting down again, his sudden fit of fury spent. "Whatever you like, but get me a drink of water and an envelope. Don't mind the envelope . . . just a drink of water first!"

"A wee drop of milk!—it's better," said Oonah. "The milk that the Grey Cow gives. Milk indeed! It's all crame. And so thick that a sheep could walk on it. I saw many a one that had good milkin' cows, but the like of the Grey Cow!——"

"For God's sake give me a drink of water, Oonah!" yelled Lanty. "To refuse a sup of water to one that has the drouth!"

"It's because it's only water you want that ye're refused it," said Oonah. "Ask for milk!" She looked at the lowering face of Lanty. "Well, if it's only water that ye want, ye can have it!"

She went towards the dresser, filled a bowl with water and brought it to my master. He gripped it and drank with mighty gulps.

"Ah'm!" he grunted. "Water! what is to come up to it!"

"I suppose it will be the belly burnt out of ye with the drink," said Oonah, sorrowfully, as she sat down. "I knew a man, a great drouth, and one day his wife saw smoke comin' from his mouth——"

"Get me the envelope, Oonah," said Lanty. His tone was asperse; the old woman tried his patience. Probably he would flare up in a moment, and Oonah seemed to sense as much, for she went to a teapot on the dresser, brought therefrom an envelope and silently handed it to him.

"Miss Maldy Ruddagh," dictated the old woman. "'Miss,' mind ye, Lanty, for she's a girl that wants her own by rights. 70 Eighth Avenue, Germanstown, Philamadelfia, Ussa."

"Ussa! Ussa!" blurted my master. "That's the devil's Ussa? Ah! U.S.A. That's right, Oonah!"

Finished writing, he got to his feet, put his right hand in air, cracked his thumb against his middle finger with a report like a whip, and went towards the door.

"This way, MacMonagle!" he said, looking back at me. In his voice was the dignity of a lord. I followed him.

III

We went out on the road again, Lanty with great assurance, though I stole furtive glances behind me along the road to see if my father were coming in sight. But there was nothing to be seen. All the countryside was asleep, and in the distance. I could see the fires of the peat-makers sending their lazy wreaths of smoke up into the sky. A few hens were rolling in the dust of the roadway. The air was filled with the scent of heather and roses.

"MacMonagle," said Lanty Hanlon, coming to a sudden halt and gripping me by the shoulder, "what was the most wonderful thing you saw this day?"

"What you were doing with the pen," I made answer. "Were you putting what the old woman told you, down on the paper?"

"That's what I was doing, Neddy," said my master.

"But I saw you doing nothing, only making black marks and wriggly things like thin worms."

"In deepest ignorance!" commented Lanty Hanlon, his grip tightening. He shoved me round in front of him and looked in my face. "Neddy, you've got to go to school and become a gentleman if"—he paused—"if a tinker's brat can ever become a gentleman."

"Lanty Hanlon, asthor, Lanty Hanlon!"

We looked behind to see Oonah racing down the road after us. She carried something in her apron, that wonderful apron which served purpose as duster, handkerchief and basket.

"Lanty, asthor, Lanty!"

"What is it, Oonah?" asked my master.

"It's that medicine that you were speakin' about," called Oonah, still running, although she was well within earshot. "Turnips ye said, and onions ye said, and nettles." She was beside us now. "How many nettles, Lanty?"

"Nettles!" mumbled Lanty, who apparently had forgotten all about the matter.

"Aye, Lanty. How many for the medicine?"

I could see that she carried a few turnips in her apron.

"Aye, Oonah," said Lanty. "About—about as many as you can stand!"

"If they are as sore on a person's inside as on the outside, I'll not be able to stand many," she piped. "And Lanty, asthor, Lanty!"

"What is it, Oonah?"

"Once at the cross-roads, and you in your

carriage, you told us that you were going to make everybody rich, everybody in the parish," said the woman. "Now, when is that coming at all?"

"One day it will come, Oonah Ruddagh," said the man. "Mind my words. One day it will come."

He assumed a grand posture; hid one hand in the priest's coat and raised the other in the air. How he thrilled me at that moment! Lanty Hanlon, Guild's Honoursman, he stood there, master of his fate, although the tail of his shirt stuck out from trousers that were not his own.

"And the day will come, Oonah Ruddagh, the day will come!"

CHAPTER IV

MEENAROO

Three things strong, and a house is blest:
The table, the fire and the hand to a guest.
—*A Ballykeeran Proverb.*

I

THOUGH great in himself, as everyone who knew him must admit, Lanty Hanlon, G.H., was of mean habitation in those days. His house (I use it as a byre for my stock this day) was a poor place, a man's stretch from earth to eaves, containing one window, one fireplace, one table, two chairs, and two rooms.

The door was too small for Lanty, who always stooped when he entered the cabin, and this stoop had become such a habit to the man that in time he bent down even when going under a railway arch.

To the left of the house, lipping the gable-end, was a midden, part of it covered with rich green grass which showed that it had not been disturbed for many a day. On the further mear of the midden was a building, a byre by the look of it, its roof sagging in where it had thatch, but bare for the most part, its rafters naked to the sky. Nothing moved about the place when we came there, all was dead, and damp as the bottom of a bog. The name of his house was Meenaroo.

We went in, and were met in the mouth by a damp breath and the stench of rotting wood, soft clay and mildewed thatch. My very clothes seemed to suck the moisture from the room. The window was boarded in front and the narrow streak of light that came through the door showed the clammy clay floor, covered by many shiny, glittering streaks made by snails. Outside the flies buzzed against the window and door, but none entered. Outside, was Summer; inside, the grave.

"Neddy, it doesn't look up to much!" said Lanty Hanlon, going to the window and pulling the boarding down with mighty hands. With every board removed a fresh volume of light came into the room. "It doesn't look up to much, but when we have a fire and the beds up it won't be so bad. Ah! it is good to be back again!"

He drew a chair towards him, sat down and explored the breast pocket of his coat. From it he brought a little statuette of the Virgin Mother. Holding it on the leaf of his hand, he surveyed it a moment, his eyes filled with reverence. Putting the statuette to his lips, he kissed it.

"You know what this is?" he asked me.

"The Holy Mother," was my answer.

"She who bore without sin," said my master. "That is man's highest thought concerning woman. It is true because millions have believed it, and holy because it is a belief that has never done harm. This has been my talisman in stress, my safeguard in rack and ruin. Without it, I would be lost!"

Having said this he kissed the statuette again, placed it on the window-sill, and perching himself on his chair he felt with his hands behind the beam that carried the roof and brought out a little tin box. Opening it, he took forth a handful of money, which he shoved in his trousers pocket. The pocket being opened at bottom, the money dropped to the floor.

"The MacMonagle men may be good fighters, but their women are bad housewives!"

As he said this he gathered up the money, and handed a number of coins to me without counting them.

"Neddy, I am going to trust you," he said. "Go out and ask Paddy Cosdhu to send me a creel of turf and two bags of chaff. Go into the town, buy yourself a suit and a collar from Mick Flaherty. Tell him to send a ready-made suit to me. He knows my measure. Also bring two pounds of bacon, a loaf, a dozen eggs, a pound of tea, two pounds of sugar. Go!"

"But where does Paddy Cosdhu live?" I asked my master.

"What do you want to know?"

"Where does Paddy Cosdhu live?" I repeated.

"If you are going to be my servant, Neddy MacMonagle, you are never to ask idle questions," he said, speaking slowly and letting every word sink into my brain. "If you are told to find Paddy Cosdhu, you've got to find him. Away!"

I went out, found Paddy Cosdhu, who lived not more than a hundred yards away, delivered my message, went to the town, got myself a suit and provisions as ordered. Never was such a suit seen! If I only had boots to go with it! How soon pride creeps into the heart, even the heart of a tinker's brat.

Back at nightfall, Lanty Hanlon, G.H., gave me instructions in cooking. He was not above doing small things, a sign of the truly great.

"A good cook comes from God," he said as we sat to our steaming repast. "Green things are an abomination. The race was cursed through a green apple. Even bad food is good if well cooked. A red herring gets flavour from a snug fire, potatoes laugh when browned in a pot oven. And eggs, eggs"—he was at his fourth, I at my third and nearly choking—"they are the foundations of a race, even a race of roving tinkers!"

It was grand to see him with flushed cheeks and eager eyes, his jaws moving as he spoke and ate at the same time.

"To-morrow," he said, when he had finished and was using his tongue for a tooth-pick, "to-morrow you will go to school, and I will set about getting the place into order." He spread out his hands and the gesture was eloquent. Five acres his holding, but the out-throw of his arms hinted of square leagues, the whole barony. "To-morrow I will get a horse, a bee-hive, hens—dozens—and stock, cattle. Honey and milk and eggs, what is better?"

"Whisky!" I said. "My father says that there is nothing like it."

"Neddy MacMonagle, your father is a fool," said Lanty Hanlon, G.H. "A fool unhung, a fool and a half!"

He got to his feet. So did I, placing myself near the door so that I could scoot through at the least sign of danger. Blows were my everyday up till then, blows without stint or sparing, blows from my father, drunken or sober, blows from the fist, the boot or the stick. I had not reached my years of retaliation; evasion was my perquisite.

"Sit down, Neddy," said Lanty Hanlon. There was something commanding in his voice. I sat down.

"You are entering on a new life, and you go to school to-morrow," he said. "I want to speak a few words of instruction to you which you are to bear in mind ever and always!

II

"A fool can speak wisdom, though he may never practise it," he began. "Call me a fool, if it's your fancy, but listen to what I say. I have had money, crocks of it, and it is all gone. I put it into a whisky bottle and stored it in my belly, where it left nothing but heartburn and a sore head. So take precept from my life, Neddy, and what you see wrong in me, mend it in yourself.

"Never drink beyond thirst, nor eat beyond hunger, and always leave a decency bit on the skimpiest plate to show that you have a mannerly belly.

" Look above your station for counsel and beneath it for solace, and don't envy those above or scorn those below, but be tolerant to both.

" Choose the good man as friend, but don't make the bad man your enemy.

" See not the faults of the wicked or you may forget your own, and the man who forgets his faults is ten times worse than the man who hides them.

" I may be severe to you in private, Neddy, though you are a MacMonagle and of a breed that never took advice, but I'll commend you in public, if you're worthy of it.

" Make good men your friends, Neddy, and they'll be few.

" A good man is better than a wide estate, and wide estates are few and far between. Don't judge him by his substance but by his deed, and if you find his deeds worthy, never stand on his colour or name.

" Three things will stand for ever: the kind purpose, the kind word and the kind act; and a man's life is not counted great for the foes, but the friends, he makes.

" When you are in company keep your eyes and ears open, but hold your tongue.

" Though quarrels are better than solitude, don't quarrel; but if you quarrel, hold your own, for the dog with its tail between its legs is chased over the mearings of the parish.

" Have a bold face in a row and it is as good as a closed fist.

" Help the poor with caution, but don't forget that the hungry beggar often throws his crust in the ditch.

" See the end of a job before you begin, for the man who drives a nail in the dark has often bleeding fingers.

" When you are at school, agree with your master, whatever he says. Even if he says a cow has five legs, agree with him, for he has a stick in his hand and there are only two buttons between that stick and your naked bottom.

" Never gab, Neddy," Lanty went on, warming to his subject. " If you have a secret, keep it. Speak it to a friend at night and seven town lands will know it in the morning. And, Neddy ? "

" What ? " I asked, for I saw that he waited for an answer.

" Did you ever see a man in a red petticoat ? Don't answer for a minute ! " he almost shrieked at me as I was about to reply. " A man, a good strong man, who was not slow in showing himself to be a man when it was necessary. Now I want you to answer that question, thinking what a shame it would be for a man to wear such a damned thing as a red petticoat round his legs. Now, Neddy MacMonagle, did you ever see a man in a red petticoat ? "

" Indeed and I didn't," was my answer.

Lanty Hanlon looked pleased.

" Now we understand one another," were his words. " But bear in mind, if ever you say that you've seen a man in a red petticoat, I'll hold you on my knee, wrong side up, and linge you to within an inch of the grave. Now, off to bed with you ! "

III

So to bed, the first bed under a roof in my life. How far from the ground the bed seemed, how soft, and oh! how uncomfortable. All air was shut out, the roof settled on my head. I could not breathe. To shuffle about, to arrange myself amidst gnarled roots and knobbly stones, was now quite unnecessary. The bag filled with chaff was soft, easy to the skin, the blankets were too warm. The sweat streamed from my body, ran down my forehead, into my eyes. What was to be done?

I sat up, took off my coat and trousers, put them under my pillow so that nobody would run away with them when I slept.

Prior to this I had always worn my trousers and coat at night. Now, although I wrapped the blankets round me, I felt utterly naked. Suppose my father came and pulled me out, what would happen? Where was I? Was it a dream? If I had only a stone against my body I would have felt more at ease.

I fell asleep, but only for a moment. I awoke in terror. The room was entirely dark; the roof closed over my face, suffocating me. From the adjoining room came a queer noise, half whistle and half hiccough. I sat up and looked into the darkness. I stretched out my hand into space, put it downwards and encountered nothing. Down still, and my fingers rested on something damp and slimy—the floor.

A great terror laid hold of me. Rising, I went to the door, tried to open it, but could not. I was locked in. I might as well be naked for all that I wore, a shirt, or the mere remains of one.

Going back, I clothed myself in my new suit and again tried the door. Its surface was blank as a newly-planed table.

Not altogether as blank! On one side was a thong. This I pulled and the door opened. I went into the next room. From the bed in the corner came the sound half hiccough and half whistle, Lanty Hanlon, G.H., deep in his snoring.

I opened the outer door and went into the world. The air was soft and fresh, the land filled with the scent of heather and wild roses. A moon, a silver bill-hook without its handle, showed over the hills. The garment of green which the dung-heap wore was covered with sparkling dew-drops and looked like a beaded dress at carnival. I lay down on the midden, curled my feet till their heels rested on my hams, placed my hands in the shelter of my coat, and fell asleep.

CHAPTER V

NORAH HANNIGAN

A man without learning, wearing good clothes,
Is like a gold ring in a pig's nose.

—*An Old Song.*

I

IT might even be in keeping with the story which I tell to say a little of my days at school, very little, if I can help it. But it is hard to be sparing in words when I talk of those days, for surely an old man needs a bit in his mouth when he runs to the pastures of his youth.

Lanty Hanlon took me to the school the next morning, resolved that my entry into the abode of learning should not be without the formalities which he deemed the occasion required.

"Before me!" he ordered when we came to the door of the school.

What a crowd of tousled heads, cunning eyes and dirty faces! I stood at the door, afraid to go any farther. I could hear a great buzz of voices before I went in; now, when inside, all was still, and a midge could be heard winging in air, a pin dropping in milk.

"What do you want?" asked a man who sat by a desk in the corner.

My eyes rested on the speaker. He was the master, a man of ungainly build, bald as a basin.

Lanty Hanlon came to my rescue. He was afraid of nothing.

"Good morning to you, Master Malley," he said.

"Good morning, Mr. Hanlon," replied Master Malley. "I didn't expect to see *you* back again!"

The master spoke as if he were vexed, as was really the case when he found himself in company of a man cleverer than himself. For had not Lanty Hanlon once pulled Master Malley up on the declension of a noun, twice on a problem in compound interest, and thrice on a political question, and proved that the master was wrong. But that was before my time and in the house of Oonah Ruddagh when she was waking her dead man, God be his comforting!

"Back again, like the broken-winded horse," said Lanty Hanlon. "But I've brought you a scholar, master; Neddy MacMonagle, who wants to be a gentleman."

The master looked me up and down in front, then, getting to his feet, he came towards me and looked me up and down behind. His belly was big and, moving, he gave one the impression of a duck running to a meal.

"MacMonagle," he enquired. "One of the MacMonagles?"

"One of them," said Lanty Hanlon.

"Never been at school before?" the master asked me.

"Never," I said.

"Then you are starting late to become a

gentleman! Eh? Well, you can stay here, and I'll see what I can do with you!"

As he spoke he lifted a knife from the table and handed it to me.

"Go out and cut a nice green ash-plant in the wood, a plant with a swing in it, mind you, a supple one, and don't let the grass grow under your feet till you come back. Now, hook it!" said the master.

"I'll show him where he can get the best," said Lanty Hanlon, and accompanied me outside. The wood stood near the school, a wood of holly and hazel, ash and rowan. The birds were nesting. Lanty Hanlon came to a halt in a shady place and looked me up and down.

"The rod is necessary for a boy's education," he said to me. "In school it is applied for many reasons. You'll get it if you are stupid and you'll get it if you're clever, so you must strike a happy mean. It is applied to many places, so be careful that you don't wear out the seat of your trousers. From a boy's point of view a short rod is better than a long one. Never pull your hand away from the rod, for the farther it travels the harder it hits. Now, cut your rod and off to school again."

Back at school again I felt very ill at ease, and no wonder! I was the biggest in the place and there was not one word of learning in my head. The alphabet and its twenty-six letters! I had never heard of them. Could I spell cat? Spell! What was that?

"Norah Hannigan, come here and teach this Man his alphabet!"

Shy little Norah Hannigan took me in hand. How my heart leapt when I saw her, for she was the girl whom I met on the road two days before, Norah Hannigan, in her tweed frock with her brown hair falling in soft ringlets on her shoulders, sweet as a wild bog-blossom. How pleased I was to be attired in my new suit! If I had a pair of boots!

"You don't know the alphabet?" she asked in her sweet voice, and I shook my head.

Then she began the A B C, which I repeated after her, and because it was so novel and my memory so tenacious, I knew the whole alphabet by heart at the end of an hour. How proud I was! Soon I would be the best scholar in the school!

But what a fall had my pride when the hour of religious instruction arrived. We were ranged in a class round the Master. I stood at the bottom of the class, so tall that even those farthest off had to look up at me.

"Who created you and placed you in this world?"

The question was put to me. Created? What did that mean? Immediately every hand in the class went up, and thinking that this was part of the game my hand went up as well.

"Who?" the master repeated. "Put down your hand!"

All the eyes in the place were on me. Norah Hannigan was watching. I was quite easily seen! Why was I such a big lout?

"Your size, and you don't know who made you!" exclaimed the master. "Do you know your prayers?"

"No."

Oh! how I hated the master, the school, the scholars, Lanty Hanlon, everything. That was why he had bought the suit and sent me here. Just to make a fool of me!

"Stay where you are," said the master, seeing that my eyes turned to the door. "Listen to the answers that the others give and try and learn. There is nothing like learning, my boy. Nothing. Listen to this!"

He brought a tablet from the wall, held it in his hand and looked at me. Something was printed on the tablet, and this he read:

> Labour for learning before you grow old,
> For learning is better than silver or gold—
> Silver and gold they will vanish away,
> But Learning, proud Learning will never decay—
> And a man without learning, wearing good clothes,
> Is like a gold ring in a pig's nose.

"And you have good clothes on you," he said, and this being a very sly dig at me, made me feel very uncomfortable.

For three days afterwards I stood in the class and merely by dint of hearing others repeat I came to know the answers to a number of elementary questions. On other matters I made great headway. In a fortnight I could decipher the names of people over the doors of the shops in the village. I forgot nothing that I was taught. Even the master marvelled at my memory.

In addition to being gifted in this way I had the desire to get on. When I came away from school in the evening I carried my lesson books and conned to myself all that was taught me earlier in the day. Instead of forgetting, as most youngsters did, I kept all in my mind, and there it stuck fast like ink on a white tablecloth.

The weeks flew by and all the time I kept studying, putting something in my head that a comb wouldn't take out.

"Have you found out yet how stupid you are?" Lanty Hanlon would ask me many a time, and this question always troubled me, especially in view of the fact that I was making such progress. Stupid, indeed! I knew the whole Catechism from beginning to end, and simple addition, subtraction and division were no problems for me.

Now, however, when I come to think of it, and me an old man of eighty, neighbourly to all, I see that there was more than a grain of sense in the question. For what does anybody know, even the most learned? Why does the rain fall? the day come and go? the tree blossom and bear? Why is there a season of seed-time and harvest?

Why do men come and go, passing like a wind on the hill? Why does God in His great mercy watch over the unworthy? Surely the foothold of wisdom rests on knowing how little we really know.

II

Meanwhile Lanty Hanlon procured a swarm of honey-bees, housing it in a straw skep which he placed in front of his door, the door of Meenaroo. In this swarm he took great interest. For hours on a sunny morning he would lie on his belly by the skep, watching the bees come out.

"Good luck to you," he would cry when the workers flew away on their daily search. "Go to the heather. Honey from the heather is the sweetest!"

One sunny evening when he and I were a mile away from our home he heard a bee drone by.

"One of mine!" he exclaimed, and a smile showed on his face. "Burdened like a stallion. Good luck to you and a safe journey home," he called as the little worker disappeared amidst the branches of a neighbouring rowan.

He treated his hive as if its occupants were human beings. Perhaps it was in the personal interest which he took in his occupation that his business success lay. If the curse, his curse and the curse of many others, had not been so heavy on him, what a fist he would have made of his life. The personal interest. In that lay his secret.

But man does not live by bee-keeping alone, especially when his stock consists of one solitary hive. Money was running short, the tinker brat whom he had adopted needed food, drink and books, and he himself with his great appetite, the appetite of a giant, needed food as few other men need it. Something had to be done.

"The time is not ripe yet for the great change which is fated to come to Ballykeeran," he said to me one day. "I have given my promise, and my word is bond."

"What promise?" I asked in my idle and curious way.

"The promise I gave to the good people,"

was his reply. " But the hour is not yet. Meanwhile a cart, Neddy, a cart and horse."

Two days later the summer fair of Ballykeeran! To it hied Lanty Hanlon, the purchase of a horse his object.

Amidst the stock in the market-place, the Kerry cows, brindled mountainy heifers, shorthorn bullocks, drifts of sheep, Shetland ponies and donkeys, was to be seen a horse, a raw-ribbed animal, angleberried and spavined, doing its paces, the walk, the amble, the rack, the trot, the canter and the gallop. A horse for sale, the salesman Kevin Roe, a returned Yankee who had just opened a butcher's shop (the first) in Ballykeeran.

" How much ? " asked Lanty Hanlon.

" Whoa-p ! "

Streaming with sweat, Kevin Roe stopped the animal in its mad career and put eyes on Lanty Hanlon.

" Six pounds ten ! "

" Five pounds ! "

" Six pounds ten and cheap at the price ! "

" Did you hear me say five pounds. Yes ! Well, five pounds it is or nothing ! "

These were the words of Lanty Hanlon, a strong man. His look was straight. His thumbs were hidden in the sleeves of his waistcoat. He had spoken and would stand on his word.

The horse became his, and barebacked he rode it home. Reins ! What did he want with them ? Reins were common ! Everybody used them ! Bravely he rode the highway, now and again pressing the animal beneath an angleberry and above the kidney just for the pleasure of seeing the steed arch its neck and flash fire from its eye. Lanty Hanlon knew the point of pressure. He knew horseflesh.

But unfortunately the animal did not arch its neck and flash fire from its eye. Instead its head sank to the road as if it were scenting the gritty highway for a wisp of hay.

"It's not such a bad horse," said Paddy Cosdhu, who met the rider. "Not so bad if it hadn't them damned angleberries."

"Angleberries are a sign of high breeding," said Lanty Hanlon.

Nearer home Lanty became conscious of a slight disturbance in the animal's respiratory organs. The rider leant his head on the animal's mane and listened. Not much to be heard; just a slight cough, nothing more!

He urged the steed to a canter and it creaked forward like a wooden goose. The breathing became laboured, the nostrils dilated, the eyes became bloodshot and blue in colour—blue as a duck's egg. The out-breath was performed in double action; one jerk from the lungs up, another jerk from the throat out.

"Broken-winded, Garibaldi, broken-winded," was Lanty Hanlon's remark, and his generous heart went out in pity to the poor dumb beast.

On Garibaldi he turned the corner where the Ballykeeran road curves to the National School, and there he encountered Norah Hannigan and me. We had just left the school and as the spot was shady we paused for a little to speak to one another before we went to our homes. Under the trees the bluebells were in blossom. I pulled a little bunch and handed it to Norah.

"What is this for ?" she asked.

"For you to wear," I said.

"And isn't it the silly boy that you are !" were her words, and a great blush came on her cheeks. But she took the bluebells. At that moment we saw Lanty Hanlon on his steed, Garibaldi.

"Ah, this is something that you do not learn at school," he said, with a funny turn of his eye. "Too young to begin, Neddy MacMonagle, too young. And you, Norah Hannigan, home with you and help your mother at the washing !"

That evening, when Garibaldi was stabled and supper was eaten, Lanty Hanlon asked me to take a chair, "Because," he said, "I have something to say to you, which, being a MacMonagle, may do you no good, but it will certainly do you no harm."

I sat down.

"You have started too soon, Neddy MacMonagle," said he, and there was sorrow in his voice. "If you forget your lessons for love when you're bare-footed, you'll be a gadabout in shoe-leather. I have sent you to school so that you may, when the hour is ripe, be able to take your post as my trustworthy henchman. Now I see what may be the first step in your undoing. Women are to be kept at a distance, Neddy.

"They'll steal your heart first, then your money.

"Like bird-catchers they lay their snares and geese are caught every day.

" When you see them in their outward show and brave attire, think how they would look bare-footed in a quilted petticoat.

" The man who takes a woman before thirty is a fool, before forty is an ass. The graveyard side of forty is a fitting season, because no man lives for ever.

" Her mother is a hard worker. The daughter of an active woman is a bad housekeeper.

" When her face is her portion it's a poor look-out for the man.

" Wrinkles and hard work are fellows in misery.

" Look for her warranty at the washing-tub, not on the dancing-floor.

" Women take up their education where a man leaves off.

" Neddy, you're a fool."

Having spoken, he rose and stretched himself, looked round the room, and fixed his eyes on the teapot.

" Put the kettle on and make a bowl of tea," was his order.

As he drank his tea with a great noise and made headway with his heavy chunks of buttered bread, he spoke of his horse.

" Garibaldi its name," he said. " I bought it from Kevin Roe, and the price five pounds. Broken wind is his ailment and Kevin Roe made it swallow shot before he showed off its paces in the market. Shot in the stomach hides the symptoms. Kevin Roe is a crook ! I shall be even with the man yet. Now, Neddy, off to bed with you ! "

III

Next morning I was up early, pulled from my bed by Lanty Hanlon. An angry look showed in his eyes.

"Run down to Oonah Ruddagh and tell her that I want her up here at once," he ordered me. "At once. Off with you!"

Ten minutes later I returned with the old woman. What was wrong? When Lanty Hanlon had set his teeth in business he was a changed man.

"Good morning, Oonah!" This was a growl. "How's the health?" This was a snarl.

"I have a word to say to you, Oonah." He was now getting to business. "When I went away from here, the time before last, I left a cart in the corner of the byre——"

"A cart, Lanty?" Oonah stammered.

"A cart, Oonah Ruddagh, an ordinary cart with two wheels, two shafts, a splatter-board, a tail-board and two wings——"

"Two wings?"

"Two wings," said Lanty Hanlon. He was very explicit. "Two wings, and these are used when the cart is loaded with hay or straw——"

"Straw?" asked Oonah. She was very uncomfortable.

"Ordinary straw," Lanty explained. "When a corn-sheaf is thrashed, that which is left is straw."

"That's true, Lanty," Oonah made haste to say. "And it's the great boy for the truth you were, even when you weren't the height of two turf. And many's the time it was myself that said——"

"Now, Oonah, I don't want to hear what you said then, but *I* want to say this now! To yourself of course and don't let it go any further," said Lanty. "I left the cart in the byre when I went away, and since coming back I have not gone in to see whether it was still there or not. Now I have got a horse and I want the cart, and the cart is gone."

"Maybe it was the rain falling in through the roof that rotted the cart," said Oonah. "The rain that fell in the last six months would rot anything. I mind once thirty years back it was——"

"Listen, Oonah," said Lanty. "I want that cart. And if it doesn't come back here to Meenaroo this night, I will arise to-morrow morning, go round the whole parish and look for it, and if I get it, God help the one that has it; and if I don't get it, I'll ask Father Dan to put a curse on the thieves that took it."

"I have told Oonah Ruddagh not to speak a word about this," said Lanty Hanlon to me when the old woman had taken her departure. "Now seeing that she is a woman, the whole parish will know all that I've said in an hour's time."

At the shut of day, when the sun set and the full moon heaved high over the fields, I sat by the door watching the lamps being lighted through the parish. The corncrakes were loud in the meadows. Lanty Hanlon came to the door.

"Neal Hannigan's people haven't lit their lamp yet," he said.

"Haven't they?" I asked. Why should I know when their lamp was lit. My lessons fully occupied my hours. Had I time for anything else indeed!

"There!" exclaimed Lanty Hanlon. "The light's on! It's out again! '*Up the light, down the light! Once, and she hates you!*' There! it's lit again and it's out! '*Up the light, down the light! Poorly she rates you!*' Again, Neddy! Up and down! '*Up the light, down the light! Three. Who's above you?*' There it is again. Up and down, Neddy, you rascal! '*Up the light, down the light! Four. She does love you!*'"

He came close to me and, squeezing my arm, looked in my face.

"Who is playing tricks with the lamp?" he asked.

"Norah Hannigan," I said. Only that day Norah and I had decided to pass messages of love. And he knew! What a man!

"I've done it myself, Neddy. I've done it myself!" he remarked. A far-away look came into his eyes as he spoke, telling me that ancient memories thronged his mind. "But now you've got something else to do. The cart is coming back to-night, and I want you to watch and see who brings it. Come in and get dressed for the job!"

IV

The watches of the night! Attired in my master's greatcoat I took up my post amidst the rafters of the byre. To a person looking up from the ground nothing was visible save my face, and my face being blackened with soot took on the hue and colour of the oaken beams. I was invisible.

"Just watch, and not a word," said Lanty Hanlon. "Report at dawn!"

He went inside. Presently the lamp was turned down, and in a little while I could hear his snoring, half hiccough and half whistle. Far over-head a flight of wild geese careered through the night; the corncrakes called to one another in the holm. The parish lights went out one by one. The house of Neal Hannigan was steeped in darkness. Good night, Norah!

Time passed! Was it now one o'clock or two. My feet were getting cold and a shivery feeling ran up and down my spine. This sensation was unknown to me when I was on the road. How quickly does the soft bed take away the stuffing of a man! I would have given a lot to be able to clamber down from my perch and warm my limbs by running about through the dew-beaded grass.

I was on the point of coming down when I saw something move in the field and come towards the house. To your post, MacMonagle! That which moved came nearer. A human being, a woman, Oonah Ruddagh, and in her arms Oonah bore the splatter-board of the missing cart. The wet weather had not rotted it!

She placed it on the ground by the gable end of the byre; looked round for a moment as if seeking something. But not finding that which she sought she stretched herself, shook her fist at the door and made off, legging it like a hare.

Next came Eamon Larrimore, a hard-working man and a decent man. He brought a wheel. Not that he would keep it, of course, when Lanty Hanlon needed it, but it was better used stopping a gap than rotting in a byre.

Paddy Cosdhu came with the other wheel. He ought to have sold when offered a price three days before, but now he brought it back because Lanty Hanlon was a wild man and Paddy did not want Lanty Hanlon to find it in his house.

Manus Glynn brought the body of the cart. Bare-footed, he had carried it on his back for four miles. The strength of Manus was known to all.

Kevin Roe brought the other wing; Neal Hannigan (not a word!) the tail-board, and Master Malley, in his collar and tie, came and placed a little poke on the ground beside the wheels. Next day we discovered that the poke contained half a dozen washers which the master used as weights when fishing. Of the others who came I will say nothing, as they have little to do with the story, but I may mention that before my watch came to an end, all cart and harness, parts and particles, were restored.

Next morning I gave full report of the affair, mentioning the names of those who came and what they brought. All names I mentioned, with the exception of one.

"Neal Hannigan did not come?" my master asked me.

"No," I said.

"Well, seeing that it was such a clear night, it was maybe his daughter who took the tail-board back." He spoke with a down curl of his lip, which, if it meant anything, meant that he considered me a liar.

Lanty Hanlon, G.H., saw more than his bees.

V

Three days later he left the parish with his horse, Garibaldi, and his cart, the latter newly greased and painted.

"You have begun steady at school. Keep hotly at the work and soon it will be time for action," were his last words to me. "Read everything you can lay your hands on, and by the time I return you will in all probability know how ignorant you are. Have a civil tongue in conversation, keep away from the girls and say your prayers. I will send money to Mick Flaherty and every week he will give you a little to buy yourself food. If you are short of money sometimes, do a day's work for the neighbours, and they will give you a bit to eat. Choose your master. Eamon Larrimore is generous, Paddy Cosdhu is close, Oonah Ruddagh is penurious. That is all."

He went out into the world. For weeks he remained absent. The potatoes lost their blossoms, the heavy-eared corn knelt to the earth, the scythes were loud in the land, and still he did not come back.

Now and again a whisper came to us. In

some far town he was seen selling second-hand clothes at the market; in other parts he had a booth where he sold scapulars and blacking brushes. Drink! He shunned it.

And weekly I called at the house of Mick Flaherty and received my dole, one week half a crown, the next week a crown piece, flat and shiny like the bottom of a new tin dish. And once I got seven shillings and sixpence. On that occasion I bought Norah a comb for her hair and a bunch of green ribbons.

But I was not forgetful of my studies. Nothing could be done without education, I knew. And therefore I kept hard to the work, and the more I studied, the more did I become conscious of my own ignorance. And that was well.

Lanty Hanlon returned with the first frost. He unyoked Garibaldi, put it into the byre under the corner where the roof was whole. For me, at the start, he had not one word; that I knew would come later. From the byre he went to the door of his home, stood there for a moment and sniffed the air like a dog on scent. Then his eyes rested on the beehive.

"Sleeping," he said in a whisper. "Neddy"—he had noticed me, and as he noticed he pulled a crown piece from his pocket,—"Garibaldi is hungry. Take this crown and go to Eamon Larrimore. He has a strong haggard and his corn is always the best."

This was an observation and an order. I went to Eamon Larrimore and bought provender for Garibaldi.

VI

The Winter passed with very little incident. In addition to my work at school, I fed Garibaldi morning and night, brushed him down and cleaned out his stable, now a snug place; for a new roof had been put up, and this, being thatched with rushes, was nice and comfortable.

For a while after his return Lanty Hanlon mooned about the place, ate his heavy meals and drank water. Whisky! Away with it. Never touch it again to his own undoing.

This was his remark, and one thought led to another.

"But why not to our (his and mine, mark you) profit!" he thundered one evening as he sat by the fire and brought down his fist on the arm of his chair, brought it down with such force that the delf on the dresser danced a hornpipe.

Quick the thought to action! Two days later he bought a load of hay and came through the village with this load so insecurely roped that it was in danger of falling down in front over Garibaldi's angleberries. The twelve straight policemen of Ballykeeran came to the street and laughed in silence at Lanty Hanlon, his horse Garibaldi and the load of hay.

And Lanty Hanlon, who could see much from a corner twist of one eye, saw the twelve straight policemen smile. But he did not mind. In fact, when he was out of eyesight and earshot a great smile came over his face, reached his ears, went down his very throat into his stomach. He came to a stop, put his hand on his kidneys, swayed, and then it came forth, a stream, a torrent—thunder, the laughter of a giant. He reeled backwards, almost losing footing, straightened himself for a moment but again succumbed, and, falling to the roadway, he rolled in the dust like a bull at play.

When he came home he stored the hay in the stable and that which the hay concealed in the corner of my room. And this was what the hay had hidden: bags of barley meal, vat meal, meal seed, sugar; hop-juice, yeast and soap; a vat, a still and a worm.

"Our (mine and his, mark you) distillery," he said to me. "But not a whisper about it, Neddy MacMonagle."

For nights afterwards he remained in the steaming room, the window-blind tightly down so that not even a ray of light fine as a spider's web got out into the darkness. There Lanty Hanlon worked, stripped to the waist, streams of sweat running down his mighty chest, while outside, with my nose on the keyhole sniffing the subtle odour, my ear on the roadway waiting the foot of the police, I stood as sentry. In my keeping was the well-being of the home distillery. What a proud position! Had the great day really come?

That Lanty Hanlon, G.H., was a master distiller was decisively proved by the fact that in not less than six weeks his blend was considered full of merit by the countryside. Even the Ballyroon carters who came to Ballykeeran on market days went back unhappy to their native place if they did not possess a jar of Hanlon's prime mixture. And appreciation from Ballyroon was appreciation indeed.

Who was it who tipped the wink or slipped the word to the police? Who knows? But it happened that on a night when I watched I heard a rustle outside, a hand on the door knob, and the door was pulled from its hinges. Outside in the night, helmets a-tilt and batons drawn, stood the twelve policemen of Ballykeeran.

Twelve! And Lanty Hanlon, G.H., was only one. But such a one!

With ponderous dignity, the sergeant (a father of ten children, all born in the month of June) wrote down the details of the case, the amount of liquor recently distilled, the amount in the process of distillation, the stores: two bags of barley grain, three of meal seed, a gallon of hop juice, half a hundred-weight of sugar, two bars of soap, four pounds of yeast, and appurtenances, vats, barrels, still, worm, buckets and jars.

Three days later came Kevin Roe, process-server. This man had his finger in many pies and, in addition to being butcher and process-server, was land-agent, gamekeeper and water-keeper. He was not liked by the people.

He handed a blue paper to Lanty Hanlon.

"What is that, Kevin Roe?" asked Lanty Hanlon.

"I guess it's a summons," was Kevin Roe's admission. "You have to appear before the authorities and show cause, why you had on the thirty-first ultimo certain illegal and illicit——"

"It's school time," said Lanty Hanlon to me. "You'd better go there."

His voice was calm and showed not the slightest trace of rancour. I stood at the door and looked at my master. I wanted to speak to him about a little matter.

"What are you wanting, Neddy?"

"My copy-book is filled," I told him. "I've lost my lead pencil, and my nib is broken."

"Ah, you're wanting some money, then," said my master. "Just wait a minute and I'll give it to you."

Perching himself on a chair, he brought forth the tin box which lay behind the oaken beam. This was our safe and no one knew where it was concealed. But why did he let Kevin Roe see the hiding-place? My master must have been a little excited. But he did not show it!

"Here is your money," he said, and handed me a shilling.

As I went out I noticed that Kevin Roe's eyes were on the door, and in those eyes there was a great longing.

Afterwards, by a piecing two and two together, I was able to picture the scene that ensued following my departure.

Lanty Hanlon bolted the door and, with the grand courtesy of a strong, silent man, enquired if Kevin Roe had had his breakfast. And Kevin Roe had had. But walking such a long way on such a cold morning would certainly make him hungry again! (Hanlon's suggestion.)

His stomach couldn't stand as much now as

it did when he was a younger man. (Roe's assertion.)

"There is a little sup of tea left in the teapot," said Lanty Hanlon. "Dry blue paper needs something to wash it down and I am not a man to begrudge anybody a cup of tea, even a summons server."

And there in the privacy behind the locked doors of Meenaroo, Lanty Hanlon, G.H., prevailed upon Kevin Roe to partake of a second breakfast consisting of cold tea and paper blue and dry.

A week later Lanty Hanlon was fined twenty pounds for illicit distillation, but in view of the fact that this was his first offence, the fine was mitigated to six guineas.

VII

Apart from this episode, the Winter was one of little note. Now the air of the parish was never disturbed by one whisper of the great time that was to be. Not one further atom of belief was held in the promise of the man whose word had heretofore been bond in any market! His fame dwindled in the neighbours' eyes. "It's hard on him," they said. "And the brains he has!"

Before, they honoured him, now they pitied him.

"And if he had only married daughter of mine, he'd be a great man this day," said Oonah Ruddagh.

But in the village of Ballykeeran, where quality was high and shoe-leather worn Summer as well as Winter, disgust and not pity was on the tongues that mentioned his name, high pride was in the eyes that looked on him in mass or market.

"And this is all he shows for the chance I gave him!" sighed Mick Flaherty. "And with the learning that he had he might even be a priest of God!"

"And the airs that he gives himself, even now," said Genevieve, daughter of Mick, she whom of old had waited in shine and shower for the mail-coach. Now in gold-rimmed spectacles she walked out with Kevin Roe.

When this young lady met Lanty Hanlon on the road or street, she did not see him. He was as nothing in her eyes. Oh! woe that day that saw my master slighted in this manner. But wait! One day, and God send it soon, he would show them!

But the poorer neighbours were leal and loyal, and at night his house was crowded. The hearth never lacked turf on the fire, a kettle on the crook, a teapot on the hob. In would come the neighbours, the clod-breakers, farmers, carters, jobbers, housewives, the commonalty of the parish, with a day's work well past them, and sit down to their tobacco and snuff and talk of the events of the day.

What numbers of things were discussed, things little enough in themselves but of real import to the people. A child was born; a cow near note was giving milk; sheep were heavy with lamb; a fox had been seen on the hills—the first in twenty years; a ghost had knocked at Oonah Ruddagh's door at midnight, gave three knocks and then went away—a common thing, for Oonah often saw ghosts.

And there I would sit listening, my heart filled with the wonder of the world. Perhaps Norah Hannigan was near me, for she always came with her father, and he was a constant visitor.

Oh! the nights that were; the white nights when the heart was young.

But the thing I liked best in those days was Lanty Hanlon reading the newspaper on a Saturday night when supper was over and the pipes lit.

It is strange to look back upon those days, especially now, when papers come not once a week to one, but every day to all. And are we as clever and up to date? I ask. I do not think so. The biggest head can only hold a little, and if a lot is put in a lot must go out to make room. It's in on one ear and out on the other, as the saying is. Everybody gets the papers now; even if one goes out to buy a red herring, that fish will be wrapped in a newspaper, and if the paper is more than a day old nobody will look at it.

But in the old days we had only one paper and it came by post. On Saturday evening it arrived at my master's house. And on its scent came the people of the country, some even eating their suppers as they walked so that they would be in time. The belly hunger was as nothing compared to the hunger for news.

I would light the paraffin lamp, trimming the wick, so that the globe would not become sooty. Under the lamp was placed my master's chair. He tore the wrapper, brought the paper out. The heel of a lighted turf went the round of the house, pipes glowed, eyes lit up, and puff, puff, went the guttering tobacco. The women tucked their bare feet under their quilted petticoats.

"What will it be first? Politics?"

Politics, of course, for the older men—Paddy Cosdhu, Eamon Larrimore, Neal Hannigan. The half-witted Manus Glynn was strong on politics, as he should be, having put four Irish miles behind him to come and hear. But, if the truth must be told, he understood little of what was read.

Oonah Ruddagh knew nothing of politics, and being a woman proud of her own limitations, she was not slow in owning up to her deficiency. She would keep busy turning the heel of a stocking, until Lanty came to the murders and the grand people getting killed. Then she would listen, and keep knitting, though the stitches dropped were beyond all telling.

Eamon Larrimore would sit behind Lanty Hanlon, so that nothing might be skipped. He was the man for the job, one who would read a little "in to himself," but would not read aloud. Still, he was the man to hold the point of vantage behind my master's chair, the man who would call the reader to account if anything were skipped or evaded.

My master would start, speaking in a loud, ponderous voice. A hush fell on the assembly; nothing could be heard save the sharp click of needles and the slow shuffling of bare feet on the floor. Pipes ceased guttering, went out, and were not lit again.

"Aye," the old men sighed, when Ireland was mentioned. "It's always the way. The poor country never gets what it wants."

"The body of a woman was taken from the river Thames," Lanty Hanlon would read. "She was well dressed and wore jewellery to the value of several thousand pounds."

"To think of that," Oonah Ruddagh sighed, dropping several stitches in the excitement. "Diamonds and jewels in the dirty water!"

The reading would go on. Rumours of war were in the air; murders had taken place; a woman had died of hunger in London.

"For all their jewels and diamonds in foreign parts, they are not all well fed," said Paddy Cosdhu, who smiled as if he liked to hear such deep philosophy from his own lips. He was a man whom I never liked.

"And what about the fashions?" Mary Hannigan, Norah's mother, would enquire. Fashions in clothes were her little hobby. Why? It was hard to say, as her fashion altered only once a year, in the Winter season, when two petticoats took the place of one, when leather was worn, a stomacher donned, and she placed a woollen cloud over her head and ears.

"There are no fashions this week," my master would answer. He had no time for such idle matters.

"But there's a whole big column," Eamon Larrimore would affirm. Nothing escaped his eye.

"Very well!" stuttered my master, smiling without parting his lips, and digged down into a medley of directions that concerned the making of a camisole.

Camisole! What was that? Nobody knew,

but a look of supreme bliss showed itself on Mary Hannigan's face and remained there until the reader had finished.

"And that's that," said my master, curling up his paper. The night's reading was at an end.

"But there's one bit you didn't read yet," Eamon Larrimore made haste to say. "At the very start."

Lanty Hanlon looked at the paper again.

"Only an advertisement, Eamon, only an advertisement. A cure for corns. One and three-ha'pence a bottle, and cures in one night."

"All that money," Oonah Ruddagh gasped.

"It's always toe-rags for me when I have the corns," was the remark of Manus Glynn. "And corns! Well, I never have them now at all."

Once more pipes were lit and, wreathed in their own tobacco smoke, the men went out into the night. The women followed after. Outside the moon shone over the hills. A fine night, surely, thanks be to God.

Lanty Hanlon would look round to find I was the only one in the room.

"Ah, Neddy!" he would exclaim. "Not in bed yet! How much do you understand of it all? But it doesn't matter," he would go on without waiting for an answer. "Put the kettle on and make us a bowl of tea."

CHAPTER VI

THE LOST LEADER

There never came a gatherer, but a scatterer followed him.
—*A Ballykeeran Saying.*

I

OFTEN I find myself, in these days of thin blood and old memories, thinking of the times that are far off and no more. What faces come thronging into my mind, what almost forgotten voices whisper in my ear in a quiet hour, the faces and voices of the people whom I knew! And all are gone, gone like the wind of yesterday.

"Old Oonah Ruddagh," I say to myself. "Do you remember old Oonah and the way she suffered from her corns, the honest Eamon Larrimore, the cute Paddy Cosdhu, the simple Manus Glynn?"

I am making myself this question; myself, and no one else. Round me is a world that is growing up. Those who grew up with me are dead. And those that live have no memory of Oonah Ruddagh, Lanty Hanlon, Mick Flaherty, Eamon Larrimore and the rest, folk once alive, my compeers, who are now lost on the world like the tune of yesterday's fiddle. To live to a great age is a sad thing, surely!

These thoughts come to me as I recall that

happy Winter and Spring, but alas! like all things earthly, that time had to come to an end.

"MacMonagle!" said Lanty Hanlon to me one morning.

The date was early June, the weather warm, and the corn in blade. My master looked me up and down and cleared his throat. He was going to speak. Had the great day come?

"Going to school?" he enquired.

"I am," was my answer.

"You are not," said he, and I realised that my schooling days were at an end. No more to sit beside Norah Hannigan, to press her hand under the leaf of the desk, to touch her toes with mine as if by accident and see the red come into her cheeks and know that the swift light which showed in her eyes was not the light of anger.

And all this would end now.

"For breakfast this morning we had a salt herring between us two," said Lanty Hanlon in a voice of sorrow. "That is a pauper's fare and not for us. Garibaldi is unfed. This is my worldly wealth!"

He took a florin from his pocket, placed it in the palm of his hand and closed his fist over it.

"What was it?" he asked.

"A two-shilling bit," was my answer.

"Where is it now?" he enquired.

"In your fist."

He opened his hand. The florin was not there!

"Where did it go?" I asked.

"Here it is," said Lanty Hanlon, and brought the piece from my ear.

Wonder of wonders! How did it get there?

And I felt nothing. The neighbours said that Lanty Hanlon was in the pay of the devil, and at that moment I believed it. How unjust one can be to a friend! But I was young.

"The time has come," said my master, fixing a steady glance on his clay-lined thumb-nail, his habit when in the maze of a problem. "The promise must be kept. Go out, MacMonagle!" —his voice rose—"go out and steal a bundle of hay for Garibaldi!"

"Who will I steal it from?" I asked.

"Who!" repeated Lanty Hanlon, and a puzzled look showed in his eyes. "Eamon Gerahty? No; he's a decent man. Paddy Cosdhu? No; he's a cunning man. Oonah Ruddagh is out of the question; she's red-haired. Neal Hannigan is the man. Ask him for it, Neddy, ask him. Tell him to send in his account at the end of three months. All accounts are paid quarterly!"

Accounts are paid quarterly. What did that mean?

He came with me to the door. On the other side of the valley rose the green fields that lost themselves amidst the heather on the braes. Higher up was the broad-spreading moorland, unpeopled and unstocked, anybody's property and all going to waste. Above the moors rose the eternal hills, heavens high, the outer mearing of the parish. Down from these hills rollicked many foam-heavy torrents that looked white as snow in the distance.

"Leagues of land all wasted, water calling to be harnessed," muttered Lanty Hanlon as he viewed the prospect. "I can see every house becoming a hamlet one day, every hamlet a town, the tide of emigration stemmed, rivers bridged, roads made, houses erected, education flourish. This must be. I have given my promise, and the time is now. Neddy "—he had suddenly noticed me—" run to Neal Hannigan. Get a bundle of hay and tell him that accounts are paid quarterly."

In ten minutes I returned with a bundle of hay, a small one, because Hannigan did not understand what Lanty meant by "accounts paid quarterly," but concluded it meant that he would never get a penny-piece for the bundle. He gave the bundle because Lanty Hanlon was a neighbour, and a Ballykeeran man will never see a neighbour in want.

Coming back, I found Garibaldi yoked in the cart, waiting to start, and Lanty Hanlon sitting in the cart waiting for me.

" Throw the hay in here," he ordered. " Get in yourself and sit beside me. The time has come, MacMonagle. The time has come ! "

So saying, he gave Garibaldi a clip over the ear with his whip and went down the laneway leading from Meenaroo while I, clambering over the tailboard, got into the well of the vehicle and settled on the bundle of hay. Now we were off ! Where to ? How was I to know ?

We got out on the highway and took the road to the village of Ballykeeran. Nobody was on the road, but now and again we saw a face appear at a near window and watch our departure. What was Lanty Hanlon, G.H., up to, now ? Something great, surely. Maybe the day had come !

We passed Neal Hannigan's house, a lime-washed house, snugly thatched, and standing on the brae across the river, a gunshot from the public road. On that day Norah was at home. She had not gone to school. Was she thinking of me? I looked for the sign!

There it was and no mistake: a white handkerchief placed on the holly tree which grew outside her door. This was to be the token of a broken heart; we had arranged for this when I went for the bundle of hay. Norah was not to be seen. If Lanty Hanlon saw her looking he would make fun of her and me.

But his thoughts seemed to be otherwhere at that moment. With head bent down he fixed his eyes on the moving hindquarters of Garibaldi. The day was new and the steed had not, as yet, given any symptoms of its chronic ailment.

"That's a poor washing the Hannigans have on the holly bush," Lanty Hanlon suddenly remarked. To think of him seeing it! "Is it the girl—what do you call her—that does the washing?"

"I don't know, indeed," was my answer.

"*A white cloth on a holly tree: my heart is sore when gone you be,*" chanted Lanty Hanlon. Could anything escape his eye? He might have been listening to us!

For a moment he was silent.

"Neddy MacMonagle," he said at length, "I suppose one day she'll wash your shirt for you. For a woman, it's a poor washing that has no shirt. But I want you, when you take a woman, to have a good shirt; not one, Neddy, but half a dozen.

How to procure these is to work hard, keep at your studies day and night, and remember that your education begins when you leave school. . . . Who's that trying to get in front of us? Is it Oonah Ruddagh?"

"'Tis, then," was my answer, for I had already noticed the old woman running across the braes, and she seemed bent on overtaking us.

We were now entering a wood, and I could see the woman change her direction, by taking a near cut through the trees. In this way she would meet us when we came out of the wood.

"Meet us face to face!" groaned Lanty Hanlon. "And her a red-haired woman. We'll turn back!"

Immediately he turned the horse round and drove back to his home. Such was the man, past all understanding.

Oonah Ruddagh arrived at Meenaroo five minutes after us. She was bare-footed and drops of sweat stood on her withered cheeks.

"And the race all for nothing!" she groaned. "If I stayed here you would come back and save me all this trouble."

"I wouldn't, Oonah," said Lanty. "'Twas you and your red hair that drove me back."

"What's wrong with my hair?" screamed Oonah. "Isn't it the hair that God gave me, and when I was young on it was there any hair to beat it at mass or market? Answer me that, Lanty Hanlon, now, and at once!"

"Concerning your tresses of the past, Oonah, I have nothing to say, of those in the future I won't hazard an opinion, but at the present moment if

I meet a red-haired woman on the road when I'm going to business, I turn back," Lanty Hanlon informed her, his air that of a man who would stand on his word if the heavens fell. "Now, Oonah Ruddagh, what do you want to tell me?"

"This is what I wanted to tell you," said the old woman, her eyes agleam as if some great item of information were presently to be thrown to the world. "She's writ me!"

"Who?"

"Herself."

"Maldy?" asked Lanty Hanlon in a voice of interest.

"If I say it isn't I'd be telling a lie," Oonah replied. "She writ me and says that the foreign parts are not agreeing with her, the poor soul, and that when she has enough to pay her way home, she'll be coming back again to me. I saw you going away, and I thought the great day was coming, and the good times that you promised, and I ran after you to tell you this, for I thought that maybe if you knew that Maldy never forgets you in her prayers it would give you heart in the job, whatever it is, that you're taking up. Maybe you'd think of it when the temptation would come over you, and then you wouldn't let the drink get the upper hand of you. But all the thanks that I get for it is the hard word because I've the red hair, and it once the pride of the parish, too, and that long before you were christened in whisky. To be christened over again, that's what you need, and when you get that, the curse will be took off you. I had a dream last night, Lanty, asthor, and what was it ? Nothing much at all ; only I dreamt that you were a married man, and it was to herself, to Maldy, that you were married. Wasn't that a funny dream, Lanty, asthor ?"

"Worse things might happen, Oonah," was Lanty's answer, as he took the old woman's hand in his own. In his eyes there was a look that I never saw there before.

. . . . .

At twelve o'clock that night we yoked up again, and dawn saw us beyond the mearn of Ballykeeran.

II

Ballykeeran ! What place under the sun to equal it !

Come by its high-roads on a forenoon in early September, when the mellow odour of the aging year is in the air, and see the sun standing high in a cloudless sky, the cows lowing, a symbol of Ballykeeran prosperity ; the hens with their devil-may-care, rollicksome spirit rolling in the dust of the roadway ; the ducks with filled craws, wobbling along with a real Ballykeeran wobble as if they too realise that they belonged to the first parish in Ireland.

The hay was up, the corn down, and a good harvest and all, thanks be to God. And we were coming back again, back after three months roving, our hearts light and pockets heavy. Business had prospered.

Our means were slight when we started. Ballyroon was our first stopping-place, Ballyroon, with a fair in full swing. Garibaldi was unyoked, Lanty Hanlon took up his stand on the bed of the cart and produced his florin.

"This is a two-shilling piece," he told the crowd, placing the coin on the leaf of his hand and closing his fingers on it. "Now I bet that nobody in the audience will be able to tell me where the coin is! A shilling the bet!"

He opened his fist to show that the coin was exactly where he had placed it.

"That's easy enough to tell, that," vowed a man in the audience.

"A shilling you cannot do it," said Lanty Hanlon.

"A shilling I can," was the answer.

"Name the hand," said Lanty Hanlon when the money was laid down.

"The right!" and on the word, Lanty Hanlon opened his right hand and showed the man that he was wrong. In this way did our business start.

Before night fell Lanty Hanlon, with three thimbles and a pea, was asking the young men of Ballyroon to watch closely and see him move the thimbles. The pea was under one of the thimbles! Which thimble? Did the young men of Ballyroon know? Heads, close-cropped and curled, nodded. The young men of Ballyroon knew a thing or two!

"Bet a shilling you don't find it!"

"Bet a shilling, I do."

And sometimes they found, and won, and sometimes they did not find, and lost. All was above-board, the play was fair, and those who found, won, and those who did not find, lost, for that was the way of the game.

The fair had been a good one, but a strange thing was noted that night by the publicans when they counted the profits of the day. Never had they made as little at a fair. Of another fact the girls took notice. Never before had the young men been so slow in treating them to soft drinks, pearly beads and ribbons.

If Lanty Hanlon had been asked his opinion on this matter he could have given it in all truth. Those who found, won, but those who did not find, lost, and the latter were in the majority.

In the days that followed we travelled over leagues of country. In the busy fairs we set our pitch in the market-place, rested the cart on a box, yoked Garibaldi to the shafts, and made money by the gentle art of thimble rigging.

One day we chanced to come to a big town, and here we arrayed ourselves in new garments, appointments in keeping with our profession, as my master said, strange outlandish garments, the like of which seldom showed themselves on the highways of Ireland.

Now the business took a new turn. When he came to a fair he stood on the floor of the cart and spoke down to the assembly. "Speak down to the ears that listen and the game is won," he often told me, for in that, as in everything else, he knew how to deal with the crowd.

Speaking down, he would offer his wares: a purse containing a chain, a watch (jewelled movement) and money, gold and silver which he threw into the purse with a lavish hand. All for a pound! He promised nothing except the watch and chain. There was money, of course. He would not say how much! But they saw what he did! Only a guinea, too! And the watch, chain and purse were worth more than a guinea, twice as much; nay, ten times as much. And the people bought, and we became rich.

III

Ballykeeran was the last place. Then he would go home. Then I would see Norah Hannigan again!

The date of our return was the first of September, the day on which is held the harvest fair of Ballykeeran. Kiln-dry was the street, glass-clear the sky, that seemed to have been washed for the occasion. The whole country-side was in attendance; every townland had sent of its prime in young and aged, in men of mettle and girls of grace. The best in beauty and brawn had come in from the outer mearings of the parish.

The heavy-handed farmers were wetting the bargains made earlier in the day, when we three arrived in the high street of the village, three, a little tired, for we had left many a hard league of dry roadway behind us. Such a trio had never been seen in the place before and came in for no little share of attention.

We had come back, Lanty Hanlon, G.H.; his henchman, Neddy MacMonagle; and the poor spavined, angleberried Garibaldi, the same old cart, the purse of fortune, three thimbles and a pea.

Attired as we were, the crowd marvelled to see us, and no wonder. In front was Lanty Hanlon, G.H., in a tight-fitting jerkin with brass buttons, corduroy breeches buckled at the knees, a wide-brimmed felt hat topping his mighty head, which hat in turn was topped with a white cockade. A strange, outlandish costume, to which my master gave dignity.

A little to rear strode I, a boy that knew my place, clad in sailor apparel, the trousers seat a little worn, the name H.M.S. ORION standing out boldly over the peak of my cap. Barefooted, I was, but what did that matter? Trafalgar was won by a blind eye and no shoe-leather.

Came next the horse, Garibaldi, always hungry and half asleep, his mane gay with coloured ribbons, a harvest plait tied to his tail.

Ballykeeran harvest fair, as everyone knows, falls on the first of September. Seasons may be unseasonable, crops may prosper or fail, tides may be Spring or Neap, for of seasons, crops or tides there is no surety. But one thing is as certain as death for all and damnation for the wicked, and this is that the harvest fair of Ballykeeran is held on the first day of September.

"Whoa, Garibaldi!"

The horse came to a dead stop like thrown mud that strikes a wall. It opened one eye, then the other, and looked round. Probably the poor animal had been walking in its sleep, but the thought of the nosebag had wakened him.

Unyoking, I tied Garibaldi to the shafts, sorted its nosebags, while the crowd gathered round. Lanty Hanlon, G.H., was back and nothing else mattered. Had the great day come ? The public-houses emptied themselves like pricked bladders, porter-fringed beards sorted themselves round the cart, young men gave their love-making the go-by. Green ribbons and necklaces, what did they matter ? The Ballykeeran wenches clustered round the man with the felt hat and the white cockade.

Lanty Hanlon, with a purse in one hand, a watch and chain in the other, was on the cart, speaking. How strong was his voice ! Its echoes rolled down the dry street, startling the tethered sheep, shaking the apple stalls, cracking the fly-blown windows.

There they were, Mick Flaherty, his daughter Genevieve, Eamon Larrimore, Paddy Cosdhu, Neal Hannigan, Kevin Roe, Oonah Ruddagh, the twelve straight policemen, all the quality, commonalty, rag-tag and bobtail of the parish. Was the good time coming ?

"Men and women of Ballykeeran, natives of the first town in Ireland," said Lanty Hanlon. "I come amongst you to offer you a bargain, a bargain such as has never been offered you before. Here I have in my hand a purse, a weasel-skin purse, and you know what a weasel-skin purse is. The luckiest thing you can have."

"There's not a word of lie in that, Lanty, asthor," said the old red-haired, bare-footed Oonah Ruddagh from the depth of the crowd.

"And in my other hand," Lanty Hanlon went

on, " I have a watch and chain. The chain is good, and the watch is better. Jewelled movement ! Isn't that enough ! Worth ten guineas, if worth a penny ! I put these, the watch and chain —jewelled movement the watch, remember—into the weasel-skin purse "—he did so—" and the price is one guinea. Not enough, did you say ? I grant you that, but I am not a man to be mean when I do business with the good people of Ballykeeran. Not alone will I give you the watch, chain and purse for a guinea, but I give you more. I give you this, and this, and this."

Rattling a number of silver pieces in his hand, he started showering them into the purse.

" I promise you money, I won't say how much, but all is for a guinea—a guinea ! "

There are hard heads and tight purses in Ballykeeran : but never had such an opportunity come their way. Those who had done well at the fair drew out their purses, loosened the strings and bought. Oonah Ruddagh coughed up a guinea.

" A red-haired woman ! " whispered Lanty, and gave me a sidelong look. " I don't like it. Why the devil did she come here ? "

We sold all our stock-in-trade : not a purse was left, not a watch, not a chain.

" We'll be off home, now," I said to Lanty Hanlon, for my mind was filled with Norah, my sweet little girl, she who one day became my wife. Not that I thought of marriage then, which was not to be wondered at, seeing that my years were not sixteen, and small for my age into the bargain.

" Not us," said Lanty Hanlon, with such a

violent nod of his head that he almost shook his cockade from its setting. "There's more than one full purse here, so we must make the best of our stay. And it's our last day."

Enough! He took the side-boards from the cart, brushed the bed of the vehicle with the sleeve of his jerkin, brought forth his three thimbles and his pea, put the pea under a thimble, moved the three. Where was it?

"Those who find, wins. Them that doesn't, loses! Where is the pea?"

"This is something new! Come and see it! A shilling you don't know where the pea is?"—"A shilling I do!"—"Put down your money!"—"Cover it!" And a young man, a strapping buck, in high attire, put down a shilling and won. He knew where the pea was concealed. A second time he was successful, and a third. Others crowded round. We know where it is. Under that one! No; the other! The third! Money was put down, and Lanty Hanlon, G.H., started reaping a steady harvest—the last harvest for many a day.

Oonah Ruddagh, who had purchased the watch, was back again. I saw her take her place on the fringe of the crowd, her eyes set, hard as glass taws, her lips shut, her fingers working as if she were throttling a hen. Lanty Hanlon sensed her, and his fingers shook a little as he showed a sportsman that the chosen thimble did not really hide the elusive pea.

"And I would put my soul on it that it was under that thimble," the man remarked.

"You never know your luck." Lanty Hanlon

had one eye on Oonah. " The next time it may be easier. Never say die. Those who find, wins. Them that doesn't, loses."

" It's always losing one is, if he has anything to do with a dirty vagabond like that ! "

How cold it can be, the hard word of a hot, red-headed woman. She came nearer the cart, clearing the way, her elbows sufficing when her tongue was of no avail.

" What has upset you, decent woman ? " asked Lanty Hanlon, his bearing superb, his voice innocent.

" Decent woman ! " Oonah snorted. " I am that, and every decent man and woman in Ballykeeran will back me in what I say. But rogues and vagabonds I cannot stand, never could and never will, here nor anywhere else. And once you had the high talk of bringing fortune to the place, you rogue, you dirty rogue, you rogue unhung——"

" I'm afraid I cannot understand you, my good woman——"

" You'll understand me before I'm done with you," roared Oonah. " I came in here to-day and sold my cow, a good milker, and then when I get the money you come with your outlandish clothes, like a workhouse scarecrow, and sell me a watch. A guinea for it, and it only brass like the knob of a door."

The crowd looked ugly. Those who had not bought watches, laughed, those who had, looked glum.

" It's gold, my decent woman ! "

" Like the gold of a whin bush ! " Oonah

shrieked. " And the money that you threw into the purse, where is it ? "

" I promised nothing," said Lanty Hanlon, who was not slow in noticing that the crowd had sympathy with Oonah Ruddagh. " But I'll tell you what I'll do. I'll buy the watch back from you and give you what you paid for it."

" You said that it was worth ten times as much as I gave you. Give me twice as much as I gave and I'll be content," said the woman. " Then you can have the purse and the chain into the bargain."

" I'll give you a guinea," Lanty made answer, and the turn of his voice showed that he meant it. " So hand me up the watch and chain, and here is your money."

He held out two coins, gold and silver, to the woman.

" But I'll keep the chain and the purse," she said, and her voice gave tone to her feelings. Possibly the watch was worth ten guineas ! She turned to a man who stood beside her, Kevin Roe, Yankee in cut of clothes and shape of shoe wear.

" How much are these watches worth in money, Kevin Roe ? " she asked him.

IV

What a moment of triumph for Kevin Roe ! Appealed to in a crowd and all ears hungry for his word ! And Genevieve, the daughter of Mick Flaherty, grand in her gold-rimmed spectacles and proud attire, was near him.

"Well, I guess they're worth about a dollar apiece," was Kevin Roe's answer to Oonah Ruddagh.

"A dollar! And how much will that be now?" Oonah enquired.

"Four shillings," said Kevin Roe. "The chain is worth about ninepence, and the purse sixpence."

He was very near the truth in his estimate of the price, but at that moment, God forgive me, I wished that he had been choked when he had had the blue summons for his breakfast.

"Four shillings, ninepence, sixpence: five and a penny." Oonah Ruddagh was doing the tally in a loud voice. Having finished, she looked up at Lanty Hanlon. "Here's your dirty watch. Give me back my guinea!" she screeched.

"Here it is!"

Lanty Hanlon, handing down the money, spoke to me in a side whisper: "Yoke like hell, Neddy! Yoke like hell. The sooner we're clear of this place the better!"

"Cheating a poor widow woman like that," grumbled Oonah Ruddagh, who had now got her money. She handed back the watch, but retained purse and chain. "Is that to be allowed in a decent place like this?"

She clicked her ankles together like a soldier on parade, threw out one arm and appealed to the crowd. "Is it going to be allowed here," she entreated, as she stuffed the chain and weasel-skin purse into the pocket of her quilted petticoat. Her words covered her action.

"He's cheated us all," was the answering shout,

and Kevin Roe, who had not bought anything, was as loud in his condemnation as the others. "Give us back our money!"

"I'll see you in hell first," was the grim answer of Lanty Hanlon, master of his soul in any adversity.

"I guess it's easier to take it from him," said Kevin Roe, and accompanied by half a dozen young men, Freelys by name, a bad breed, he rushed the platform, overturned it and fell upon the thimble-rigger. Effort was futile. My master was laid flat as a sack on the ground, his pockets rifled, his thimbles crushed in the grit.

"And I was wanting a thimble," said the red-haired Oonah, endangering her fingers in trying to grab one.

Things went hard for Lanty Hanlon that afternoon. All his money, the savings of his tour, was taken from him. A few, the first in the scrimmage, filled their pockets; the late comers receiving nothing, and filled with a just resentment, they took Lanty Hanlon in their arms and deposited him in a steaming midden which occupied a prominent place in the village street. His felt hat and cockade vanished.

Some young ragamuffins took my cap (H.M.S. ORION in golden letters, you will recollect), tore my trousers and left me two black eyes as tokens of the tragic day. A tramp, not being slow to profit by the auspicious occasion, unloosened the horse, took position amidst the angleberries, and rode Garibaldi out of town.

Three heavy-helmeted policemen, straight as telegraph poles, marched gravely to the midden and fixed their eyes on the man stuck therein. To help him was out of the question. Their trousers were newly creased, their tunics spotlessly clean. Soil their appointments in such filth! What would the Ballykeeran girls say! Besides, the policemen had bought watches half an hour ago. Feeling they had been done they grieved that the hard discipline of the Force forbade looting. (This was in the old times.) Now, however, there was a chance of getting a bit of their own back.

"What are you doing in there?" asked one.

"Bathing," growled Lanty Hanlon, making an effort to pull himself out. This was a difficult job. The crowd stood a good distance off; even the police force drew back a pace and drew their batons.

He drew himself out and stood upright. Fire and fury was in his eye as with dung-strewn magnificence he sized the crowd.

"Ballykeeran, traitors and toe-rags!" he muttered between close-set teeth.

That was all, one simple assertion, "traitors and toe-rags," which at that moment only reached the ears of those nearest the speaker, but which, with that faculty which belongs to the words of the great, rolled onwards like an echo, not alone outwards but downwards through the years that came after. At the present time it is only necessary to repeat that phrase, "traitors and toe-rags," anywhere in Ireland, on highway, by-way, field or farm, to anybody from merchant to muck-sweeper, priest to pig-sticker, and the one who listens will cock up his ear and say with a knowing air : " Ballykeeran ! where Lanty Hanlon lives ! "

Lives indeed ! He has been under clay for twice fifteen years, and a grand funeral his ! But perhaps he does live even yet, for the great never die.

Having given voice to his famous utterance, Lanty Hanlon looked round him. What a sad sight for the parish, the parish and its glory, and for the Guild's Honoursman in which that glory was impersonated.

Glory has many faces. There is glory in a tattered flag, but none in tattered breeches. Lanty Hanlon, G.H., had fallen from his high estate, as was to be plainly seen when the Quality passed by, the Quality with its finger on its nose and its eyes the other way.

Amongst the assembled crowd there was laughter and jeering. Once he was honoured and now there was none so poor as to do him reverence. In fact, nobody would touch him with a six-foot pole.

But to this day I will give myself credit for not having denied him.

" We'll go home," I said in a whisper. " I have saved a little, and it's hid in my coat. I'll get tea and sugar and something to eat."

" Where is Garibaldi ? " asked my master.

" Gone he is," I told him. " Stole by a tramp ! He was taken out to the Ballyroon road."

" Then I must follow ! " said my master. " Go home and wait my return. And one day "

—his voice was hard as iron—" one day I will make Ballykeeran ashamed of the injustice which it has done me."

Standing well out of arm-reach the populace watched him passing. Down the kiln-dry street he strode, growing smaller and smaller in the distance. Presently he turned a corner and gone from sight was Lanty Hanlon on the trail of Garibaldi.

V

Where was Lanty Hanlon ?

A day went by, two, three, a week and he did not return. I waited, my eyes weary watching the road in the bright day, my ears strained at night waiting a heavy foot on the doorstep, a strong hand on the latch. The door of Meenaroo was never bolted. The house was his, and who was I to deny him right of entry ?

I kept house in my own way, patched my clothes, ate sparingly and at my hours like Garibaldi. I must admit I was a little lavish in one way. I bought me a pair of boots, nicely nailed and strongly welted. Well, the weather was getting cold, to be sure, and Norah Hannigan wore boots.

Nevertheless, I did not spend all my money, all that I had saved from the scrapings and drippings of the business which came to such an untimely end. Five pounds ten shillings I had in my keeping, and the fact that my master never missed it when he tallied his winnings showed the strength of the business. Now perhaps he would need it on his return, so I kept it in a safe place and waited.

What had happened him? Nobody knew, though up and down the roads within the mearing of the parish his name was on everybody's tongue. Old doating Father Dan, eighty if a day, who had forgotten his *Paternoster*, had still one pat question for each of his flock: "Heard anything about him yet?"

One day Eamon Larrimore and Paddy Cosdhu met on the highway, running in opposite directions, Paddy to put out his corn-stack which had caught fire, Eamon to fetch the midwife to his good woman, who suffered from an ailment common to wedlock. They passed like swallows in mid-air, but in passing they had time for one question: "Any word of him?"

Him! Where was he?

"It'll go hard for Lanty when he comes back," said Neal Hannigan to me one day. "The young vagabonds that bought the watches and didn't get their money back are going to set about him, and the Lord knows what will come of it! Kevin Roe, that sandy-haired, bandy-legged pup of perdition, is putting bad notions into their heads. And he never bought a watch that day, but he wasn't slow in the picking up piles of the money that they took from the poor man before they threw him in the midden. Dear me! and the money that he had on him, and I was late! Got nothing! But for all that, I've a soft spot in my heart for poor Lanty! And Kevin Roe! Well, Neddy MacMonagle, he's a pup!"

The true word, and doubly true when spoken

by Neal Hannigan, a man civil in word and generous in deed, who never begrudged a rich neighbour congratulations, nor a poor neighbour consolation.

True were Neal Hannigan's words. Kevin Roe was a pup, a mean pup, a pup of the third generation.

Kevin Roe, process-server, land-agent, game-keeper, water-keeper and butcher, belonged to the third generation. "Ragged breeches to ragged breeches in three generations," as the saying has it, and the truth of the saying has often been made plain to me in my eighty years.

First there was Kevin's grandfather, who built up a big fortune. "Slow at the start and keep hotly at it," was the rule of his life. And slow was the start of Kevin Roe's grandfather, Phelim his name, for if the truth must be told his father died leaving him nothing but his name, a mud-walled cabin thatched with rushes, and as much ground of the world as could be held under the finger-nails.

But by dint of hard working, a quick eye in marketing and skill in getting the best of a bargain, Phelim, when he died at a ripe age, was able to leave money behind him, so much that his son, Farley, could count guinea against guinea with the best in the parish, and have a rich man's fortune when the count was finished.

Farley was a clear-sighted man, good-natured, affable, with a strong sense of duty and position, a pillar of the Church, on intimate terms with the landlord, upheld law and order, was a little severe to those who were poorer than himself, and was respected by those in a better position. He wore a starched collar, donning a new one every week. He married well, taking the daughter of the village doctor as wife. One child, the man now known as Kevin Roe, was the result of the union.

Kevin Roe was given his own way from the very start, and this means that he was badly brought up. His mother mollycoddled the boy, combed and curled his hair, trimmed and tidied his clothes, taught him to knock at an open door and use a knife and fork at a meal where his fingers would have sufficed, collared him like a priest, apparelled him like a doll, until he became the laughing-stock of the whole parish.

His mother got a pony for him ; he was taught riding, and in course of time his legs, a little bowed, were proudly shown by his mother to the people. Riding on horseback makes bow-legs, you know. A sign of quality ! The statement contained everything but the truth. There was an inward curve in the legs of the Roe family from the beginning of time.

Ballykeeran was not the place for such a doll as Kevin. When he came to the years of discretion he was sent to the big town of Dublin and thrown into college, there to prepare himself for man's estate. After a while, for some reason or another, the college became too warm for him and he was thrown out.

"He was the great boy for learning," his mother explained. "They could not teach him any more ! So why should he stay there ?"

Why, indeed?

In course of time his father and mother died and the young man came into the property. It was worth five thousand pounds at the lowest estimate. But Kevin belonged to the third generation. One to make, one to hold, and one to scatter. And he scattered. Money in his hands was sand in a riddle. In eighteen months, when he had not a penny piece, he went to America, and remained there for two years. Then he came back, not of his own free will, if accounts are to be believed, but because America had no further use for him.

Back in Ballykeeran he turned his hand—his knife, I mean—to butchering. But alas, there was little to be butchered. Who was going to eat meat when the cows were in milk, and the butter prime, and the hens laying. The day when there is neither butter nor eggs is a bad day, surely!

Still there was a little work for the man. The twelve straight policemen of Ballykeeran sat round a roast on Sunday, tourists came for the fishing, the priest had a kindly eye for a chop on the day that was not a fast-day, and the aroma of a rump-steak could be smelt in Flaherty's house on a Sunday. And Kevin Roe fed in Flaherty's every Sunday afternoon.

Well, it was lonely having nobody to cook his dinner, and for all his wild raking past Kevin Roe had the education of a gentleman. It was Genevieve Flaherty who said this, once in my own hearing, and more than once in the hearing of others.

The ranting season was in full swing now. Every holly-bush in the parish sheltered a pair of lovers nightly. Never was a time like it for soft whispers and kisses. Christmas would be a great time for marriages—and Kevin Roe paid court to Genevieve Flaherty.

Although his love suit prospered and the portion of Genevieve was a big one, the man was not happy. Why ? A word, a down droop of the eye, a curl of the lip and a question from a gamin in passing, addressed to no one in particular, made his days heavy, his nights sleepless.

"Who ate the blue summons ?" was the question. And pondering over this question, Kevin Roe passed his hours in a sweat of worry. But stronger than anything in the man, stronger than his conceit, his vanity, stronger even than his love of Genevieve and her portion, was his hatred of Lanty Hanlon.

Hate ! What is stronger ? Love of mother, of wife, of money and fame, are as nothing compared to a deep-rooted hate. The hand that gives a crust may be forgotten, but the hand that gives a blow is always remembered.

Meanwhile Lanty Hanlon was afar, on the trail of Garibaldi. The chase was a trying one, as it well might be, for Shank's two-legged mare had little hope in the chase of a four-legged steed. Several times Lanty Hanlon came in at one end of a far village to see the mounted tramp going out on the other side. But in this, as in everything else, Lanty Hanlon had his own grand dignity. A word to the police force and the tramp would have been tracked down ! But my master was not the man to have recourse to the law.

"Dastardly minions!" his word when he spoke of the police. "Not Hanlon to have anything to do with them!"

And so, on his own bent, disdaining assistance, Lanty Hanlon followed Garibaldi, while I, Neddy MacMonagle, waited his return to Meenaroo.

CHAPTER VII

THE WILD RIDER

A beggar on horseback will ride to the devil.

—*Proverb.*

I

I SAT in the house by the roadside, the home of Paddy Cosdhu, a comfortable house with a good fire and a stirabout pot spluttering on the crook.

A few neighbours were in, softening the evening with tobacco, snuff and gentle discourse. Eamon Larrimore was there, hearty after the event. (Mother and child were both doing well.) Paddy's good woman sat near the fire, taking turns at knitting and stirring the pot. Nothing like stirabout for burning if you do not keep your eye on it.

Oonah Ruddagh came in just for a minute, because she was passing by and saw the light, and wasn't it a cold night, surely! At six o'clock she came in; it was now nine, and the " minute " was not up yet.

Round the room were the various Cosdhu youngsters, seven in all, healthy children, keepers of the grace which their mother had lost in bearing them.

Paddy himself was busy at work seating a pair of bottom-worn trousers, trousers that held so many patches that not even a vestige of the original cloth remained. Patches had even been put on to hold the buttons, and even patches were in many cases patched three times over.

"No word of the bucko yet?" asked Paddy, fixing a black cute eye on me.

"No!" I said in a cold tone. I did not like to hear my beloved master termed a bucko.

"He's a gadabout," said Paddy after a short silence. "He can't be trusted. I've known the bucko since he wasn't the size of a pig's tail. And always into mischief. And the money that he's put through his hands and into his belly! Dear me! And an honest man like myself working from the screech of dawn to the shut of night, and as poor at one year's end as at the end of another. . . . But he'll come back again from wherever he is and be the same as ever."

"He will that," said Oonah Ruddagh grimly. "I knew 'twould be bad for him, and the way that he got whisky on him instead of water the day that he was christened. Some say that it was because old Andy, God rest him! was drunk that morning, but I know better."

"Surely you do." Eamon Larrimore was strong in his support of Oonah's assertion.

"'Twas because it was to be, and there's no other reason," said the old woman. "And it was a waste of good stuff too, the best that ever went into my belly. Not that I'm a judge, for what do I take!"

"Nothing worth talking about," said Eamon.

"Not as much as that even," said Paddy Cosdhu, winking at me.

"But them that never took much are often the best to judge," Eamon affirmed in his calm, quiet way. "For there's a reason."

"So there is," said Paddy, with a knowing look, though if the truth were confessed he did not know of any reason. But the wise look often carries weight in a council.

"Whatever the reason is I liked the wee sup I had that morning. And there's a reason in everything," said Oonah, with a heavy nod signifying that the truth on which she stood while begging polite confirmation could very well damn contradiction.

"The reason is this, that them that's used to it can take it no matter how bad it is, for their insides are hardened to it," Eamon ventured to explain. "But them that's not used to it will get their stomachs turned if it's bad."

"I suppose it would turn one's stomach if it is bad," said Paddy's wife, Ellen her name, with the air of one who really knew nothing about the matter, and felt it would not be amiss to hazard an opinion.

"If it's bad," Paddy affirmed with emphasis. "And the state that their stomachs bees in, them that's always tight," he added with an upthrow of his arms.

"It's said that their bellies gets like leather, God help them!" said Oonah, with a sigh. "When I think of that it always makes me glad that I take the pledge so often. And I'm not the one to take it and break it the next day as some people do. The only time I would think of breaking a pledge is when there's a drop to be had for nothing."

"If I could get as much as I want for nothing I'd never be sober," Paddy confessed. "But for all that we get in this arm of the world we might as well have the pledge all our lives. All the times that I've been proper tight in my life I could count on the fingers of one hand, and have the most of the fingers to spare."

"I can back you in that, Paddy Cosdhu," said Eamon.

"There's drunk and drunk in it," said Oonah philosophically. "And some can stand it better than others. Him that's away, now!"

"He could put down a whole bottle of the best, gulp down a whole barrel, even without a shake of his Adam's apple, and be as sober at the end as at the start," said Eamon. "And a man to do that must have a constitution like a bullock."

"He'll have a leather belly, as Oonah says," Paddy remarked.

"Leather couldn't stand it," said Eamon wittily. "It will be made of iron."

At that moment four neighbours came in and sat themselves down on various chairs, Neal Hannigan, Norah's father, whose flocks had many acres of mountain land for pasturage; Denis Freely, quick-eyed and wiry, a drover whose purse was good for a score of stock in the highest market; Manus Glynn, the easy-going simpleton, bootless, although a heavy frost was on the land; and Kevin Roe, the sandy-haired, bow-legged butcher. Genevieve was doing the Nine Fridays at the time, and one cannot leave devotions to the Mother of Perpetual Succour for idle merry-making under a holly-bush.

II

" We were just speakin' about him that's off there, and the way that he could put it down," said Paddy, shoving the needle in the lapel of his coat and addressing the visitors collectively. " And Oonah here says that it's an iron belly that he must have with what he can hold."

" Leather, I said," Oonah corrected, straightening her spine and assuming a defensive pose. " Leather and nothin' but that, and not my own words, but what I've heard people say. I can always stand on my own word, and if I said leather it was leather. And I did say it too, that I admit, but not about Lanty Hanlon, but about them that bees always tight."

" One can't be very tight here," said Neal Hannigan, spitting into the fire. " It costs that much."

" Aye! it's a funny world and all!" said Manus Glynn, looking at his toes. The humorous aspect of the world always impressed him.

" For all that we get here we might as well have the pledge all our lives," Paddy broke in. " That's what I said before you came in, and that's what I say just now."

" I guess that's quite right, Paddy," said Kevin Roe. " And as to a pledge, well, I've never let them put it on me. No pledge, no temptation, is what I say. If a man with a pledge gets drunk it's two sins, getting tight and breaking his word with God. No pledge on Kevin Roe, thank you."

"And you, Manus, what do you say?" asked Paddy, looking at Glynn.

"All that I can say is that it's a funny world anyway you look at it," replied the man, smiling so broadly that the corners of his lips almost reached his ears.

"Well, it's not for me to be going against the opinions of anyone," said Oonah Ruddagh. "But I think that the pledge never does harm. Mind you, that's only my own opinion, but I'll stick to it all the days of my life, and they're not to be many now, for I'm creepin' over seventy as it is."

"But you don't look it, Oonah," said the house in unison.

"Smart on your feet now as you were twenty years ago," said Eamon Larrimore in confirmation of the popular expression.

"And the way that you carry yourself," said Neal Hannigan, amplifying the statement already made.

"The wonder of the world the way you can go about," said Manus Glynn.

"There's no wonder in it at all," said the old woman, proud of being the centre of interest. "It's the way that I've lived all my life. It wasn't me gadding about even when I was a young one and the boys after me. 'Twas the back of my hand to them after ten o'clock at night and no sitting in a haystack nor on a stone ditch. That's the worst thing in the world for giving pains and rheumatics in the legs. One doesn't mind and one young, but it's when they get on in years that they feel it. And even when himself, God rest him, turned his eye on me for good, see all the childer that I had be him! But if I was a gadabout! Thank God I never was that, and now past seventy, see what I am! Able to hold my head up with the best of them!"

"That's what you have to bear in mind when you start going about with the girls," said Paddy Cosdhu, looking at me. "Never keep them out at nights sitting on a stone ditch."

Neal Hannigan laughed. What did he know?

"No one can grow up decent with a man like Lanty Hanlon watching over him," said Oonah Ruddagh. "He's a blackguard, that same man."

"An old rascal," said Kevin Roe, and a white laugh was on his face.

"And the ones that he robbed in his life," Denis Freely interposed. Denis had bought a watch at the harvest fair. The watch did not go and he did not get his money back. "But wait till we get him back here."

My heart boiled with indignation. To hear these people speak of my beloved master like this, my defender, my hero. The tears welled up in my eyes and I got to my feet.

"That such a creature as that can make money, lashings and leavings of it, while myself have nothing and am working from morning to night all the year round," Paddy was saying. "Having nothing but the leisure of the smith's helper, from the bellows to the anvil," said Eamon Larrimore.

"That's what he is," said Denis Freely with a laugh. "An old drunken pig. Trying to make fools of his neighbours! We put him into the midden at the harvest fair and let him get out. He'll not be let out the next time!"

"Guess it will serve him damn well right," said Kevin Roe, and the hate in his voice would break a rock.

"We'll all set on him, my Uncle Ned, my brothers Tom and Jack and a dozen others, and Kevin Roe as well," said Denis Freely.

I could see that the times would go bad for my master when he came back. The Freelys were all hard fighters and no row was complete when they were not in it. Still, I was not going to see my master run down. I strode across the floor and faced Kevin Roe and Denis Freely.

"You're two pigs," I shouted, not in a loud voice, of course, for the tears were choking me.

The house looked at me in surprise. Kevin Roe tittered. Oonah Ruddagh shut one eye and surveyed me through the other. The remainder stared at me, Paddy Cosdhu with anger, Eamon Larrimore with pity. Everybody was silent.

"And if he were here you wouldn't have so much to say against him!" I cried, quivering. "He's too good to you, that's what's wrong with Lanty Hanlon. When the cart came back he saw everybody that took it back. And he could have you all in prison if he wanted it. There, now!"

I stopped. Not one word was spoken. Nothing happened except that Oonah Ruddagh got to her feet, went to the door and fumbled with the latch. Her "minute" was up, surely.

"Well, Paddy Cosdhu, this is a latch," she said at last. "There's a hasp of some kind, but I cannot open it at all!"

"It's getting old, of course, Oonah, old like us all, for that is the way of the world, and a funny way it is," said Paddy, running to the door. He caught the hasp.

"This is the way of it. All that you need to do is to give a wee pull and give a twist of the wrist, like this," Paddy went on as he fumbled with the hasp. "Just like this, Oonah—Oh! Mother of God, help us!"

The door came inwards against his nose, almost throwing him down, and after the door came Lanty Hanlon, bare-headed and bare-footed, his head caked with clay, his trousers plastered with refuse as if he had rolled in the mulch of a wet farm-yard. All got to their feet, the women crossing themselves. Paddy Cosdhu drew back a few steps, holding his nose in his hand. Kevin Roe and Denis Freely went out.

"And it's Lanty that's in it," said Oonah Ruddagh. She looked him up and down. "And this is the way that you come back. But what is one to expect with the christening that you had on you! Gallivanting into a house in this way, too!"

"Well, maybe it's just coming in that he is and will be going off in a minute," said Paddy Cosdhu, sniftering like a dog with pepper in its nose. It was as well to speak the soft word now, though Paddy had termed Lanty Hanlon a drunken pig a moment before.

"I have just called in to see you, Mr. Cosdhu," said Lanty Hanlon, reeling a little. He steadied himself by embracing a bag of meal which stood on a form. "Home I have come with Garibaldi. Home I am, but where is my henchman?"

"Here I am," I answered, coming close to my master.

He held out his mighty hand and gripped mine.

"Neddy MacMonagle, I have returned, tight as a drum, tight as a drum. And Eamon Larrimore, how are you?"

"Middling, Lanty, middling, thanks be to God," said Eamon.

"And Paddy Cosdhu is the same old threepenny," said my master. "And Oonah Ruddagh! Well, there will be guineas growing on the gooseberry bushes before she's anything but what she is, the same old Oonah!"

"Old I may be, Lanty Hanlon!" Oonah was on her dignity. "But for all that I am as smart on my feet as some of the young ones. If it was not for the corns, Lanty, I'd be able to foot a six-hand reel with the best of them!"

"And Neal Hannigan! H'm!" My master had noticed Neal in the corner, and with outstretched hand swayed towards him, first getting entangled in a medley of pans and porringers which littered the floor, then getting mixed in a hank of yarn. Breaking free, he surveyed his position. In front lay a boundless spread of floor, having neither hold nor stay for an uncertain traveller. Far in the distance he could see the face of Neal Hannigan, beaming in the lamplight like a friendly beacon.

Out upon it! He twirled round like a top whose spin is coming to an end, and as he spun, his outstretched arms kept warding off the attack of the advancing walls. And the walls crowded in upon the daring traveller, throwing him back two paces when he advanced one. What a conflict! what grit! what muddled magnificence! Only when he found himself with his back supported by the meal-bag from which he had started did Lanty Hanlon realise the hopelessness of the struggle. The walls had won!

But not the Guild's Honoursman to acknowledge defeat! The meal-bag his support, he weighed the pros and cons of the situation, and lo! the decision. He lay coffin-flat on the floor and, bare-headed and bare-footed, he rolled himself across to Neal Hannigan. The objective was attained; the roll had accomplished what the spin could not perform.

"Neal Hannigan, a trustworthy man," he said with a voice of feeling as he got to his feet. "Ever true to your principles, are you not?"

"I am indeed, if there's no harm in it," said Neal Hannigan, a civil and obliging man who was loth to annoy anybody, especially one with the drink, God help him! Principles! What were they at all? He did not understand Lanty Hanlon.

"But there is one thing that you do not know, Neal Hannigan," said my master.

"I am afraid there is many a thing I don't know," admitted Neal, who was never a man to boast. "But about sheep or cattle——"

"Enough!" roared my master. "But about your own daughter, your own flesh and blood! Ahem! One day you will give her away in marriage to my henchman, Neddy MacMonagle—a scholar. Neddy, where are you?"

"Here he is!" said Manus Glynn, catching me as I made for the door. How I wished to get away!

"Neddy," said my master, "who discovered America?"

But before I could answer we were all aware of a commotion outside. Nailed boots rasped on the camber and the night air was filled with shouting. Angry voices were calling for Lanty Hanlon. My master ran to answer the call, but Oonah Ruddagh shoved him back, an easy job in his condition. He flopped helplessly to the floor. Oonah bolted the door.

"Is Lanty Hanlon in there?" came a voice from the roadway.

"Brrr!" said my master. "I know that ring. It's Kevin Roe."

"That is Kevin," said Oonah. "He's looking for yourself, and God help you if he knows that you're here. There's a hundred of the Freelys outside as well, led by Kevin Roe. Ever since you made him eat the summons he has had his eye open for you."

"Let him be careful that I don't close it for

him," stuttered Lanty Hanlon, and made a swing of his mighty fist. "Let me get out!"

"Bare-futed like that," said Ellen Cosdhu, sinking helplessly in her chair. "Oh! Mother of God, what is the world comin' to at all!"

"We don't mean any harm to anybody else, but if Lanty Hanlon's in there, let him come out!" came the roar from the roadside. "Selling us penny watches for a guinea."

"Let me go!" growled Lanty, trying to throw off Manus Glynn, Neal Hannigan and Eamon Larrimore, who were holding on to him. Even Oonah Ruddagh was assisting, while I held on to my master's leg.

"If he wants to go, let him!" said Paddy Cosdhu, a man of peace in hours of danger. "If he has put his head into trouble, it is his own fault."

"H'm! the true spirit," said Lanty Hanlon, with a superior curl of his nose. "Let me go!"

A stick struck heavily against the door and a voice hissed through the keyhole:

"If the door isn't open at once we'll pull down the house!"

"Mother of God!" wailed Ellen Cosdhu.

"Unhand me, Oonah," roared Lanty.

"Stay where you are," said Oonah, tightening her hold. "And don't be a fool, Lanty Hanlon. The door will stand them that's outside!"

"Not with the hasp that's on it," moaned Paddy through chattering teeth. His face was as white as a sheet of note-paper.

"The hasp won't stand it, Paddy Cosdhu

says," grunted my master. "Unhand me, Oonah!"

"Open the damned door!" came the ultimatum from the outside.

My master, thrust back against the rear wall, made a determined effort now. With one wild burst of Berserk passion he broke the bounds that held him. Neal Hannigan went to the floor, Manus Glynn followed, but Oonah, with a head for any emergency, despite her years, gripped a pitchfork from the roof and with her back to the door stood at the point, facing her godson.

Here was a problem confronting the man. Though very much excited, he paused for a moment and considered the matter, which bristled with properties that were quite new to him. Women are strange cattle. And an angry woman with a pitchfork! These circumstances called for caution.

He looked at the wall at his back. In it stood a window, through which it was possible to make exit if there were no panes there. But there were two panes. However, he wanted to get out.

"That's all I want! To get out!" he grunted, and bracing his weight on tiptoe, gave a wild whoop and took the window head foremost. There was a crash of breaking glass and the last of my master, his bare feet, vanished into the moonlight.

At that moment the old hasp went to smithereens, and a party of wild men, led by Kevin Roe, filled the doorway.

"Where's that strap of the divil?" roared Kevin, swinging a knotted stick over his head.

"Who do you mane?" asked Oonah, turning round, so that she had the fork between herself and the Yankee.

"Lanty Hanlon!"

"He's not here," said Oonah. "And here I've come in and only for a minute, and me a widow woman too! And this is how I find myself with a fork in my hand."

"Mother of God, what's the world comin' to at all," asked Ellen Cosdhu, crossing herself. "All the men in the parish goin' mad."

"Lanty wasn't here at all the night. If he was, he's not here now, and none iv us know where he is," said Paddy Cosdhu. He spoke quite impersonally, though his face, white as a paper sheet a moment ago, was now stamped with a stamp that was red. His nose was bleeding.

"He was in here a minute ago," said Kevin Roe.

"He's hiding in the room," said Denis Freely.

"And we'll search the place and see where the rip of the devil is hiding himself," said a Freely, the brother of Denis.

"And if we find him there will be one house empty in the parish," said another Freely.

"He'll go into a midden this time and he'll not get out!"

"God look on us with all this madness in the world," moaned Ellen Cosdhu.

"No harm will be done to anybody except

the man we want," said Kevin Roe. " Turn up the house and see where he is ! "

Acting on Kevin Roe's instructions, the Freelys set to work, turning up the beds, the lumber in the corners, the heap of turf near the door. Oonah Ruddagh made a show of resistance, but was soon overpowered, and with both arms held by the doughty Freelys she watched the sack of the household. If it were only her house, what a fight she would have made !

The Freelys were past masters of the work which they set themselves to do. Pillow-cases were searched. What might they not contain ? Shawls hanging from pegs on the wall were taken down. What might not be hiding behind them ! Nothing was left to chance, and the Freelys, under the leadership of Kevin Roe, were thorough in their search.

" If we had only left a sentry at the door ! " said Kevin Roe when the examination was completed. " I'm sorry to have troubled you in this way, Paddy Cosdhu. But war's war, you know. So have a drop of this to show that there's no bad blood between us even though I had to tear down your house."

With these words Kevin Roe took a bottle of whisky from his pocket, drew the cork and handed the bottle to Paddy Cosdhu. Paddy, a man of peace, drank heavily.

" And have a pull yourself, Oonah," said Roe, handing the bottle to the old widow woman.

" I don't often," said Oonah, catching the bottle and sniffing it. " I don't often, but seein' it's yerself and the night such a cold one . . ."

With these words she put the bottle to her lips and had a good hearty pull. Then she handed the bottle back, made a wry face and puckered her lips as if it were salt and water she had drunk instead of pure undiluted whisky. This, however, was only a mere feminine formality.

"And you, Mrs. Cosdhu, wantin' a drop?" asked Kevin Roe. "Just say the word——"

The word might have been one of acceptance, but the word was never said. From the outside came the clatter of horses' hoofs at that moment, and mad whoaing and halloing as if the animals of Ballykeeran market, bullocks, ponies and donkeys, were stampeding. And loud over all came the strident shriek: "A Hanlon! A Hanlon to the rescue!"

"Mother of God look on us all!" gasped Nelly Cosdhu. "It's Lanty again!"

Lanty indeed it was, bare-headed and bare-footed, riding bare-backed on his steed, the angle-berried, broken-winded Garibaldi.

"To the fray!" he roared. "Come on, Kevin Roe, and cross swords with me!"

A Freely who happened to be on the road at that moment crossed sticks with Lanty and to his undoing. A blow on the head delivered by the frenzied rider brought the attacker to the ground. Upon this happening, Hanlon gave the horse a lash on the neck with his stick, seized the animal's mane, and with a cry of "Hanlon to the rescue," jumped the roadside fence and careered to the door.

"Let me get at him!" Kevin Roe was

roaring at the moment though no one was detaining him. " Let me get at him ! "

" Come on ! " roared a voice from the doorway, and there looking in was the horse Garibaldi, its nostrils steaming, and lying across the animal's mane was the face of Lanty Hanlon. In his hand the rider held a knobbed and knotted stick, a stick seasoned and supple with a head as big as the fist that held it.

" Come on ! " he roared. " To the rescue of the unhappy women ! Come on ! "

Kevin Roe looked to the window space at his back and dived through it like a shuttle. The others followed. Seeing this my master pulled back his steed by the mane (he had no reins) and galloped to the rear at breakneck speed.

He was in time to see the last of the Freelys come out, and helped this man to the ground with his stick. Then, frenzied and furious, foaming at the mouth, he struck his horse across the head with his fist and was off on the trail of Kevin Roe.

That night the parish was late in going to bed. Twelve o'clock saw all the lamps still lit, one o'clock saw all the doors open. Dark figures could be seen on the road. Here and there men and women gathered in little parties and spoke in whispers. The door of Ballykeeran Church was open and one lone figure was in there making intercession to the Mother of Perpetual Succour —Genevieve Flaherty.

And louder than all things, louder than the whispers and intercessions, than the wind on the hills, than the rumble of the sea, rose the clatter of flying hoofs on the roadway and the thunder of my master's loud voice echoing through the hills. We stood shivering by the door of Paddy Cosdhu's house as he flew by, his wild steed striking sparks of fire from the roadway.

"Where is the caitiff?" he roared, but before our lips could frame an answer the master was far out of sight, so far that the sound of hoofs could not be heard and the sparks of fire were invisible.

And meanwhile Kevin Roe sat safely in a ditch under a drooping beech, listening to the sounds of the great rider who made the night hideous with his yells. Great was Kevin Roe's wisdom, the wisdom born of fear!

At three o'clock the chase was given up. My master came to the door of Meenaroo, dismounted and placed Garibaldi in my charge.

"Back again!" he said. "Back again, Neddy MacMonagle!"

Yes, he was back again. And such a home-coming!

III

I was up early the next morning, and at ten o'clock had breakfast ready for my master who was still asleep. And what a breakfast!

I had scoured the whole parish that morning, got half a dozen newly laid eggs from Oonah Ruddagh, two pounds of prime bacon, not too fat and not too lean, from Mick Flaherty, two fresh trout from the river, catching them myself, a half-pound of China tea, two loaves of bread and a basin of cream-heavy milk.

He was still asleep, his snore, half hiccough and half whistle, filling the room. The oatmeal stirabout, thin and a little burnt, the way he liked it, was simmering in the pot, the trout were frying on the coals and the grand mellow scent of the tea filled the air.

He awoke, threw the blankets aside, and getting from the bed, dressed himself. He paused, buttoning his coat, and sniffed the air.

" Never have I smelt such a repast," he said, and the look on his face was thanks enough for five years' hard work. " Where did you get all these things ? "

I told him.

" But the money, Neddy, the money ! Where did you get it ? "

I told him.

It was good to see him five minutes afterwards smacking his lips with pleasure at that which he had eaten and looking with longing on that which was to come.

" Trout ? "

" Surely, but one yourself, Neddy ! "

" Eggs ? "

" Half and half. The big ones for yourself. Man stands on three things, Neddy, butter, eggs and stirabout."

Like himself I made a good meal. Hunger was my sauce and happiness my relish.

" Neddy MacMonagle," he addressed me when we had finished, " there is much that you have not learned at school. Knowledge of books makes a scholar, but knowledge of a knife and fork makes a gentleman. You have never used a fork in your life, you eat with your mouth open, you pick your teeth with your finger-nails. To do these things shows that you are a tinker. You bolt your food like a dog, and you eat and drink at the same time. This shows that you are a fool, and a fool of this kidney never makes old bones. Now run out, Neddy, and give provender to Garibaldi, then go to Ballykeeran and get two knives and two forks. And, Neddy, what did God send Eamon Larrimore ? "

" A girl," I said. " He was expecting twins."

" He should be thankful that he got only one worry instead of two," said my master. " And the amount you have in pocket, Neddy ? "

" Five pounds four shillings and sixpence ha'penny," I made answer. " I bought a pair of boots ! "

" Why ? " asked my master. " Don't answer for a moment. Your breed seldom wears boots until they reach the age of twenty. That is the men. The women never wear boots. You did not feel cold, for your breed never does. Why did you get the boots ? "

" Well, everyone else has boots."

" Manus Glynn has none."

" But they were so cheap, and I wanted to have a pair when you came home, and——"

" These remarks of yours, Neddy MacMonagle, have everything in them but the truth." He filled his pipe. " Do you know what truth is, Neddy ? "

"I do, indeed."

"Well, you're the first! Now, if I said that you got these boots because you wanted to wear them when you met Norah Hannigan, would I be telling the truth?" asked my master.

"You would," I said, for the man knew the deepest secrets of my heart. Nothing could be hidden from him!

"Now we'll get to more pressing business," he went on, putting a lighted turf-end to his pipe. The pipe gurgled; he spat into the fire and rubbed his lips with the back of his hand. "Now we will discuss the future. We went out some time ago with the object of making a little money, to launch the great business which has been the dream of my life. Unfortunately, and on account of a red-haired woman and a bandy-legged Yankee, the speculation failed in a Ballykeeran midden. I was separated from my friend and henchman, my horse was stolen and I went on the track of the missing steed, I, the Ulysses of Ballykeeran. . . . Neddy, are you a poet?"

"I don't know," was my answer.

"Homer wrote about Ulysses. You've heard of Homer, Neddy?"

"Master Malley told us about him," I answered. "He was a beggar."

"Aye. And you are a tinker," said my master. "This beggarman, Homer, wrote a poem about Ulysses, who padded the hoof for ten years in Greece. I padded the hoof on the search for Garibaldi. It's your work to write a poem about me, Neddy. And what a search it was! I got my steed in the town of Ballymote, where the whole market was round him, inspecting his angleberries. Berries, Neddy? Mountains! I found the man in charge. Trounced him and took the horse from him. Unfortunately for himself he was the owner of the horse, having bought it two hours before. But the tramp was found and—— Well, it's a long story, Neddy, but the upshot of it is that Garibaldi is here and prospects are bright for the future."

"Is the great day near?" I asked, in an eager whisper.

"Nearer, Neddy, than you anticipate," my master informed me. "I have considered everything, what is necessary and what is unnecessary, what is feasible and what is not, and the way is clear. This project of mine is going to benefit the people of Ballykeeran, and why should not the people pay a little at least to start the concern? The railway to Ballykeeran was opened a week ago and this is a hopeful sign. And Ballykeeran has potentialities. There is wealth in it, Neddy MacMonagle, wealth, and so I go forth to see my dreams realised. Meanwhile, go out and give Garibaldi of the best!"

"There's no best," I said.

"No best! What is there?"

"Nothing," I told him.

At that moment the door opened, and Oonah Ruddagh in frilled bonnet and shawl entered the room. Following her came Eamon Larrimore, Paddy Cosdhu and Neal Hannigan. The eyes of my master beamed in welcome on the visitors. He stuck his feet under the table and remained on his seat. This, however, was not due to lack of friendliness. He did not want the neighbours to see him bare-footed.

"Welcome, all of you," he shouted. "Sit yourselves down and be comfortable."

"Feeling all right on it this morning?" asked Neal Hannigan.

"Fit as a fiddle," my master admitted. "And yourself, Neal?"

"Middling, praise be to God, but the cold weather that's in it is awful."

"Awful indeed it is," said Oonah Ruddagh, and she sat down. "It's hard to know what the world is like at all. And it used not to be like this in the old times. But ever since my man went, God be his comforting, I feel the cold more and more."

"It's cold with only one in a bed this weather," said Paddy Cosdhu, rubbing his nose tenderly. It showed sore from the blow which it received the previous night.

"There isn't much news in the paper this weather," said Eamon Larrimore. What had the paper to do with the visit?

"It was grand to hear all the news that was in the papers last winter," remarked Oonah Ruddagh. "And you were the grand reader, Lanty, asthor. There's nobody that can read like you, not even the schoolmaster."

"I never thought much of the schoolmaster," said Neal Hannigan.

"Nor myself," said Paddy Cosdhu. "No, never!" He was certain of this point.

"I can read myself," said Eamon Larrimore.

"But when it comes to the big, long words I'm as ignorant as the child unborn."

My master smiled as he listened. He knew what the visitors were up to! They wanted to speak of the incident of the previous night, but as yet none had the courage to broach the subject. Could the talk of newspapers and great readers lead to it.

"I have heard you read," said Neal Hannigan, fixing an admiring eye on Eamon. "And the way you would take out every word so plain was a wonder. And maybe when you came to a big word you'd make no pretence of understanding it like some. You would just say, 'Here's a word as long as my arm, and I'll give it the skip, for I haven't the learning to know what it means.' Wasn't that the way with him, Oonah?" He appealed to the old woman. Having made such a long assertion Neal was frightened and wanted somebody to back him up.

"That was the way, Neal Hannigan," said Oonah. "But there are ones that can read, or think they can read, and can they?"

"Aye, that is it!" said Paddy Cosdhu. "Can they?"

"Well, speaking as a man that can read a little, but not as much as some, and not half as well, I say they cannot!" said Eamon Larrimore.

"There are ones that think they can," Paddy Cosdhu remarked. "Let's see who they are!"

"Let's see," said the cautious Neal Hannigan.

"Now there's Master Malley." Eamon Larrimore was biting his finger-nails as he spoke.

"And there's the quality of Ballykeeran," said Oonah Ruddagh. She saw the way to the desired end, but looked round for assistance.

"Aye, there's the quality," said Paddy Cosdhu, but not having the courage to go further his remark was of little help.

"Quality!" said Eamon Larrimore with a nose curl of disdain. "Commonality, I call it."

"The true word," said Oonah Ruddagh. "It's the back of my hand to them, to the Flahertys, anyway. And I remember the old father, now with a gold chain across his belly every day of the week, when there was more of him to be seen through the back of his trousers than decency would allow."

"And I've heard of the same," said Eamon Larrimore.

"Heard it!" said the woman. "I remember it! And the way he has got on," she sighed regretfully. "Some people make money and the dear knows why! And the quality name that his daughter has! Genevieve. Not me for a name like that when children of my own came. 'Norah or nothing,' I said with the first, and 'Oonagh or nothing,' I said with the next. 'But,' says himself, God be his comforting, when I said Oonah, 'could we not call her Bella?' 'And what is wrong with Oonah, Peter?' I asked him. 'Wasn't it good enough for me and wasn't it good enough for you when you married me? So it's Oonah or nothing,' I said, and the look that I gave him! 'Well, please yourself,' says he, God be his comforting, and that was the only time that there was a hard word between

Peter and me. But that's neither here nor there, but Genevieve is a name I do not like. And the news that's up and down the parish about her and her marriage!"

"Everybody's talking about it," said Paddy Cosdhu, his eye on my master.

"But it'll be a poor match," Neal Hannigan remarked.

"Better have a red herring than no fish, as the saying is," was the word of Eamon Larrimore.

"But red herrings are not in his line, are they now, Mr. Hanlon?" Paddy Cosdhu enquired, as he looked at my master. The gathering had come to a head and the brave Paddy had lanced it.

"In whose line?" my master enquired. This was his first word in five minutes.

"Well, who do you think now?" asked Neal Hannigan, taking the matter in hand. "Who but——" He stopped at the word, and could not proceed further.

"Kevin Roe," said Oonah Ruddagh.

"Kevin Roe!" exclaimed my master in all innocence. "He is in the country yet, is he?"

"In the country yet!"

"I thought he had gone away a week ago," said my master.

Such ignorance! Did he not know? Did he not remember? Last night on Garibaldi! The house was all voice, all explanation. They would tell him!

"I now remember what happened," said Lanty Hanlon, before the speakers got very far with their chatter. "I was rather excited, and put Garibaldi through his paces——"

"And the coughing of the poor beast and the sparks flying!" gasped Oonah Ruddagh. "You should be ashamed of yourself."

"Lanty Hanlon is never ashamed of anything he does," said my master with a grand wave of his hand. "If I rode my steed it was to show the vigour of the animal. Now I want to sell him. You are needing a horse, Neal Hannigan. How much for Garibaldi?"

"I wouldn't take him as a present," said Neal.

"Well, suppose I give him to you as a present."

"Well, Mr. Hanlon, if you put it that way——"

"I don't put it altogether that way. I'll make a business deal. You can have the cart, the harness, the whip—and the horse, all for six pounds. I never bargain; I sell, and my price is six pounds or nothing."

"Six pounds is a lot of money," said Neal Hannigan.

"All right. You're not buying, then," said my master with the grand air of a man whose verdict was beyond appeal.

"If it was only five pounds ten," said Neal, who in his heart knew that the cart was worth the money asked by Lanty Hanlon.

"You're not wanting a horse and cart?" The question was addressed to Eamon Larrimore.

"I'll give the six pounds," said Neal Hannigan. The bargain was sealed by the smacking of hands.

"And a beehive for sale," said my master. He alluded to the skep outside. "Now who wants a beehive? Ten shillings, the price!"

" I would run ten miles to get away from it," said Oonah Ruddagh. " If there's anything I'm afraid of it's bees. The way they sting! When I was a wee girl, not bigger than two turf, I was stung three times in the leg——"

" Which leg ? " asked my master. " If it was the left leg you'll die of the drouth, and if it was the right leg you'll die in the workhouse."

" Not me to go to the workhouse," said the old woman. She was on her dignity immediately. " You'll be more likely than me to finish your days in the workhouse, Lanty Hanlon. Without a boot to your feet too ! "

" Neddy MacMonagle, the hour is at hand," said Lanty Hanlon to me, when the visitors had departed. " Get a ream of foolscap. If you cannot get a ream, get a dozen sheets. Get pen, ink, note-paper and envelopes. Ask Mick Flaherty to send me a ready-made suit. He knows my size. He also knows the size of my feet. Ask him to send a pair of boots. I need other things, but I will go down there myself and get them. Now go, Neddy ! "

He stood upright, his bare feet holding strong purchase of the earthen floor. Fire was in his eyes and a great look showed on his face. He seemed to be looking far into the future, and even in rags he was magnificent.

" Go, Neddy MacMonagle ! " he repeated. " The hour has come ! "

CHAPTER VIII

THE DAY IS DAWNING

Sweet is the song in the morning.
—*A Ballykeeran Saying.*

I

THE great day of which Lanty Hanlon spoke was not a day in the ordinary sense of the word, a day of twenty-four hours, starting with breakfast, finishing with supper and having a stretch of night thrown in like a tail to a dog.

His Day was a metaphor, so to speak, consisting of boundless time, weeks, months, aye, even years. The Day, his Day, was something past understanding, as it should be, for was he not Lanty Hanlon, Guild's Honoursman, the shining light of the greatest parish in Ireland? Not him to be content with a day of twenty-four hours, and why should he?

A week he worked in his house, office he called it now. Dawn saw his head bent over books, dusk saw his pen moving on white paper. Letters were written and posted to far places, letters came in, were read, digested and nailed to the wall.

I moved about the house, silent as a ghost,

going when he said "Go," coming when he said "Come"! I cooked his meals, laid them out on the table amidst the papers and told him when the food was ready. He ate in silence, his mind on his work, and broke no word with me. Neither did I speak, and being a gentleman now, ate with my mouth closed and made no sound. Of this he took no notice. His head was filled with other things. But his appetite suffered no hurt. In fact it had improved.

"I am not at home in future for any callers," he told me. "If anybody comes here, tell them that and don't let them in!"

To convince Oonah Ruddagh that my master was not at home when she called was a difficult job.

"And I saw him standing at the door a minute ago," said the old woman, when she first came. "Standing with his pipe in his mouth!"

"But he's not at home," I said.

"Not at home! How can he be not at home when he is at home," she grumbled. "I never heard a lie like this, Neddy MacMonagle."

Of course she did not. But I had my instructions.

"He says he's not at home, Oonah, and when he says he's not at home, he's not at home," I told her.

"Then if he's not at home, it'll do nobody any harm to let me in to rest my feet that are almost off me with the corns," she pleaded.

"He won't let anybody come in," I said,

feeling that I was getting the worst of the argument. What a hard job is that of a henchman!

"And that's what he's up to now!" she shrieked. "Making a fool of a poor widow woman. And there's not another house in the parish that I wouldn't be allowed into. Even Mick Flaherty, for all his pride, has the kind word for me when I go to his shop. But here, on the doorstep of a next-door neighbour that I stood sponsor for, I am turned away——"

My master opened the door.

"Good morning to you, Oonah," he said. "Come in and rest yourself! I had a bad headache and I was trying to sleep. But it's all over now."

And Oonah Ruddagh came in and talked for an hour on one thing and another, corns, the white scour which was ravaging the young cattle of the parish, births, deaths, lovemaking and the return of Maldy, who was surely coming back next summer when she would have enough money to pay her passage. And my master sat, ground his teeth and listened, not in the least interested in her chatter and not having the bad grace to turn her away. When she had gone he summoned me to his presence.

"Neddy MacMonagle, I am at home to Oonah Ruddagh in future," he told me. "It's better to speak to her in the house than to listen to her at the door!"

A fortnight later he received a large parcel from the offices of the *Ballyroon Sentinel.* The

Ballyroon Sentinel? Yes, Ballyroon had a newspaper in those days, a newspaper that had big print where it should be small, print where no print should be, and no print where print should have been. Everything was mixed up anyhow, like yarn in a stirabout pot. Just think of this that once appeared in the paper:

Mrs. Mulligan and family desire to return live stock selling well to Edward McNulty married to Mary Bryce, of a daughter in their recent sad bereavement.

Who would give hard money for a paper which, under the heading, "Perils of the Deep," printed the above jumbled notice of a death, a birth, a marriage, and the monthly fair of Ballyroon. Ballykeeran never bought the *Sentinel.*

In the parcel which my master received there were a number of little bills, and on these bills there was a picture of a man running for his life and chased by two women.

And in big letters beneath the running man and the pursuing women was the message:

THE DAY IS DAWNING!

Dawning, mark you! The Great Day, and for a fortnight it had been dawning. What would it be at noon!

That night Lanty Hanlon and I went out in the dark hours and placed the notices where people should see, one on the gate of the graveyard, one at the church door, and one on the barracks where the twelve straight policemen slept. We placed them everywhere.

And when the next ordinary day dawned,

Ballykeeran showed a bold front to the sun, Ballykeeran with its placarded bridges and boulders, its festooned trees and hedges, its great message of the future and the grand time ahead.

The day was Sunday, the day when the people who pray to God in the church congregate outside afterwards and talk of the doings of their neighbours. I joined the crowd, keeping my ears open and my mouth shut in obedience to my master's orders.

"On the door of my house when I opened it I saw it," said Mick Flaherty, speaking to a crowd of common people, a thing which he did not always do. But a strange happening always makes for fellowship.

"'The Day is Dawning' was what was on the placard, wasn't it?" asked Neal Hannigan, who could not read. He had heard the message fifty times already, but still sought assurance of its purport. Might they not be making a fool of him, eh?

"'The Day is Dawning,' that's what was on it," Eamon Larrimore made haste to affirm. "As one that can read I will give my word——"

"But the two women chasing a man!" said Oonah Ruddagh in a voice of surprise. "Never seen anything like it myself. And he's not much to look at, either. Black whiskers, he has, and I hate men with black whiskers. I wouldn't like to wake any morning and see a face with black whiskers in the bed beside me! And I suppose it's Lanty Hanlon that's up to his capers again."

".But what day will be dawning?" asked Neal Hannigan. "A day dawns every day, but the morrow never comes, as the saying is."

"It's the day he promised," said Paddy Cosdhu. "And God send it soon if it's going to be as great as he said it would be!"

This and much more was the subject of their conversation, and coming back I made report to my master, giving him the whole gist of the people's remarks.

"Splendid!" he remarked when I had finished. "It interests them and that is half the business done!"

"They all say there's a great time coming," I made haste to remark, seeing pleasure in my master's eye and feeling he would not consider it amiss if I asked a question. "They say that this great day will make the fortune of Ballykeeran and everybody will be rich in a year's time. In what way will they be rich?"

"Neddy MacMonagle," said my master, and his brow darkened, "ask no question and you'll hear no lies!"

II

In that week I turned away many people and had much trouble in proving how my master, who was in his house, was really not there, because he was "not at home." On Monday I was ordered to stand five yards away from the door and make explanations. The noise of voices disturbed my master at his work. Even at five yards the sounds troubled his seclusion. On Tuesday I stood ten yards away, on Wednesday twenty, and twenty yards was the distance for the remainder of the week.

On the last day of the week (Sunday it is with us, though abroad they tell me that they start the week with Sunday—resting before toil and not after!)—a fresh notice appeared on walls, boulders and bridges, and this the wording of the notice:

TO ALL WHOM IT MAY CONCERN

To Those resident within the Townlands of Meenalore, Meenaran, Kingarrow, Kilfinnan, Dooran, Cushendoon and Cushendall:

To Those Property-holders of mature years, who are Natives of the Parish of Ballykeeran:

To Those Ratepayers of Ballykeeran who have slept too long and now feel that it is the hour to waken—

Whereas a New Era is in sight and the Hour is at hand.

And Whereas an Hour lost can never be regained.

Now, Therefore, take notice that on this date, October 29, 18—, at the hour of 3 p.m., a meeting is arranged to take place in the Ballykeeran National School, situate within the Parish of Ballykeeran.

And Now Therefore take notice that all Property-holders and Ratepayers of mature years who are on the electoral list of Ballykeeran are invited to attend this meeting, which is convened for 3 p.m., on the date above mentioned.

Given and set forth under my hand this day, October 29, 18—.

LANTY U. HANLON,
Guild's Honoursman.

BALLYKEERAN FOR EVER

Lanty U. Hanlon! U? Ulysses, of course!

I was at church on that momentous day, but left when the last Gospel was read and the good Father Dan was starting his sermon.

"My Dearly Beloved Brethren——"

I bowed to the Divine Hidden Presence and, with head high, walked down the nave. All eyes turned towards me. How great to be henchman on that day! How they must have envied me! wishing that they were even door-keepers in the house of the mighty. What great secrets were within my breast! And did they not wish that they were I!

But my pride gave way to surprise when I got home and saw my master. What a change had taken place in the man. What had happened? My master he was, of course, but so changed that I hardly knew him.

He was dressed as I had never seen him dressed before, and I had seen him in many guises. I had seen him as a man of means, a man without means, shod and shoeless, in a red petticoat, jerkin, felt hat and cockade, in the quiet clothing of a financier and the shirt-sleeves of a clerk.

But now his appointments were different from any he had ever worn in my presence before, and this the manner of them. On his head was perched a castor hat, higher than the priest's and glossier than the coat of a stall-fed bull. His starched collar stood ear-high. Bright were his polished cuff-links, but not as bright as his tie-pin. His boots, which I had polished that morning, shone like a looking-glass in the sun. The legs of his trousers were creased back and front. The creases were straight and perfect; the trousers had lain for three nights under the bed-tick on which he slept, and my master's weight would have creased a plate of zinc.

"Neddy MacMonagle, gather up all the papers you can find," he ordered me. "Take them to the school-house. Put them on the master's desk, and wait there until I come."

I made haste to gather the papers.

"How many have you?" he asked, when I had finished.

"Thirteen papers," I told him.

"Thirteen is unlucky," said my master. "Make it fourteen. The more to be seen, the greater the show!"

III

I got to the school. The parish was there waiting at the door, Mick Flaherty one of the first comers. His heart was able to stand it, but nothing more, mind you. Paddy Cosdhu and Eamon Larrimore were there, talking to one another in whispers, smoking short clay pipes, spitting at intervals and rubbing that part of the world on which they spat with their hobnailed boots. Master Malley and Neal Hannigan were in attendance, Norah Hannigan also. She was not of mature years, and might be turned away. But, again, she might not, so she would await and see what happened. Two were not there, Kevin Roe and Genevieve Flaherty. Love-making needs a quiet place, and they were not married yet.

The Ballykeeran band, fife and drum, played national airs. *The Wearing of the Green* was struck up when I arrived.

" And what is this going to be at all, at all ? " Paddy Cosdhu asked me when I came to the door of the school. I shook my head and looked wise, as if I really knew all, but was not prepared to divulge the secret.

" It's money for everybody and a good job, as far as I can make out," said Eamon Larrimore.

" Everybody here has a job," answered Paddy with a cunning smile—" a job to make both ends meet."

The master opened the door and let me in, and the band, which had ceased playing, struck up again. A cheer rose from the assemblage. " Ballykeeran for ever ! " was the loud cry of a hundred lusty voices.

Lanty Hanlon, G.H., cuffed, collared and hatted, was seen approaching.

I had arranged the papers as directed before he came in. And when he came in it was not in the usual manner, but borne on the strong shoulders of his neighbours. Honour where honour was due, and Ballykeeran was princely in its recognition of the great.

When he was freed he perched himself on the raised platform. He was a figure of importance, with one hand in his trousers pocket, the other holding a sheet of foolscap curved like a roll of music. I placed a glass of water on the table near his elbow and took up my place immediately behind.

His calm eye took stock of the crowded room. He coughed. Quiet there, at the back! Lanty Hanlon, G.H., is going to speak!

"Gentlemen——"

Paddy Cosdhu looked at Eamon Larrimore as if doubting whether that man could be included in this category.

"Gentlemen: Before you can rear a pig you must first procure it," my master began. "Each and everyone of you know that, which is as true as death. Aye, and truer. It's an old saying, but in it there is common sense. Before you can rear a pig you must first procure it.

"That gets me to my business, so, from now, nothing irrelevant. I know where a pig is to be procured, and this pig is one that everyone here will take pleasure in rearing; and the name of the Pig is to be called 'The Ballykeeran Development Society.'"

"Hear! Hear!"

Whereupon Lanty Hanlon, G.H., gave utterance to the plans of a project which he contemplated launching.

"Here we have here, miles of country, mountain and moor, good for nothing except feeding moor-fowl; streams falling from the hills, good for nothing bar rotting the crops that you've set in the braes; young men of muscle, good for nothing but going abroad and working, shovelling dung waggons in Scotland or falling from sky-scrapers in New York; and girls—ah! that is the saddest story of the lot! Are they good for nothing?"

"No!"

"Yes!"

"Well, all that they are good for now is going to the States, these fair Irish girls, the flower of the land! And when abroad they are shoved into fetid kitchens to cook food for money-hogs who are not fit to tie the boots of these girls. There is where your daughters go, into these foul haunts of sin and shame, where they lose their health and sometimes—how sad to say—their very souls!"

As he said this, there was a slight commotion near the doorway.

Oonah Ruddagh had just edged her way into the assembly, and being the mother of three daughters, all Yankees, by virtue of their long sojourn in the United States, she was interested in the speaker's remarks. But hearing him speak of the pitfalls into which girls fell when abroad, Oonah became angry.

"Do you mean my girls, daughters of my own?" she called. "Is that what you're after meaning, Lanty Hanlon?"

"Whisht!" whispered Paddy Cosdhu. "Let him have his word!"

"You're just as bad as he is, Paddy Cosdhu," said Oonah. "And you with your sisters away there, and they've never sent word or money to your old father—God rest him—all his life. But of mine, it's another story. Every Christmas it's ten pounds apiece from every one of them. The Bank can stand surety for my word, and if——"

"Of course it can," said my diplomatic master. "And I can stand on your word as well. But if you just wait till I have my say, you'll see what I mean. Just take a seat and make yourself comfortable. It's a long walk that you've put past you coming up from the church."

"A long walk, and that's true, Lanty Hanlon," said the old woman, now somewhat mollified and taking a seat. "And the corns that's on my feet!"

"Corns!" said the speaker in a tone of concern. "They're the devil's own curse, and with the weather going to change, they're always bad."

"I've one between the big toe and the one next it," said Oonah, putting one leg across the other and touching her boot with a gnarled thumb. "And it's the worst I have."

"A one between the toes is always the worst," said my master in a voice of feeling. "But we'll soon have a day when there won't be a corn on a foot on the country road. And that will be when"—he hurried on as Oonah gave a cough as a preliminary to saying something further—"when we have established the Ballykeeran Development Society, when everyone in the place will have the quality toss, when poverty will be a thing of the past and money without stint or sparing will be in every pocket.

"Here, Oonah"—he spoke as if for the sole benefit of the woman—"here we have miles of mountain and moor going to loss, waters going to loss, the whole country going to the dogs. But if it is taken in hand, all will change. The mountain and moor will become white with wool, the water-power of the streams will be harnessed. Every stream will have its woollen mill, every hand its shuttle. Ireland once was called the Land of Saints and Scholars; now, with the Ballykeeran Development Society, it will become the Land of Shuttles and Shears.

"But to get such a thing in working order will require much work," said my master, and thereupon commenced enumerating the difficulties which he (my master was going to shoulder the whole concern at the start) would encounter—the propaganda, planning, and the writing of letters to the great and sympathetic. All sources would have to be tapped; a question asked in the House. Michael Davitt would be asked to do that. He knew Michael Davitt. Possibly an act would be passed. Yes, it certainly would be passed, and then it was law, as sure as the bank.

But money was required, now, on the spot, at once.

There was a certain uneasy shuffling of feet and timorous coughing. Uneasy eyes looked towards the door. Even Oonah Ruddagh brought both feet to the floor as if she had determined to face the road home despite the pain of her corns. My master sensed the mood and hastened to temper it.

"Before going any further let us appoint a committee," he said hurriedly. "A President, a Secretary and a Treasurer. A President! Who can fill that post better than our friend, the good and estimable Eamon Larrimore, a man known to us all and held in repute near and far. I propose Eamon Larrimore as Chairman, and all who agree to that put their hands up."

My master put his own hand in the air, and immediately every hand in the building, even Larrimore's, followed suit.

"But what am I to do?" asked Larrimore, pulling his hand down, when he realised what he had done.

"Easy job, man," said Hanlon. "Easy job!"

"I can dig pratees and carry a creel of turf," said Larrimore. "But as for the job of a chairman——"

"The easiest job in the world," said my master in an offhand manner. "And now, as Secretary, I propose Paddy Cosdhu; a man of ability, who writes a good hand and can keep tally of figures with the best of them. All who favour Mr. Patrick Cosdhu, up with their hands."

All hands, with the exception of Oonah Ruddagh's and Paddy Cosdhu's, went in air. Paddy knew that he was doing the correct thing in not voting for himself and gloried accordingly. Oonah did not like Paddy, but feeling that it was safe to remain while the money question was in abeyance, she settled herself in her seat again.

"So far, so good," said my master. "Now comes the job of electing a Treasurer. This is a horse of another colour. The work of a treasurer requires insight relating to financial concerns, credit and debit, the mystery of chartered accountancy, algebraic equation, interest, simple and compound, the rate of current exchange and the fluctuations of the world's markets. I'm not going to dwell any longer on this, but I would ask if there is any man here whom the meeting can propose to fill this onerous post? Now, whom do you propose, Mr. Cosdhu?"

"Me!" said Mr. Cosdhu, the secretary, and his eyes wandered round the meeting, taking stock of all the faces. There was a certain air of uncertainty over the whole assembly.

"If a man knows algebraic equation, remember," whispered my master.

"Does any of you know that?" asked Paddy, spitting on the floor and curling up the corners of his eyes with a very knowing look, paramount to saying that though he himself had no time to waste on such a minor matter as algebraic equation, other members of the party might possibly know something about it.

With imperturbable front my master waited. "Algebraic equation," perhaps, was a mere phrase to him, sound without meaning, but, despite this, there was a hidden purpose in its present use. Mystification was needed for the occasion.

" No one willing to take the job, Mr. Cosdhu ? "

" Not a one at all," said the Secretary, with a downthrow of his arms. He had done his best.

" Can you suggest anyone, whom you think suitable, Mr. Larrimore ? " Hanlon enquired, looking at the chairman. " One who has done a bit of clerking and knows the ins and outs of trigonometry ? "

" Bar the schoolmaster," began Larrimore. " I——"

" He has his hands full with the young spalpeens in the school," said Hanlon. " What stupid creatures ! " he added, under his breath. No one heard this except me.

" Well, what about yourself doing the job, Mr. Hanlon ? " asked the Secretary. " You have the learning."

" Well, it's a difficult job," said my master. " But . . ."

" You're the man for the job," said Larrimore, " You're the old dog for a hard road."

" But if anyone else," suggested my master.

" No one else has the head for the job," said the Secretary. " So up with your hands, all of you."

His words seemed to contain a threat. All the hands in the room went up.

" Thank you all," said my master modestly. " So I am, from now forward, your servant, and I will do my utmost to make the Ballykeeran Development Society a success. Not alone will Ireland hear of it, but the whole world. Ireland has been steeped in slumber for too long. We must waken it, pull it from the bog in which it is lying, and first and foremost in the van will be the Society which we have formed to-day, the Ballykeeran Development Society."

"Hear, hear! Ballykeeran for ever!" came the shout of the assembly. The band outside struck up a few bars.

"Ballykeeran for ever and always," said my master, catching the mane of the mood. "For ever and always! But money is needed at the start. A small collection. A shilling a head! It's a matter of putting out a shilling to draw in a sovereign. We must have funds."

From the corner of his eye he saw that Oonah Ruddagh was again restless. Both her feet were on the ground, her eye on the door.

"A shilling per head," he went on. "And soon we'll have money coming to the place. Wool will be worth its weight in gold, work will be paid for, butter will go up in price. A field worth ten pounds now will be worth fifty pounds and much more when the Ballykeeran Development Society is put on its feet.

"And another thing," he hastened to add, seeing that Oonah Ruddagh was standing. "I'll do my work free, not asking a penny for the labour. And when it becomes a profitable business, when a treasurer will be paid a thousand pounds a year for his work, I'll hand the job over to some younger man and let him do it. So now, all that you here have to do is to pay a shilling apiece, and that money will be placed in the hands of the Chairman and Secretary until such time as it is needed for stamps and stationery and incidental expenses."

As he was not taking control of the funds, and as Larrimore and Cosdhu were the soul of integrity and probity, the meeting agreed—all, with the exception of Oonah Ruddagh.

"Can we not wait until the time that we have plenty of money from this whatever-it-is-going-to-be?" she asked. "Then, if it gives a lot to me, I'll not pay one shilling, but two."

"But it's wanted now," Paddy Cosdhu, with a very self-important air, informed the woman. "And it's only a shilling."

"But a shillin's a lot," said Oonah.

"You've got to buy your pig before you can rear it," said the Chairman. This was one point of Hanlon's speech that he particularly remembered. In fact he remembered nothing else. "And a shilling won't put anyone to the workhouse."

"I'll tell you what I'll do. I'll give a pound of butter," said Oonah, who by some strange sense of valuation thought a shilling in kind was not as much as a shilling in cash, though this was the price of butter at that time. "A pound of good fresh butter and the like of it never marketed in Ballykeeran!"

"I never heard of a Society starting on a pound of butter," said the Secretary. "It's not a creamery that we're going to open."

"But there's money in butter," said Oonah. "I can call to mind the day that Mick Flaherty of Ballykeeran had to steal the rags off scarecrows to put patches on the bottom of his trousers. But look at him the day with his quality toss and his wife in silks and satins and his girl that won't come out on the street unless she's in shoe-leather. Shoes in the cradle means none in the stubble for many's a one, but not for Mick Flaherty, with his light weights and short measures. And the fortune that he has made, and all on butter."

Did the old woman realise that Mick was in the room? Probably she did.

"I'm glad to see that most of those here are making a brave show," said my master, cutting across Oonah's utterances and fixing his eye on the hat that passed from hand to hand through the assembly. Into this hat silver coins were falling. "Just pass it along here and as treasurer I will add my little quota."

The hat was handed to him and into it he put a silver crown-piece. At that moment he had not much more in his possession.

"We are all doing our best," he said, seizing his act of the moment as an example for the rest of the company. "Those who can give a little will do so, I know, for such an opportunity seldom occurs in this arm of the world. And those who cannot pay, cannot, and that's an end to that. Asking those who can't cough up a little to pay is the last thing in the world the Ballykeeran Development Society would think of doing."

"If it comes to that," said Oonah Ruddagh, shoving her thin, claw-like fingers into a bag which she had drawn from the pocket of her quilted petticoat. The bag resembled a woollen sock, as it probably was at one period. Now it was Oonah's purse. "If it comes to that, I can pay as well as any family in the parish."

With these words she handed a shilling to Lanty Hanlon.

And in this manner did Lanty U. Hanlon, G.H., inaugurate the Ballykeeran Development Society.

IV

To me the days that followed that momentous Sunday were a delight. My master, so long fallen in the estimate of his neighbours, came into his own again. When Oonah Ruddagh, on the high-road, passed by our dwelling, she was always seen to bless herself! She was praying! What for? For the success of the Ballykeeran Development Society and for the Treasurer of the Society and for her young daughter, Maldy, who was surely coming home in the Summer. But what had Maldy to do with the Ballykeeran Development Society? Who knows?

At night, when the lamps were lit, the men of the neighbourhood gathered together on the roadside, and at a point from which the light of my master's lamp was visible. The light was a beacon foretelling prosperity and the good time. And when these men spoke it was in whispers, for maybe if he heard their voices it would disturb him at his work.

Genevieve Flaherty was interested, it was said. But this perhaps was only the idle talk of the roadside. Sufficient to state, however, that she no longer walked with Kevin Roe.

Sobriety, honesty and industry were my master's three outstanding characteristics in those days. If when passing a public-house, attired in his best from glossy castor to shining leather, someone invited him to enter, he would raise both hands shoulder high and shake his head. Sobriety was his watchword now ; nothing would move him from the path of rectitude.

But he seldom entered the village. He was far too busily engaged, drawing out plans, schemes and projects relating to the new society, which was now as much a part of the parish as Mick Flaherty's licensed premises or the police barracks.

My master was the life and soul of the movement—treasurer, secretary and chairman combined. Eamon Larrimore and Paddy Cosdhu possessed honorary offices—nothing more. Without duties, too, for what did they know about the ins and outs of the business ?

My master's lamp was lit into the late hours, and there in his room, with the blind down so that it was impossible for passers-by to see him from the street, he sat immersed in papers, his coat off, shirt-sleeves rolled up, fingers ink-stained, a lead pencil stuck in his hair and a pen behind each ear.

Industry was his prerogative ; soon the achievement would blossom and shears and shuttles would be heard from one end of the parish to the other.

His honesty was above censure. The funds

of the society were safe in the keeping of Mr. Patrick Cosdhu, secretary, and Mr. Eamon Larrimore, chairman. And these two were surety sufficient to the last penny.

Now and again my master would send me to the chairman or secretary, with a request (in writing, and signed) for a small sum to be expended in stamps, a small sum in paper and a small sum in ink. Nothing worth speaking about, and for every penny received due acknowledgment was made in writing and thuswise :

Received for stamps the sum of 1/3 (one shilling and threepence).

LANTY U. HANLON, G.H., Treasurer, B.D.S.

Honesty his perquisite, how could he stand otherwise than as a man of esteem in the eyes of the society ?

" Aye, and may he keep like that always, the good soul, till we get the grand times that he promised us," said old Oonah Ruddagh.

V

The Spring sped by and came the Summer, the lean season when June merges into July, when the old potatoes are all eaten and the new crop is not ready for the spade. At this season the affairs of the Ballykeeran Development Society were in a precarious condition. At that time the famous Manifesto was written, that Manifesto which came to be known across the face of the world. It was written at that date, but not printed.

" Neddy MacMonagle," said my master to me

one morning, " go to the secretary and ask him how much money has he in hand."

I made haste to the home of Paddy Cosdhu and asked the question, and Paddy took a delf teapot from the dresser and poured its store on the table. A small pile it was, surely, and most of it coppers. I am certain that no coppers were put in the hat on the momentous Sunday.

" Well, this is what is left now," said Paddy. " It was going away all the time, with nothing coming in, and it's a big purse that will be able to bear that now, isn't it ? "

" It is," I answered.

" 'Tis, indeed, and there's no lie in it ! " Paddy picked up a shilling and sighed as he did so. " Now 'twas a lot of stamps and ink and paper that you got, the two of you. Every second day it was money going, and remember, there was not so much in the collection at the beginning. Three times you came last week, and it was four shillings and sevenpence you took one day. Wasn't that so, Neddy ? "

I nodded, for that was so.

" And the week before that you came four times. Wasn't that so, Neddy ? "

I nodded, though there was a slight mistake.

" And the week before that again, 'twas seven times you came, and always asking for money and getting it. And wasn't that so, Neddy ? " Paddy asked.

" No," I said. I had never come two days in succession.

" Aye, aye. That's right," said Paddy. " What a good memory you have ! 'Twasn't that week, now that I remember it, but the week before. The memory that you have for your size!"

He built up the money in two neat piles, silver in one pile and coppers in the other. And while he built he discussed money in all its aspects: the difficulty to procure it, the difficulty to hold it, the way it goes when there is nothing coming in, the way it comes in for some and not for others, and the thin season that was in it now, the cows near note and little or no milk—the potatoes, too, were looking well, and by the grace of God, if the weather stood and the blight didn't come, we would surely be able—that is, with the Society—to live like lords and high gentlemen.

And much more to the same effect and purpose, all having very little to do with the matter in hand.

"How much is left?" I enquired at last. "My master wants to know."

"Well, Neddy, the straight question looks for the straight answer," Paddy admitted. "You remember a week three weeks ago, and the week before that and the week before that as well. Well, Neddy, how many times did you come that week for money?"

"I don't remember," I said.

"That's it," said Paddy, very much relieved. "You don't remember that week at all, at all. And why should you, indeed, Neddy? Why should you, indeed?"

"Why shouldn't I, indeed?" I made answer.

"Well, this is the way it is now," said Paddy. "I'm the secretary. I put the money in the teapot when I got it. And a good place for money it is, not like a pocket, with the silver falling through the linings. I put the money there and paid out when you came with the wee slips of white paper. And you don't mind all the times you came, do you now?"

"I do," I said.

"You don't!" said Paddy angrily. "With you only the size that you are, how can you remember as far back as me? And if I say you have been here for money seven times in one week, you have been, and my word will stand against yours if it comes to the point."

"But my master put down the money that he received from you, put it down every day that he got it!" I explained.

"And I put down every penny I paid as well," said Paddy. "And if I gave money to you and marked it down, and if Lanty Hanlon did not mark it down, what does it mean?"

"I don't know," I told him.

"Well, I know!" Paddy Cosdhu rubbed his hands and raised the corners of his lips in a cunning grin. "It's because the money left my hands and never reached his. Neddy, that's the reason, the true reason. But I'm not blaming you for it. One of the MacMonagles, you know. As the old cock crows, the young cock learns. Eh, Neddy, my boy, eh? One of them, Neddy. That's the reason."

"That is not the reason. All these mistakes are due to a fault in book-keeping. A teapot is a poor safe. Any hand can crawl in. How much is left, Mr. Cosdhu?"

It was my master who spoke. He was standing at the door in his glossy castor and shiny shoe-leather, a roll of papers in his hand. He never went out now without this roll, a symbol of his work.

"Nine shillings and sixpence," said Paddy, who merely counted the white money. Take heed of the coppers! Not the Secretary of the Ballykeeran Development Society!

"That will do for the time being," said my master, lifting the silver and putting it in his pocket. "We'll go back to the office now, Neddy."

When we got outside, my master took a letter from the breast-pocket of his coat, and handed it to me. As he handed it to me I glanced at the address on the envelope and read:

MISS GENEVIEVE FLAHERTY,
Ballykeeran.

"Financially, the Society is at an end," my master remarked. "The Secretary's hand went too often into that teapot. The present is a critical moment, and I sink my pride and prestige in approaching a woman for assistance. What is the latest news concerning Kevin Roe, Neddy?"

"Genevieve Flaherty doesn't speak to him now."

"Since when?"

"Since you've been the talk of the parish, and everyone said you're the greatest man in Ireland."

"Then go and give that letter to Miss Flaherty," said my master. "Put it in her own hands, remember, and don't let her father or mother see it. Now, off with you!"

CHAPTER IX

GENEVIEVE

Boots for the cradle mean none for the stubble.
—*A Ballykeeran Saying.*

I

I CAME to the shop of Mick Flaherty. Over the door a sign with blurred lettering told that the house was licensed for the sale of liquors for "consumption on and off the premises."

Mick was a thriving man, thrifty by nature and on principle, simple and well-disposed in his intercourse with the world. He had started poorly (the first generation, remember), but now he was the wealthiest man in the village, a J.P. and a District Councillor.

He gave out the Rosary at church every Sunday, went round the seats collecting the plate-money, putting down his own donation first, which was always a silver piece save when a special collection was the order of the day and his poorer brethren gave silver. Then he gave gold.

His wife could speak French, his daughter French and German, but neither could speak Gaelic. The old tongue was not fashionable in Ballykeeran.

Amongst the people Mick's sufficiency brought him great esteem. But more famous than his worldly wealth was his heart. This we all knew would stop beating one day, perhaps when he was enjoying a good substantial meal. For some reason or another everybody considered that breakfast would be the fatal meal. In the end, however (God be his comforting), he died of a bad cold.

When I went in I saw him sitting at his desk, his head bald as a bladder, his eyes scanning a ledger. For a while he was utterly unconscious of my presence. In the end, however, he sensed me, raised his head, shut his eyes for a moment, then opened them.

" Well, my little boy, what can I do for you ? " he asked.

" Mr. Hanlon has asked me to give a letter to Miss Genevieve."

" Genevieve . . . h'm ! Mr. Hanlon . . . h'm ! "

He spoke in a meek and thoughtful voice as if considering something.

" Mr. Hanlon ? " he enquired. " What is he doing now ? "

" Everybody," I said. At that time I thought this was a very clever remark. I had heard it used on the roads.

" What do you mean, boy ? " asked the man in a severe voice. " Mr. Hanlon is a good, upright man. He may be foolish at times, but that's a thing of the past. The head he has ! "

Upon saying this he shook his bald pate and was silent for a moment.

"A letter!" he enquired. "Show it to me?"

I took the missive from my pocket, held it between finger and thumb, ready to pocket it again in case he reached for it.

"Give it to me," he commanded.

"I was told to give it to Miss Genevieve and no one else," I told him.

"No one else . . . h'm!" he said. "Well, away into the kitchen with you, and you'll find the women in there . . . h'm! And what is your name, my boy?"

"Neddy MacMonagle," I told him.

"Would you like a liquorice ball, Neddy?" he asked.

"I would," was my answer.

He took a liquorice ball from a glass jar and handed it to me. I took it and put it in my mouth.

"Boys are very fond of liquorice balls nowadays," he said. "But in my time, in my young days, it was different. We might get some at Christmas if we were lucky, but even if we didn't get any at all it didn't hurt us. We were smarter on our feet than some that's in it at the present time. Now, Neddy, what have you done with that liquorice ball?"

Saying this, the grocer assumed a knowing look, an almost mischievous look I might say, and shook a podgy finger in my face.

"I ate it," I replied, although I had not, for the sweet and greasy ball still remained inside my cheek.

"Well, that is what it was meant for," said

the man affably. "You'll be able to eat another, I'll warrant."

"I will."

He took three more from the jar, thrust one across the counter towards me, keeping two in reserve.

"And your master?" he enquired. "Is he hard at his work now?"

"Hard's not the word," I said. "At it from morning till night."

"And what do you think of this Society?" he asked. "You, yourself. You look a smart boy and you can see things . . . h'm! Now put that liquorice ball in your mouth, for there are two more here and I don't know what to do with them!"

At that moment I heard a noise behind me, a rustle like a rabbit in wet grass. I looked round to see the grocer's wife coming from the rear apartment. She was dressed in her best, bonnet and ribbons and satin, a real quality attire.

"Dear me! dear me!" she sighed. "The girl out and I don't know where she is. You haven't seen her here, *mon cher*?"

"Didn't see her since dinner-time," said the man.

"The girls that's in it nowadays!" The woman shook her head helplessly. "Gadding about from morning to night! And me on the Nine Fridays, too, and it time to be in the church. Only one to be done, too, and if I miss this one I shall lose all the Indulgences."

"She'll be in in a minute, maybe," said the man.

" And you," the woman queried, noticing that I occupied a position in the apartment. " What is your name, *petit garçon* ? "

" Neddy MacMonagle," I replied.

" He's working with Mr. Hanlon," said Mick Flaherty. " And he has a letter from Lanty for Genevieve."

" Oh, indeed ! " the woman exclaimed. " A letter ? "

" A letter . . . h'm ! " said the man, and he coughed meaningly. " But he hasn't to give it to anyone bar Genevieve. And he won't, either."

" Oh ! indeed ! " said the woman. " Well, I don't blame him ! And he's a good boy, too, I'm sure ! Aren't you, now ? "

" Middling," I admitted with becoming modesty.

" Then come in with me, here, to the room at the back, and have a bowl of tea," said the woman. " You like tea, don't you ? "

" I do," I confessed.

II

We went into the room at the rear, a stuffy, sooty apartment, its window-panes fly-blown, its furniture placed anyway and anywhere. Hanging from a soot-encased crook over the fire was a simmering kettle speaking to itself. A cat lay asleep in the ashes.

The woman put some tea in a delf teapot, poured water on the tea and placed the pot on the hob. This done, she cut a thick slice of bread, spreading butter and jam on it.

"Come now, my *petit garçon*, and make a meal of it," she commanded, ushering me into a chair at the table. I sat down.

"Make yourself as comfortable as you can," she advised. "And a bowl of tea! There's nothing like it when ones are growing. I'll just have a bowl, too, for it's my one weakness, tea. I'm ready for a cup any time, day or night. It must have been hard on them when there was no tea at all in the country, mustn't it, now?"

"It was, surely," I declared.

"And Mr. Hanlon is fond of his drop of tea, isn't he?"

"He is that."

"That's all he takes now, the poor man?"

"That's all," I told her.

"This is drawn now," she went on, taking the teapot from the hob and preparing two bowls of the beverage. "And, between you and me, it's a good drop." She spoke in confidence and took a sip, rolling it round her teeth with a loud, sucking noise. "Good, yes. Very good. And who makes the tea for poor Mr. Hanlon?"

"Sometimes I make it and sometimes he makes it himself, but he's soon to have a servant-girl in the house," I informed her.

"If he was a wise man he'd be thinking of getting the woman now with this big business of his with the Society," said the woman, her lips in the tea and her eyes on my face.

"He's of that mind himself."

"You're telling a lie!"

"It's true as death," I said. "It's more than once I've heard him speak of it."

"You have, then?"

"That I have."

"But maybe it's only his fun."

"As far as I can see, he means it," I told her. "And then the girls that are setting their eyes on him."

"But the great question is—Who is he after?"

"That's it," I said, assuming a wise pose and shaking my head knowingly.

"Have another bowl of tea." There was entreaty in the woman's voice. "That one that you had was such a wee skimpy one. And do you like liquorice balls?"

"I do."

In regard to liquorice balls Mr. Flaherty was generous, but his wife was lavish. She went into the shop and returned with the half-filled bottle.

"Open your pocket," she said, pointing to the one on the left of my coat.

"There's a hole in it," I told her.

"Then, that other one," insisted the woman, pointing to the pocket on the right.

"There's nothing of that one left."

"Then take the whole bottle," she said in a burst of overwhelming generosity. "And you can eat them for a week."

I took the bottle, placed it on the table by my side, and continued to eat the bread and butter. I was very much at my ease now, feeling in a measure that I had the woman in my power.

"And another sup of tea?" she asked, lifting the teapot and pouring me out another bowl.

" And," she bent her head and whispered in my ear, " and maybe it's an egg that you would like ? "

" It is," I said.

" I knew it, my *petit garçon*, I knew it," she exclaimed, her eyes beaming with joy at having anticipated my desires. Her generosity surprised me, for common report had it that she was a tight-fisted, close-scraping woman, who gave generously to God but stopped short at His creatures. " Hard-boiled, maybe ? "

" That's how I like it," I confessed.

She boiled the egg, placed it in a stand beside a salt cellar.

" Fresh laid by a red hen," she told me. " A wee red hen, but I don't like it. It crows like a rooster, and that's a sign of bad luck."

" That's what the people say," I said obligingly, though prior to this I had never heard that a crowing hen portended evil.

" Indeed, and you've heard that, too? " she asked.

" I have indeed," I muttered.

" Well, I don't know what it all means, anyway. Last night I had a bad dream about white sheets, and that's a sign of death."

" That's true," I said, reaching for the salt.

" Indeed, and you've heard that as well ? "

" Aye ! "

" Oh, dear me ! and there you've spilt the salt," she exclaimed as I caught my spoon against the side of the egg, spilling the contents on the table. " That with the other things ! What's going to come over us at all ! If I had only the dream-book to tell me all about it. But the way that books have of going. I had one book, and manys and manys the time I've read it and the tears running from my eyes all the time. *East Lynne* it is called. When you grow to be a big man, just read it and you'll see what it's like."

"It's filled with mawkish sentiment," I said, placing my yolk-yellowed spoon on the table. Here I may explain that on the previous day I had been reading a periodical where an epithet something like the foregoing was applied to Mrs. Henry Wood's novel. I had never read the volume.

"What are you saying?" asked the woman with a start of surprise.

"Filled with mawkish sentiment."

"What does that mean?"

Here I was cornered, and accordingly I felt very discomfited. What it really meant I could not say.

"Have you read it?" she asked.

"I have that," I replied, wishing that I had not ventured to make such an unwise remark in relation to the volume.

"But then you're not old enough to understand it," she said. "And it's a sin for you to read these books."

"And is it a sin for anybody else to read them?"

"Not when one's grown up and knows the difference between good and bad. And the letter you've on you?" she suddenly enquired as if in the understanding of both all our previous conversation, the soft talk, the feeding, even, had led up to this. " Is it a bulky one ? "

" It is and it isn't," I said diplomatically.

" In his own handwriting ? " she asked.

" Aye."

" Show it across to me."

" It's for Miss Genevieve," I said. " And I was told not to give it to anyone else."

" Dear me ! I don't want to eat it." The woman assumed an aggrieved air. " I just want to see the handwriting. He had a good hand long ago, a steady hand."

" It's as steady as ever."

" Well, let me see it, that I may judge." Her air was that of one who had thought deeply on this particular subject.

" I was told not to give it to anyone, only herself."

" I know, but I'm her mother."

" But you, above anyone, I was told not to give it to," I said.

" Well, to hear that in my own house," exclaimed Mrs. Flaherty in a shocked voice. " What is the world coming to at all ? But then, after dreaming of white sheets ! But I'll wait till she comes in ! "

So saying, she sat down in her chair, folded her arms across her breast and closed her eyes. She would certainly lose all her Indulgences !

III

Miss Genevieve Flaherty entered attired in her best, gold-rimmed spectacles on nose, on her breast a feather such as was never fathered by a bird within the mearings of Ballykeeran. She smelt the stewing tea, saw the teapot on the hob and poured herself out a bowl. She did not notice me, and why should she? I was only a MacMonagle, while she was the daughter of Mick Flaherty, the J.P.

She sat down, took a hearty pull from the bowl and looked at her mother.

"You're back early from the church," she remarked.

"I did not go," said the mother.

"Why?"

"Because of him," she answered, pointing at me.

"*Oui, oui*," said the girl, apparently realising that I was in the room. She had noticed me before! "What is your name, boy?"

"Neddy MacMonagle," I answered. Having met me several times, she really knew my name.

"Oh, MacMonagle!" she said with a quality lisp. "Haven't I met you before?"

"Of course you have, Genevieve," said the mother. "He came in when I was going to do the last of the Nine Fridays, and I stayed in because he had a letter——"

"A letter!" chirped Genevieve.

"From Lanty Hanlon, for you——"

"For me!" exclaimed the girl, placing her bowl on the table and taking off her spectacles. It was said that she saw better without them. But they were gold-rimmed. "Why is he writing to me? I never want to hear from him again. Not if I was a beggar on the road!"

"Well, the letter won't bite you, anyway," counselled Mrs. Flaherty. "Let's hear what he wants, anyway. Give me the letter, Neddy!"

"I was told not to give it to you," I said, taking the letter from my pocket.

"Well, give it to me, seeing that you are so particular," said Genevieve. She took the letter as if the humouring of my wishes was the only reason for doing same.

She read.

"What do you think of this Society, Neddy?" she enquired when she had finished reading.

"What everyone else thinks," I said. "Once it gets started it will be a Society."

"That's what the *Ballyroon Sentinel* said last week," the mother remarked. "Look at all the papers talking about it, even now, and it not fully started! And when it is started he'll want someone to help him, someone with education. A woman, if I may say so."

"Now, Neddy, tell your master that he will have my answer in due course," said Genevieve.

I went to the door, my jar of liquorice balls under my arm. A woman with education to help my master, indeed! How I hated Miss Flaherty on that day!

"And what is in the letter at all, Genevieve?" I heard the mother ask as I got to the doorstep.

"Nothing," was Genevieve's answer.

CHAPTER X

THE MANIFESTO

To-day is and to-morrow is not.
—*A Ballykeeran Proverb.*

I

ON the following day came a letter addressed to:

LANTY HANLON, Esquire, G.H.,
Treasurer,
Ballykeeran Development Society.

He opened it in my seeing, and from it fell a slip of paper, green, red and white—a cheque, the first I had ever seen. Worth five pounds it was and to my thinking then, and even to this day, little surety for the amount. It has been ever my way to prefer the money that rings to the money that rustles.

A week later came the wonderful Manifesto of the Ballykeeran Development Society, printed in black on a green paper by the proprietors of the *Ballyroon Sentinel.* And on the day after, it appeared simultaneously in all the papers through the length and breadth of Ireland. And this in part the Manifesto:

THE BALLYKEERAN DEVELOPMENT SOCIETY

"WE, the Ballykeeran Development Society, hereinunder set forth our aims, intentions and designs:

"Firstly, we would draw attention to the evils of emigration, which is the bane of Ireland and causes much grievous hurt and harm to the prosperity of the country.

"The young men leave her shores yearly, go out into the world, labour by the sweat of their brows until such time as they sink into a nameless foreign grave, unwept, unhonoured and unsung.

"But even more sad is the fate of the young womanhood, the fair, innocent girls who go abroad to the lands of the foreigner, who wear their lives away in the slums and kitchens of distant towns, sinking down into the dark abyss without hope or salvation. Emigration has its woes no less terrible than war.

"Now we, the Ballykeeran Development Society, feeling that we owe a duty to Ireland, propose to combat this injustice, and seeing a way of starting fresh industries in the parish of Ballykeeran, we beg to state——"

Then followed a long dissertation on wool and water, weaving and milling.. The Society spoke of the acreage of rough pasturage going to loss, and the manner in which it could be used as grazing ground for mountain sheep, then of the water-power that could be used for milling. "Every stream falling over the rocks begs to be allowed to turn a wheel," said the manifesto.

"But we, the Ballykeeran Development Society, are at present labouring under difficulties. Our members are the simple hard-working peasantry, men and women, who work from morn to night to make both ends meet, farming and knitting.

"Despite this we have responded nobly and given freely of our hard-earned money. But our all is little, and now through the Society we appeal to outward sources for help.

"All you who read this appeal, consider, and let the consideration move you to sympathy. All your subscriptions will be kindly received and duly acknowledged. If you cannot send much, send a little, for every little helps.

"And we are, Ladies and Gentlemen, on behalf of the B.D.S.,

"Yours thankfully,

"EDWARD LARRIMORE (Chairman).
"PATRICK COSDHU (Secretary).
"LANTY U. HANLON, G.H. (Treasurer)."

This appeal appeared in the first instance in the home papers, then went farther afield. American papers copied it, English papers copied it. A leading London journal gave it star-space, and the Editor went so far as to write an article on it, the article being called "Progressive Peasantry," with a sub-title "A New Era for Ireland."

A magazine, in an article "National Support for Local Industries," dwelt at length on the

Ballykeeran Development Society as a new channel of usefulness which in a little time would become a running stream of prosperity to the country in which it was founded. The two articles, " Progressive Peasantry " and " National Support for Local Industries," were nailed to the wall above my master's bed.

The following, a verbatim report of a statement made by Mr. Hanlon, G.H., to a Pressman (one who hied from a far city), will give some idea of the plans of the Ballykeeran Development Society as propounded by its honourable and estimable Treasurer.

" To erect and equip mills will require much money," said my master. " Put that aside for the present and let us start quietly. Firstly we would erect one small mill, on the most convenient site of the property. When this is shown to work properly and satisfactorily, as it will do, of course, we will engage on a more comprehensive undertaking, the thorough development of the whole parish, exploiting its resources, water-power, man-power and grazing facilities."

" Are you certain that all this power can be put under control ? " asked the Pressman.

" As certain as I am that this power is now going to loss," was the definite reply of Mr. Lanty U. Hanlon, G.H.

II

While thus, the sanguine anticipations of Lanty Hanlon, Treasurer, were bruited abroad, Eamon

Larrimore, Chairman, and Paddy Cosdhu, Secretary, carried on their lifelong labours on their roods of tilth and acres of turbary. To see them then at their various pursuits, carrying creels of manure on their backs to the fields, weeding a drill of turnips, thatching a pig-sty, or making a byre, one would hardly think that these worthy men were two of the controlling influences of the Ballykeeran Development Society.

"But to-day is and to-morrow is not," as they said, and keeping this in mind the Chairman and Secretary had to work and make the daily bread of themselves and their families.

Despite his manifold duties my master had a quick eye to see the disabilities under which they laboured, and it was not for him to heap overmuch work on their shoulders.

One morning he called them to his office, and they came in answer to the call, Eamon Larrimore bare-footed, Paddy Cosdhu in trousers with big rents and little patches like Lord Fitzgibbon's estate.

"Well, praise be to God, but it's the grand weather and all that's in it this day," said Eamon on entering. "And the way the crops are showing! It makes the heart glad to look at them."

As he spoke he smiled with great satisfaction. He was a tough-limbed rung of a man, very strong and very quiet. I had never seen him out of temper. At wakes he always gave out the Rosary, at funerals he collected the offerings. In an assembly when a job anyone could have done had to be performed, Eamon was asked to do it. A hard, decent man, able to read a little, he was very obliging and stood in the good graces of his neighbours.

" Sit down, Eamon, and make yourself comfortable. And you as well, Paddy," said my master. " And it is grand weather, as you say."

" And fine for the crops, as I said," Eamon reaffirmed. There was no harm in the repetition. Anybody could see that the weather was good for the crops.

" But what do the crops matter at all, at all," asked the Secretary. " The parish will soon be rolling with money and nobody will have to work, nobody ! "

" Well, for my own part I hope that time comes," said Eamon. " But work does nobody any harm, no matter how much money they have. And I for one wouldn't like a winter to see me without a strong house, strong in hay and corn and milk and butter and——"

" Sound common sense, Eamon ; sound common sense," said my master. " But the Society is making great headway at present, and towards Christmas we'll see everything in full swing. Meanwhile our duties as head officials are becoming very onerous."

" Onerous ! " gasped Eamon.

" Onerous, beyond doubt, Mr. Larrimore," said my master. " At the present moment, under the heading, ways and means, it is your duty to study resources and the method of raising these. This will at least take four hours daily."

" Four hours ! "

" At least," said my master.

" But I can't spare the time, and even if I could spare the time, I don't know what to do," said the poor Chairman. He was now on his feet and terror was visible in his eyes. " But maybe Paddy—Mr. Cosdhu will be able to do it. And he knows more than me, and soon it will be the time for the cutting of the hay. And heavy the hay is, I'm telling you, on the holms, and it will take a lot of saving. Well, Mr. Cosdhu," the Chairman appealed to the Secretary, " what do you say to taking the job ? "

" But Mr. Larrimore, he is the Secretary," said my master. " His duties will even be more onerous than your own. From now onward we must have a weekly meeting of the shareholders. You know shorthand, of course, Mr. Cosdhu ? "

" Shorthand ? " Paddy queried.

" The faculty of taking down conversation so that not a word spoken in the shareholders' meetings is lost," my master explained. " This is absolutely necessary, as you know yourself. From a legal point of view a company meeting is not a meeting unless reported in shorthand."

" Well, if I was a younger man, I wouldn't mind learning how to do it," said Paddy. " But like Eamon here, Mr. Larrimore, I have a lot to do——"

" Of course you have, Mr. Cosdhu," said my master in a voice of feeling. " But there is a way to surmount the obstacle. If you will allow me I will take charge of all correspondence, deal with matters, technical and financial, and get the whole concern into good working order. Patience, Mr. Cosdhu, is needed; patience and industry, Mr. Larrimore."

Both were dismissed, and pleased they were to be relieved of their stewardship.

The evening of that day saw a board placed above the door of Meenaroo, and on the board, scrawled as if with a thumb-nail dipped in tar, was the message:

BALLYKEERAN DEVELOPMENT SOCIETY

(All letters addressed to the above to be handed in here.)

"Now, Neddy, I'm going to appoint you a book-keeper," said my master that evening. "All business transactions have got to be recorded. Correct book-keeping is essential, single entry and double entry. Go to Mick Flaherty. Buy from him a cash-book and a ledger, for the Society must be run on a business footing. Run, Neddy!"

"But the shop is shut," I said.

"So it is," said my master, who had forgotten that the hour was so late. "Go the first thing in the morning!"

"And how much will they be?" I asked.

"Oh, yes. You need money. I had forgotten." My master put his hand in his trousers pocket and brought twopence therefrom. "That is not enough! But that doesn't matter. Tell Mick to send in his bill at the end of a fortnight. Now, put on the kettle and make a pot of tea before we go to bed!"

III

In compliance with the order: "All letters addressed to the above to be handed in here," the county postman handed to Lanty Hanlon all letters addressed to the Society, letters addressed to Chairman, Secretary and Treasurer. And these came, thick and threefold letters in white envelopes, green envelopes and blue, envelopes with addresses written, typed and printed, letters from Scotland, England and America. On the first day the postman glowed, on the second he sweated; the third day he brought a boy to help him, and at the end of a week he needed a donkey and cart.

My master's work became more onerous. Now on his window were the written instructions:

Hours: 9 to 12; 1 to 3. No admission except on business.

But nobody, with the exception of Oonah Ruddagh, visited him now. The neighbours were afraid of him. He was a great man, one of the nobility and nothing less. Was not his name in all the papers? He was far above common people. Go to his office and talk to him about calves and cows and crops! No fear!

Still Oonah Ruddagh was not to be daunted, and why should she be indeed? Did she not stand sponsor for him when he was christened in whisky? Coming in, she would sit down, look round the room at the papers lying on the floor, on the table, on the dresser, on the tester above his bed.

Shutting one eye she would emit a heavy sigh and lean back in her chair and fix her open eye on my master.

"Well, Lanty Hanlon, asthor, it'll maybe any day now when she's back here again," she would sigh.

"Who?" my master would enquire.

"Well, you're the one to be asking that question," the old woman would say. "As if you don't know who I mean. Ah, well, well!"

Having sighed from her stomach, her eyes would wander round the apartment, and following a second lengthy inspection of the room and its appointments, she would turn again to my master who was now immersed in his work.

"It's the grand weather entirely that we've in it now," she would say with a moan as if regretting having to live in a period when the weather was so good.

"Grand weather, great weather," was my master's reply as he gave his pen a vicious sweep across a sheet of foolscap. Even *he* seemed to resent such grand weather.

"And the flies that are in it!" was Oonah's remark. "Never saw the like of them! One cannot make butter without them being all over it."

"Damned nuisance, flies," was my master's rejoinder, pursing his lips and blowing through them as if imaginary flies were tormenting him at that moment. "Damned nuisance! Damned nuisance!"

"There's people that can't stand them at all, and there's people that don't care if the sky was filled with them," Oonah went on. "And there's people that the flies will never touch. Now, do you know what's the reason of that at all, Lanty, asthor?"

"I don't know at all, Oonah," was Lanty's answer.

"But there must be a reason," said the old woman. "Now Maldy, my own daughter, and the youngest, and who will be here any day now, was the one that didn't care about the flies at all, no matter how many were about. But they worry the life out of me and I'm her mother. And you yourself, Lanty, are never troubled by them at all, just like Maldy. Isn't that funny, Lanty?"

And thus the old woman would keep pestering my master with ridiculous comments and questions, until he would rise to his feet and on the pretext of going out to get a breath of fresh air, get rid of his unwelcome visitor.

Next day and the next she would come again. But who had better right. Was she not his godmother, the one living being who stood surety for the faith in which he was baptised.

IV

The time was ten o'clock in the morning. The heavily burdened post had been with its many letters. The world was sympathetic towards the Society and money was filling the coffers (the tin box behind the roof-beam) of Meenaroo.

My master sat in his chair puffing and perspiring, his coat off and shirt sleeves thrust up to his great shoulders. In front of him were a number of letters and a number of cheques. Letters were still being opened; cheques were still pouring out. Thanks to his enormous vitality my master was as fresh as a daisy, despite the fact that midnight had not seen him abed on the previous day.

" Neddy, look out and see if that creature, Oonah, is on her way here as yet! " he ordered me.

I rose from my work at the cash-book and did as he directed.

" She's herding her cow," I told him. " Herding it in your field."

" Damn the field! " my master exclaimed. " I'd give it to the old vagabond if it would keep her away from here."

" And Miss Flaherty is comin' up the brae! " I went on.

" Oh! Mother of the Lord! "

" In her best——"

" Her best! " he ejaculated, gripping the cheques with a mighty fist and shoving them in his trousers pocket. " That's the way in Ireland," he moralised. " Old women and old guff and young women with a gaff for catching anything that can be married. What will she be wanting? " he asked. " Has she her spectacles on? "

"She has," I said. "Shining like gold."

"If her head was made of gold, I don't want her." He spoke in a firm and decided voice. "Stay here when she comes in and be a witness to what will take place."

A rap came to the door. I threw it open in my best style and bowed as directed. Genevieve took no notice of me however. My master got to his feet hurriedly, as if he had not been aware of her coming.

"Good day, Miss Flaherty," he said in his urbane manner, and shook hands with the visitor.

"Good day, Mr. Hanlon," said she with a queer quality lisp, which was then affected by the young ladies of Ballykeeran.

"But it's so hot," said my master, rubbing his forehead with his massive hand. "It's like hell!"

"Oh, Mr. Hanlon!" Miss Flaherty gasped, assuming a slightly shocked expression. "But it is hot," she made haste to affirm.

"It's a day for the hay, anyway," said the matter-of-fact Lanty Hanlon.

"Such a day!" the girl ejaculated with a tone of bliss. "And what a truly rural scene down the valley, the sound of the scythes and the smell of the hay. Oh! it's so delightful!"

"To look at," said my master. "But the ones sweating on the job have another story to tell."

"That's true," said the girl, willing to concede a point and casting a sharp, fugitive, hawk-like eye on the papers that littered the table.

"That's true indeed. All the same, it's very delightful! . . . But one thing I miss, my parasol. I don't know why I came away without it."

"H'm! neither do I," said my master, but whether in sympathy or reproof it was hard to determine.

"I just came out and I was not coming far," said the girl, righting her gold-rimmed spectacles on her nose and looking over them. "'Twas so charming, however, that I couldn't stop till I came here. But without my parasol I'm not coming out again. You haven't an umbrella to spare, Mr. Hanlon?"

"An umbrella!" gasped my master. "An umbrella!"

"Well, I suppose you wouldn't have one, Mr. Hanlon," said the girl apologetically. "They're not for men anyway, are they now?"

"No," was the stammered answer.

"But I wish I had one," said the girl. "Anything at all to keep the sun from my hand and the back of my neck. The way it peels it this weather. Maybe the boy"—she noticed me at last—"maybe he'll run over to Eamon Larrimore's and get an umbrella for me. Tell them it's for me and say that I'll send it back tonight."

"But he's working," said my master, though since Miss Flaherty came in I had done nothing. "And the work that we have to do here! Business, business, from morn till night!"

"But it won't take him long," said the girl. "And I'll do his work till he comes back."

" Oh, yes ! What was I thinking of ? " said my master, running his fingers through his hair as if distracted. " Run and get an umbrella, Neddy. Run and get it and don't be long. Oh, my head, my head with work ! Run, Neddy, run ! "

" Come here, Neddy, like a good boy ! " said Genevieve as I got to the door. " Come here ! "

I came back to Miss Flaherty, put my hands behind my back and looked at her. How I despised her !

" What would you do with a shilling if you had one ? " she asked with a benignant and winning smile. At least it struck me as if she tried to be winning and benignant, but the fact was that it made her look very old.

" I'd keep it till the next fair," I said.

" And then ? " she enquired.

" I'd buy a knife," I told her.

" Well, here's a shilling for you, Neddy." She took a purse from her pocket and handed me the stipulated coin. " Now get me the umbrella and don't break your legs running, mind."

" Thank you," I said, pocketing the shilling and going out.

" Don't spend all day on the job, Neddy ! " my master's despairing order followed me.

V

There was no umbrella in Eamon Larrimore's home. This at least would be sufficient explanation when I returned without the article, so for the moment I went around to the gable end of the house to the orifice in which the crook-bar was stuck and placed my ear against the hole. Inside a loud-voiced tongue was in full swing, Miss Flaherty's. My master was saying very little.

"Well, I don't know, but you must," she was saying. "All by yourself from morning till night, and hard at work all the time. It's not good to be never idle, and you know that. Not for me to be saying anything about it, but there! It's bad, always working. And all by yourself! Not even a servant-girl!"

"I'm getting one as soon as I can," said my master. "As soon as I can." This repetition was always a sign of impatience.

"Well, indeed," said the girl in a tone of surprise. "But I suppose it's whatever you think best yourself. I'm not to have any say in the matter. Not that I'd want to, but if I would . . . well."

"Well, everybody has their own opinions," said my master. "But let people think what they like, it doesn't matter to me if they leave me alone. But why should we talk about this, Miss Flaherty, when——"

"Why, indeed?" asked Miss Flaherty sweetly.

"When we've a little business to do," my master went on. "The Society begs me to thank you, Miss Flaherty, for the money which you so kindly lent it and asks me to pay you back, personally——"

"Don't trouble about it, Mr. Hanlon," Miss Flaherty piped. "I don't miss it in the least, a little amount like that. And I will be very happy in the days to come when I look back on this great event and recall that even in my own little way—very little it was——"

My ear was very close to the hole in the wall. I would not have been anywhere else at that moment. Not for untold gold!

"—I was able to assist the Society. To help the poor people has been the aim of my life. And when——"

Something tickled my ear, the ear farthest away from the wall, and I raised my hand to brush away that which tickled. My hand came in contact with something soft, warm and alive. With a start I straightened myself, looked round and into the eyes of Oonah Ruddagh.

"Neddy dear, Neddy dear," said she, sitting down, her back against the wall, the upper rim of her frilled bonnet within an inch of the crook-hole, "it's bad the corns are on me this day."

She spoke in a whisper.

"Are they?" I asked. I spoke in a whisper also.

"They are that," said the old woman. "I can't go another step—and I left my stick behind me in the house. Run down and get it for me, Neddy, asthor."

"But my master won't let me," I said.

"You'd be far better doing that and helping an old woman, a widow woman too, than standing here against a wall, one hand as long as the other and neither one doing anything," said Oonah Ruddagh, stretching her back so that her ear was almost in line with the crook-hole.

"I was told to stay here, and I'm going to stay," I answered.

"And there is a nice scone on the table, thick with butter, and the best butter in Ballykeeran," said the old woman, still stretching herself. Her hams now rested on her heels; the weight of her body was borne by the toes and her ear was flush with the orifice. "Now away with you, Neddy, and you can have the scone for yourself."

"I'm not going, Oonah Ruddagh," I said.

"Well, keep quiet if you're not going!" Oonah spoke in a whisper but the whisper was an angry one. "You're all gab and guts, like a young crow!"

"I'm going in to tell my master that you are out here waiting for him," I said. "He always says that you are to be allowed in, but no other person."

"I've to thank him for that, I suppose." The old woman pressed her ear to the crook-hole as she spoke. She was a little deaf. "Nobody allowed to come in, but me! Who's in now, tell me? I'm not the one and he's paying her money! How much?"

The woman's eye replaced her ear at the hole. For a minute she looked in tense silence, then suddenly started dancing like a fiend. What about her corns now!

"One pound!" she groaned. "Two, three, four, five! Gold, Neddy. Yellow gold! Five pounds in gold and giving it to that person! And us, the poor people that have paid so much, what do we get ? Not a penny piece at all. And me a widow woman too ! But I'll show him ! I'll show him ! "

She walked off, her head high in air, her heart filled with a great anger.

" I thought you wouldn't be able to walk without your stick," I called after her.

" A stick ! " she growled, looking back at me. " That's what *you* want, a stick ! And if I had one here with me you would get it ! You're just as bad as he is ! "

I went to the door and met Miss Flaherty coming out. On her face was the look of one who has done a successful stroke of business.

" And the Society will always remember the splendid support which you gave it," I heard my master say.

" I feel honoured if my little help was of such importance," lisped Genevieve. " And what a charming view you have from here." She spoke with a deep breath, as if soaking up the aroma of the country-side. " And your bees ! Are they doing well this year, Mr. Hanlon ? "

" Splendidly," came a voice from the dark interior. " When we rob the hive in a few weeks' time I will send you a few pounds ! "

" How sweet ! " lisped Genevieve.

I passed her, but she took no notice. Had she forgotten about the umbrella ? I went inside to find my master deep in his work.

" Has she gone ? " he asked. Raising his head, he looked at me.

" She's gone."

"Did you get the umbrella?"

"There was no umbrella in Eamon Larrimore's," I told him.

"Neddy!" He looked at me. "What have you just said?"

"There is no umbrella in Eamon Larrimore's!"

"How do you know?" he enquired. I rubbed the floor with my foot and did not answer my master.

"Seeing that you have no answer ready, and ten to one the answer, if you had one, would be a lie, will you now tell me truthfully what Oonah Ruddagh said when she looked through the hole in the wall?" my master asked.

And thereupon I told him what the old woman had said.

"It is very unfortunate, Neddy," he said after a long pause. "I paid Genevieve five pounds. Oonah Ruddagh has seen me pay. Greed has made it twenty pounds by now, spite will make it a hundred pounds by night. A crumb becomes a cake in the hands of a neighbour you do not love. . . . Neddy, from now on you are to be head of the Ballykeeran Development Society Secret Service."

"And what will I have to do?" I asked.

"What you have just been doing outside," said my master. "You have to be an ear in a wall, and an eye at a keyhole. You're not to be seen nor heard! When you were outside a minute ago, listening, you were seen. I saw you! Why did I see you?"

"I don't know," I made answer.

"There was a ray of light coming through the hole in the wall, and your big head blocked the light. That was stupid, unpardonable," said my master. "Therefore, don't let it occur again. Now, these are your instructions for to-night. Are you listening?"

"I am."

"When it gets dark, out upon Oonah Ruddagh and shadow her," said my master. "She has great news and the woman will not be content till she throws it broadcast over the parish. She will possibly go to Paddy Cosdhu's or Eamon Larrimore's. All the people of the place will gather round to hear what she has to tell them. You've got to remain in hiding outside the door or outside the window, and with mouth shut and ear open take in everything. And report to me when you return!"

VI

I would have you see the home of Paddy Cosdhu (Honorary Secretary) as I saw it that night, as I saw it not as an ordinary human being, but as the head of the Ballykeeran Development Society Secret Service. B.D.S.S.S.! How it rolls from the tongue like a hissing eel. Aye, and all these letters to my name, I, who two years before, was a tinker's brat on the high-roads of Ireland.

I was one of the party, an unseen watcher, the ear in the wall, the eye at the window. The window in the back of Paddy's house was my position, that famous window which was once gateway for my master's body on the night of the rout of the Freelys, the Roes and the renegades.

(There was only one Roe, if you remember, but a little exaggeration is the sauce of history.)

Here I watched and listened, one arm against the wall, the other round the sweet waist of Norah Hannigan. My mouth was shut to everybody except my little girl, and hearing of my new position she offered to help me. As if she could help! But I allowed her to share my watch, not because of any assistance which she would give, but because I loved her. And love is a sufficient excuse for anything under God's sky.

The night was one never to be forgotten. The air was filled with the soft fragrance of July, of roses, bourtree flowers and wild honey. Coupled with this was the soft fragrance of the brown hair on which my lips rested. A spread of tiny lights showed on the dark ground, on the trunks of the rowan trees and on the lime-washed wall. These might have been easily mistaken for stars that had lost purchase of the sky and came to earth, but they were only glow-worms working out a strange pattern on the face of the perfumed world.

"Whisht, Neddy! Here comes Oonah Ruddagh!" whispered Norah, standing on tiptoe and peering into the crowded room.

It was Oonah, sure enough! The idle talk of a moment before was hushed and a strange look of suspense, timidity, and anticipation showed on the faces of those within, similar to the suspense that awaits death, the timidity that awaits a birth and the anticipation that awaits a marriage feast. And these looks blending together gave an expression to the face of the party that I did not like to see.

Oonah Ruddagh sat down in the chair under the hanging lamp, pressed her frilled bonnet to the back of her head and looked at the assemblage.

"Well, and that is the way of it," she said with a sigh.

Chairs drew nearer, and those who stood formed a circle round the woman. Faces were there that I hardly knew, faces that I knew full well; all belonging to the parish but not all to the Society. The Freelys were there, a good half-score, Kevin Roe (a bad augury), Manus Glynn, Eamon Larrimore, and Neal Hannigan.

"The true word," said Ellen Cosdhu. "And a donkey, too!" What did she mean?

"A donkey, indeed!" said one of the Freelys with a wise nod. "And the postman puts his hand to the wheel when the donkey's going up a brae!"

"Ah, Lanty's not a donkey!" said Paddy Cosdhu, spitting high over the head of one of his children and landing the spit in the dying fire.

"It's strange the way things have gone on in the last three months," Eamon Larrimore ventured, emptying his pipe of heel-tap by striking it on the floor. "And in this weather!"

"It's a funny world," Manus Glynn remarked.

"He was always a robber," said Kevin Roe. "It's not as bad when he robs people that are not his neighbours, as when it comes to robbing in his own parish. That is going a bit too far."

"Maybe he has bit more than he can chew this time!" came the growl of the Freelys.

"It's a shame the way we've let him go on so long," said Kevin Roe.

"If I was only a man," said Oonah Ruddagh. The house was all attention in a moment. Here was one speaking, one who knew something.

"And if you were a man, now," prompted Paddy Cosdhu.

"Well, this and nothing else!" was Oonah's answer. "If I was a man I wouldn't think much of myself if I was not a better man than some of them that's in it at the present day."

"What would you do, Oonah, if you were a man?" asked Kevin Roe.

"I wouldn't call myself a man if I'd let anybody rob me, anybody like him!" As she spoke she put her thumb over her shoulder, and that thumb, long and crooked and skinny, pointed in the direction of my master's house. "Robbed every one of us, even the poor widow woman!"

"The true word!" said the Freelys in a voice. They had paid nothing towards the Society.

"And what did I see this day of days!" said the old woman. "This and God is my witness! I went up to the office, and who had the better right, for wasn't I the one that stood sponsor for Lanty Hanlon on the day of his christening. The door wasn't closed, and it wasn't open, and as I was going in, slow I was on account of my corns, what did I hear but the sound of great talk, and who did I see inside through the crack of the door but *Miss* (I saw her father when he had nothing to cover his bottom) Genevieve Flaherty——"

"Old Mick, you mean?" asked Manus Glynn. He was alluding to Genevieve's father.

"Whisht, Manus," came a dozen angry voices.

"And what was my bold Lanty doing?" Oonah resumed, as if the utterance of Manus had not crossed her story. "Nothing more or less than shovelling hard gold into her lap! Not troubling to count it even, but just throwing it at her. I know what money is, and I'm not the one to boast about what I have in the bank this day——"

"The true word," sighed Ellen Cosdhu.

"The true word, Ellen, the true word," said Oonah, taking deserved due as a matter of course. "But this I will say. I wouldn't say no to taking what Lanty Hanlon gave Genevieve Flaherty this day. One hundred gold pounds it was by my counting, and here—" she got to her feet and surveyed the room—" and here this night are us, the ones that made the Society, and we haven't got one penny piece. And you call yourselves men!"

Kevin Roe studied the faces of those round him; an angry look showed in the eyes of the Freelys.

"Now, was it a whole hundred pounds?"

asked Neal Hannigan, who was a man of peace.

"May I never sit down again if it wasn't a hundred and more besides," said the old woman, fixing an angry eye on Neal Hannigan. Then she sat down, easily. Was not that sufficient surety for her word.

"Well, if there's money going, we should have it—a little of it, anyway," Eamon Larrimore hazarded.

"How does the business stand at present, Mr. Larrimore?" asked Kevin Roe.

"It's more than I can tell," said Eamon. "With the good weather that's in it, I have to be out early and late at the crops. And the way the turnips and corn is coming up! Not in my memory have I ever seen headway like this year."

"But first and foremost you are Chairman of the Society," said Kevin Roe. "And the Chairman is the most responsible person. If anything goes wrong, if funds are misappropriated, if shareholders are defrauded, and if the books are not in good order, and if the whole thing is not above board, who is to blame?"

"Not me, anyway," stammered Eamon. "What would I be doing with a thing like the Society, and me knowing nothing about it at all?"

"You are Chairman, aren't you?"

"I am, worse luck!"

"Then if you are Chairman, you are the man in a responsible position," said Kevin Roe. "And it is a shame that one man should have the whole business in his hands, and rob whoever he likes, rob everybody, even his neighbours."

"A great shame!" growled the Freelys, who had paid nothing towards the Society.

And in this way the conversation proceeded, until at the hour of twelve the party came to a decision. By piecing all scraps of evidence together, it was made clear that my master had untold money in his possession, hundreds and hundreds of pounds. In a few weeks' time he would start drinking again (with his christening, what else could be expected?) and spend every penny. Then the Society would fall to pieces; the Chairman and Secretary would be put in prison. Yes, and those who paid money at the start would go into prison as well. But would the parish stand it? No fear!

To-morrow morning the good people of Ballykeeran would go out upon Hanlon, take charge of his office and every penny in the place! This decision was carried unanimously. No, there was one exception. Oonah Ruddagh's amendment, that the office should be stormed that night, met with no support.

This the decision, but in my heart I felt neither tremor nor misgiving. What a great support is the love of a sweet girl, the love of my little Norah, my wife this day, and whose love is now as strong as on that night when we two stood on watch amidst the glow-worms and the roses.

CHAPTER XI

THE SACK OF MEENAROO

As big as the crust in the hand of a hated neighbour.
—*A Ballykeeran Saying.*

I

"MEENAROO must be held, even to the last ditch," was the calm comment of my master when I made report, placing before him the details of my first night's work as Head of the B.D.S.S.S. "Battery will not break us and fire will not budge us!" he said, and a gleam showed in the corner of his eye, a gleam no larger than a glow-worm, but greater, because it was the spark that heralded the conflagration!

"But there are so many, and maybe you will get killed," I said, and there was a great fear in my heart.

"I only ask this, Neddy," said my master, his head high, the fire of battle glowing in his eyes. "Only this! That when they storm the keep they'll find my body by the wall. Are you afraid, Neddy?"

"No; and you with me," I said, my teeth chattering when I spoke.

"The true MacMonagle spirit!" Lanty Hanlon patted me on the head. How gladly I would have died for him at that moment! "But the position must be consolidated," he said. "The doors barred, the windows shuttered, the ammunition ready!"

All that night long we sweated at consolidation of Meenaroo, belting it with girders, staying it with stillions until its strength would laugh a drove of mad charging bulls to scorn. The floors were cleared for action, the window shutters were riven securely, and all the papers were stored in a safe place. The talisman, our Virgin (ours now, because we faced a common enemy), was placed on a pedestal, the back of a chair, and glued thereto with candle wax. And dawn rose to see us ready for the fray.

We cooked a little breakfast by candlelight, and even when the hour came to ten it was difficult to see the fingers of an outstretched hand. All light of door and window was blocked and the only ray was that of the sun coming down the chimney.

Looking through the keyhole at half-past ten, I saw the hostile force advancing up the brae: Kevin Roe in front, the Freelys behind, and after them came Eamon Larrimore, Paddy Cosdhu and Neal Hannigan. The step of these three was very uncertain, and it seemed as if the job were not to their liking.

On the fringe of the party was Manus Glynn, not in the least perturbed by all that was taking place. In his hand he held a thick slice of bread, and this he munched as he walked. On the rear outskirts was a bevy of women, a straggling tail like the tail of a flight of startled partridges.

"Get ready!" said Lanty Hanlon, who did not deign to look through the keyhole. "I hear them approach. Don't strike unless they try to strike you. Don't raise your stick to a woman! There they are outside!"

"Is Lanty Hanlon in?" came the voice of Kevin Roe.

"At your service, Mr. Roe," my master made answer in his usual polite manner. "What can I have the pleasure of doing for you?"

"Open the door and let us in at once," came the roar of Kevin Roe.

"If any one of you want to come in that one will be welcome," said Lanty Hanlon. "But before one comes in the others must retire fifty paces."

"Hear him!" came the voice of Oonah Ruddagh. "Speaking as if butter wouldn't melt in his mouth after robbing everybody in the seven corners of Ireland."

"We'll toss the house and pull him out!" came the voice of Denis Freely.

"Break the window!" came the order of Kevin Roe.

Something struck against the shutters, smashing them to smithereens. The glass flew over the floor and the daylight streamed in upon us.

What a splendid sight was my master at that moment, arrayed as he was for battle, his shirt turned down at neck, his great breast bare, his sleeves thrust up over his elbows, his fist closed on a knobbed blackthorn!

"Keep in shelter, Neddy!" he called. "Keep in shelter! There is only one way of coming in, and I will take care that nobody will come that way."

A stone came through the window and landed in the fireplace. The dying fire flared a little and the sparks ran up against the soot-heavy crook.

"Maybe he will give us some money now when he sees that we mean it!" came the voice of Oonah Ruddagh.

"Not while I have a wall to shelter me!" was the answer of Lanty Hanlon, his voice as calm as that of one who prays for long-dead relatives.

"But maybe he will give in when the house comes down," said Kevin Roe. Crowbars were busy at the door.

"Never while the breath of life is in my body," was the word of my master sent out to the attackers. Speaking thus, he placed his blackthorn between his knees and lit his pipe. Nothing terrified him.

None had as yet courage enough to come near the open window. The walls were a safeguard to besiegers and besieged. The Freelys were still at the door and overhead some daring fellow was tearing at the roof with a pick-axe. We could see the thatch sag, the rafters reel, the beams strain.

"He'll be through in a minute!" said my master, as he saw the rafters creak and a shiny pick-end come through. "But it is unfortunate that they should behave in this way!"

A great hole appeared in the roof and the one who was responsible for the damage, Denis Freely, lost purchase of his implement, which fell through, landed on the shelf and smashed the statue of the Virgin.

II

Up till that moment my master kept his temper under control. He was even serene and bore the brunt of misfortune nobly. His fortitude and bearing were pronouncedly stoical. Even when his forehead came in contact with a flying stone he neither winced nor wavered, taking it as one of the risks of business.

The South Sea Bubble had its tragedies, why not the B.D.S.? But now his statue, our talisman, was shattered.

He went to the window, his shoulders taut, his lips pressed together, his jaw shoved forward, firm as the flange of a turf spade. He thrust all that remained of the paneless window apart and looked outward. Something soft flew towards him and flattened itself on his face, where it remained.

"A good aim!" he shouted boldly. "But to me other methods of war."

"May the seven curses fall on your head, Lanty Hanlon, after robbing a poor widow woman!" I could hear Oonah Ruddagh cry.

"Desist, even now, while it's time!" he called. "What ensues if you don't desist lies on your own heads."

But even as he spoke another volley of stones rattled on the walls, window, and on his head. Several entered the room, one peeling the knuckles of my left hand. My master stepped back, caught a heavy chair and heaved it through the window.

As I still remained in a safe angle I could not see if he had hit anyone. From the outside came further yells of rage and showers of stones whizzed into the room.

Battered, bloody and magnificent, my master gripped a second chair and sent it flying outwards. A third followed, then a pot, a pan, a plate, a clock, and even the masks used in bee-farming in the previous year.

A strange note suddenly crept into the voice of the multitude, a note that had peculiar qualities and properties. Rage and animosity seemed to have entirely gone, and taking its place came a cry of fear, of terror. What had happened? Was somebody killed? My heart stopped beating.

"Yeeah!" Oonah Ruddagh shrieked. "And a widow woman too!"

"What's wrong?" I beseeched in an agonised voice, looking into the battle-red face of my master. "Is one of them killed?"

"Look forth!" said he, and with a godly gesture he pointed to the window. "Look and see!"

I looked and I saw. The street was perfectly deserted and down the brae the multitude flew as from a house accursed.

Through the green grass and fair flowers in one jumble they fled, red petticoats, grey shirts, brown arms and white legs. Hands flapped overhead, outwards and downwards, beating off something.

Oonah was there and, despite her seventy years, leading the rout, legging it like a hare, her head clasped in her hands. She danced through the grass, the principal step in her dance an attempt to hit the naked calf of one leg with the foot of the other.

"What are they running for?" I asked my master.

"The rout of the Milesians!" He dribbled off into words that lacked cohesion and meaning and were little to the point.

Something sung up to me through the air and settled on my cheek and I became conscious of a sharp stinging pain, then a second and a third.

"Bees!" I shrieked. "Close the window."

"There is no window," said my master. "Let us mask ourselves."

"You threw the masks outside," I informed him.

"Yes, yes," he said, and with a deft movement he caught a bee which alighted on his face and threw it through the window. "It only stings once," he informed me, but the words reached me dimly. I was enmeshed in a blanket.

"They are still running," he said after a moment's silence. "I must quiet the bees."

He went out through the window, his sleeves rolled down, a blanket round his head. He righted the skep which had been thrown down by the chair and blew a puff of tobacco smoke amidst the angry bees. Frightened by the smoke and fearing that they were to be driven from the hive, they started gorging themselves, and bees filled with honey never sting unless hurt.

The sack of Meenaroo thwarted, Lanty Hanlon and I sat down and broke bread amidst the ruins. A fresh air blew in from the fields and in the bushes the birds were singing.

" Providence has been on our side," said my master. " Like the bees, we have made battle for our home and are successful. The bees have stung the one who protected them." He rubbed the upper part of one leg and the calf of another. " So have the people for whom I work. But I bear them no malice. The Society must not fail, Neddy. It has to stand and become a beacon to the country ! " In the stress of the moment he unshelled an egg and swallowed it whole.

" What are we to do now ? " I asked.

" Feed the brutes ! " was the strange delivery of my good master. " Give them bread. That will allay venom, blunt spite and turn away wrath. The Society made one mistake. While filling minds with hope it forgot to fill bellies with food ! "

III

How quick to action was my good master. That afternoon in his room, the door barricaded, the window broken, he sat and wrote, and what he wrote he put in an envelope, and ordered me to post the envelope and that which it contained. I obeyed, and the address on the envelope was :

THE MANAGER,
The Ballyroon Sentinel,
Ballyroon.

The following week came two-score bills printed on rose-coloured paper. This the contents of the bill which an early day of the month of August saw appear on every wall within the mearings of Ballykeeran:

TO ALL WHOM IT MAY CONCERN

TAKE NOTICE that the Ballykeeran Development Society has entered into negotiations with Michael Flaherty, Esquire, J.P., and has hired that property of his known as Homespun Hall, situate on the outskirts of Ballykeeran proper, for a period of one day, the said day being the first of September, 18—, the day of the harvest fair of Ballykeeran.

Now whereas lease and transfer have been made valid at the moneys agreed, which moneys the said Ballykeeran Development Society has paid to Michael Flaherty, J.P., the vendor aforesaid.

Now therefore on this date aforementioned, to wit September 1, 18—, the Ballykeeran Development Society requests the honour of all people of all classes to a public dinner within the confines of Homespun Hall, which dinner will from now forth be known as the Inaugural Dinner of the Ballykeeran Development Society.

Now meanwhile though the Ballykeeran Development Society does not desire to differentiate amongst the guests, it feels that the hour is due when it should show its appreciation of those who have given their help fully and freely to the great movement, and it decrees that some token or another be given to the individuals who have distinguished themselves.

Now, therefore, with this end in view the Society will issue to its shareholders: (1) to those who had paid two shillings and sixpence a green rosette, (2) to those who had paid two shillings a green rosette with a white centre, (3) to those who had paid a shilling a red rosette, and (4) to those who had paid less than a shilling a black rosette. Credentials will be handed in at Meenaroo, where rosettes will be issued to those eligible. These rosettes will be worn on the day of the Inaugural Dinner.

FURTHERMORE, provisions for the dinner on a grand scale are required. The Ballykeeran Development Society (Supply Dept.) wish to make it known that it is prepared to consider tenders for beef, mutton, bread, eggs, milk, tea, sugar, whisky, porter, ovens, teapots, bowls, buckets, peat. Best prices will be paid on delivery.

The Society, with its avowed object of helping local industry, will be pleased to buy Ballykeeran fowls, hens, ducks, geese, eggs and butter. Why should the Society let its money leave the parish?

Further details concerning the dinner will be given later. Meanwhile the Society is busy with its onerous duties and will consider it a favour if callers recollect that every minute is precious at Meenaroo during business hours (9 to 12; 1 to 3).

Set forth on behalf of the Ballykeeran Dev. Soc. this day, 14/8/18—.

EDWARD LARRIMORE (Hon. Chairman).
PATRICK COSDHU (Hon. Secretary).
LANTY U. HANLON, G.H. (Treasurer).

That, if you like, was a notice to stare Ballykeeran in the face on a bright August morning. It was enough to make the very stones ask questions!

Homespun Hall! Where was it? There was a certain ramshackle building belonging to Mick Flaherty, and which stood on the outskirts of the village. A hall, indeed! It was used as a cattle and sheep compound on fair days. Inaugural Dinner! What did that mean? Rosettes! Supply Dept.! Had my master gone mad?

All his neighbours were mystified. Even I, who knew him so well, was more than a little puzzled. But I took consolation in the fact that he slept full well and kept hold of his appetite.

IV

And the days passed! Lanty Hanlon, steeped in a great silence, broke no word with me. Nobody came near us now, not even Oonah Ruddagh. But she was busy enough at home, the good woman. Twelve hens she had, all taking their ease in sacks suspended from the roof-beam. Not Oonah to allow them to run about and lose in sweat what they gained in feeding! She was feeding them, feeding them as she had never fed them before. Surely she would get a great price for them from the Supply Dept.

The other neighbours busied themselves with the work of the season. The hay was up and the corn down. And such corn that year. Head heavy it was on brae and holm. Moonlight saw the Chairman and Secretary at their work, and the song of the scythes filled the air.

Genevieve Flaherty in high attire passed the office on her daily outing. Her eye would turn to Meenaroo when she was passing, but she never came in. Was she biding her time?

Kevin Roe's business was growing. He was gathering money hand over fist. So the people said.

Maldy Ruddagh, Oonah's daughter, was again on deep water, on her way home to her people. She would soon be here.

My master threw off his silence again and became busy in a new way. He got carpenters, four of them, and ordered them to make tables and forms, and when these were made they were placed in Homespun Hall; boards for a giant's feast, seating accommodation for the parish. And for the work which the four carpenters did they were paid in hard money. The Freelys were the carpenters.

Then in a big box came the rosettes, from a far town, green rosettes, green rosettes with a white centre, red rosettes and black. And when the people heard that the rosettes had come, they stormed Meenaroo and made application. Green was the colour sought. Black, a badge of poverty! Who would have it?

"They will have green rosettes and no other," I told my master.

"Give green to all!" was his order.

In that famous August my master came into his province again. No one in the world was like him now. The little boys of the village cheered him when he showed his face in the street. He returned the priest's salute. "My old friend, Mr. Hanlon," the doctor said when he spoke of my master. Even the Freelys touched their caps when they met Lanty Hanlon.

And wonder of wonders! Kevin Roe was the first man to tender a rate for supplying meat to the Inaugural Dinner. And Kevin Roe's tender was accepted. The Society was far above petty slight and animosity, and Roe was the only butcher in the place.

Came the evening preceding the fair and the neighbours gathered together at Meenaroo and asked how much the Society was prepared to offer for geese, turkeys and other fowls. Even the Chairman and Secretary came and put the question. Should not these two good men have known? But they did not, which shows that the controlling interest of the Society was vested in one and one alone, that one being the hard-working and estimable Treasurer.

No money could be paid for live fowls, my master explained, and so much for fowls dead and ready for board.

"It's a sad day for a fowl when it gets its feet washed," said Eamon Larrimore. That was a great joke and went the round of the parish in the days that followed.

"How much will you give me for twelve—twelve of the best?" asked Oonah Ruddagh.

"So much," was the answer of Lanty Hanlon.

"But the hens and the ducks that they are!" exclaimed the old woman, raising her hands in wonder as she thought of them. "And the feeding I put into them—meal and corn and potatoes!"

"I'm sure you were very kind to them," said my master.

"That I was," said Oonah. "I even gave them the tea-leaves. And they show for it in wing and leg. Lanty, asthor, listen!"

"I'm listening."

"There's more body on the leg of one of my ducks than there is on the whole of Paddy Cosdhu's fowls pit together, for all that he's a secretary and has his name in the papers."

"Well, Oonah, I'll give you a penny each extra, but not a word about it, mind," said Lanty Hanlon.

"I'm as close as the grave," said Oonah. "But I'll be paid on the nail?" she queried.

"Here and now," said my master, and money changed hands.

"Ah! it's great to have money," sighed Oonah, pocketing hers in her quilted petticoat. "And you're the one to make it, as I always said. And I'll always say that, and why shouldn't I indeed, and me your own godmother. And I thought of that the other day, and the wild ones trying to pull down your own house over your head. And says I to myself, says I, when I saw them: 'There, they're trying to pull down the house over his head,' and I came up here as hard as my legs could carry me, to help you if I could, Lanty, asthor. And why shouldn't I help you now, with Maldy on deep water coming home?"

"And were you out here on that day?" asked my master. How innocent he looked!

"That I was," Oonah informed him. "And when I saw it going so hard with you and the house almost coming down, I went and turned the beehive and let out the bees; wild, they were, glory be to God! and the bees soon chased them."

"I knew you always had a kind heart," said my master, shaking Oonah's hand. "And did they sting you at all?"

"They did, indeed, Lanty, asthor, stung me sharp and deep, and the money that I paid the doctor for oil to put on the swelling," said the old woman, groaning and rubbing her thighs as if the bees were stinging her at the moment. "The money it cost, Lanty, the money, and me a poor widow woman, too!"

"How much did it cost, Oonah?" Lanty Hanlon enquired.

"Well, if I said five shillings, it would be far short of what it was."

"We'll say it cost you ten shillings," said my master, who was in a great good-humour. "So I'll give you ten shillings in gold," and with these words he handed her half a sovereign.

Oonah grabbed the coin, and, holding it between finger and thumb, tested it with her teeth.

"And if I would tell you that it cost me more than ten shillings, maybe you would——?"

"I wouldn't," said Lanty Hanlon, and his voice showed that he meant what he said.

V

Homespun Hall on the night preceding the feast is never to be forgotten.

Even now I can recall the whole scene, as if it had just taken place yesterday: the great hall, lit up with lamps, naphtha and paraffin, its windows (paneless then, as they had been for years) ablaze with bunting and ribbons.

And what a great sight for the eyes when one got inside: a fire—a furnace, red and roaring—tearing up against the black soot of the wide chimney-place, and the black pot-ovens hanging in the great flame, looking for all the world like dirty-faced little boys peering out from flowering broom. But how little boys would love to be filled as those pot-ovens were filled! Flanks of beef and shoulders of mutton stuffed the pots, roasted on the spit and sweated on the dripping pans. Brown loaves, well stocked with currants and raisins, rose in the ovens. Freshly-boiled puddings were ranged in neat order on the stillion by the ingle-nook.

And here, in the midst of the smoke and sparks, were the fair girls of Ballykeeran, baking and basting, frying and roasting, doing all in their power to show that the Inaugural Dinner of the Ballykeeran Development Society would not fail through the lack of effort on the part of the Ballykeeran women.

And there, filled with the importance of a J.P.'s daughter, dressed becomingly in overalls and spectacles, was Miss Genevieve Flaherty, showing the common people how to cook. She had a diploma from some society for cooking fancy dishes, but for all that, she couldn't cook potatoes in thirteen ways, like Oonah Ruddagh, or make tea strong enough to bear a spoon, like Ellen Cosdhu.

In against the wall were a dozen jars of whisky and half a dozen barrels of porter, and on the barrels, placed out of harm's way, were boxes of bonbons, candies, chocolates and what not, rare bits for the children, the wenches and all the sweet-tooths of the parish.

One packet, resplendent in a green bow, stood above the others—the queen bonbon! Now, who was that for at all? Nobody knew, and for that reason there were many questions asked. But I knew, of course, seeing that I was the henchman, book-keeper, head of the B.D.S.S.S. But a finger on the lip through it all, though it is hard for a boy of sixteen to keep silence when the eyes of entreaty are fixed on him!

"I guess this is the biggest knock-out show I've ever seen," said Kevin Roe, heaving in from the night a cleanly-skinned half-sheep across his shoulders. He threw the mutton on the table near the fire and wiped the sweat from his forehead. A look of great happiness showed on his face. Once he had been an enemy, but now he was a friend.

"A proper lay-out," he said. "Porter and whisky, and"—he looked at the big bonbon in the green ribbon—"and who is this for?"

"Miss Flaherty," I said, and the manner in which Kevin Roe caught his underlip with his teeth showed me that I had given tongue unwisely.

"Oh, yes," he said, as if he had known it himself. "To-morrow will be a great day."

A great day! What did he really mean?

Outside the Ballykeeran band, fife and drum, was striking up:

The Night before Larry was Stretched.

Inside, the hall gave voice to the words, the girls over their basting and baking, the butcher over his cutting and hacking. Even that which fell from spit to dripping-pan kept time with the measure.

"The night before Lanty was stretched!"

It was Kevin Roe humming, humming as he hacked. Did he not know the words of the song?

CHAPTER XII

THE INAUGURAL DINNER

Share out the loot and finish with blows!
Look! Who is that soldier whom nobody knows?
—*A Ballykeeran Proverb.*

I

SINCE the day on which the rag-tag and rabble of Ballykeeran had taken the law into its own hands and consigned my beloved master to a dark and dreary midden, a year had passed. A year and a day, to be exact, for the year of grace of which I write being a leap-year, had a day added to its tally, this for the benefit of mature spinsters who could take advantage of an age-mellowed privilege and lay siege to the heart of man.

I only speak of this to show cause why I feared Miss Flaherty on that year. And now, on to the account of the Inaugural Dinner.

My master was up betimes and made a light breakfast. I ate nothing.

"You've seen the enthusiasm of the people, Neddy?" he asked as he fixed a gold pin in his tie. "You've seen how they bow to me in the streets, how they salaam and salute? Have you seen that, Neddy?"

"I have indeed," was my answer.

"The enthusiasm?" he repeated.

"Aye!"

"They're just as enthusiastic in honouring me to-day as they were in stamping me down a year ago. And perhaps this time next year it will be the midden again. Don't you think I'm a fool, Neddy?" he asked, straightening his waistcoat.

"Indeed, and I don't," I said.

"Well, I am a fool, Neddy." He sat down, stretched out his legs and looked at me. "I'm a damned fool, but listen to me. What I'm going to say may do you some good and it will certainly do you no harm. I'm a drunkard, a sot and a swindler. I'm considered to be a man with a head. You know what a head means here. It means the ability to scrape in money, to rob a little, to be able to discuss politics with a country doctor, to use a knife and fork at a meal, to wear a collar and read a newspaper, to be a quack and a rogue, to be more astute than the unlettered, to be craftier than the simple. That's what a head means here.

"But I had dreams, Neddy, in my younger days," my master continued. "And to bring these dreams to perfection I cut grooves in Mick Flaherty's counter and made money on the beer-drips of poverty. Look at Mick Flaherty's counter the next time you're in his shop, and you'll see there the first hopes of your master, carved in wood. But since then I have been a tramp, a vagabond and a scamp. Drink has been my downfall. It once widened my horizon, but afterwards clouded my vision. That is why I am now just as badly off as when I started. I have been hemmed in. That is the downfall of many in Ireland, people like myself who have a little more than average intelligence. The mearing of a parish is a stumbling-block to progress. Do you understand me?"

"I don't," I said.

"No Irishman has a chance if he doesn't clear out from the district that knows his people," said my master. He was putting links in his stick-on cuffs. "The neighbours know the man's mother and father, the mother, who never wore shoe-leather, the father who had patches on his Sunday clothes, the man's grandmother and grandfather, and back to the age when an ancestor was hung for sheep-stealing. That is a great stumbling-block to progress! Do you understand me, Neddy?"

"I do indeed!" I made answer. "Oonah Ruddagh told me that there is always thievery in the blood of a MacMonagle."

"And she may not be far wrong! Now, go to the door and see if Neal Hannigan is coming up the brae with the horse, Garibaldi!" he ordered; and I went to the door and saw Neal Hannigan coming up the brae, leading a milk-white steed.

"Neal's coming," I called over my shoulder. "But it's not Garibaldi that he has with him, but a white horse."

"It's Garibaldi in his holiday suit," said my master.

Which was true. The ruin had been made whole, the wreck repaired. The steed had been painted white from muzzle to croup. Gay ribbons placed on its trappings hid the angleberries from the eyes of man. It looked a new animal, as it well might, for its stomach was filled with shot and whisky. Its eyes flashed fire; it pawed the ground with fiery hoof and the spirit of the day had entered the gay Garibaldi.

The road was crowded as we made our way to the fair. Down the long perspective of dry highway, as far as the eye could scan, the world was moving to the fair of Ballykeeran. Carts squeaked from dry axles, carts heaped with wool and weaving, corn in sacks, potatoes in creels, butter in butts, apples and pears, spades and baskets, carrageen and dulse, mussels and cockles, all the wealth of the parish, and many a parish forbye.

In the midst of this grand abundance came the shepherds from the back hills, the creel-makers, stock-jobbers, cow-drovers, apple-sellers, ballad-singers, and thrifty wives in frilled bonnets and quilted petticoats.

And proudly in the great array rode my good master, resplendent in glossy castor and shiny shoe-leather, mounted on his famous steed Garibaldi. And Garibaldi for the time befitted its master, Garibaldi with its outer fittings of white and green and inner fittings of shot and spirits.

In front the word sped that Lanty Hanlon was riding to fair. Immediately a laneway was opened and the drovers, jobbers, shepherds, and ballad-sellers stood at attention, their hands to their hats and watched him pass. The women showered blessings on the man.

Never was bargaining done as quickly in Ballykeeran as on that day. Pounds were split, but not shillings, for who would haggle over little things on such a momentous occasion. Was there not the great Inaugural Dinner in front and a speech from Lanty Hanlon? A great speech it was to be and, in addition to the speech, my master had something up his sleeve. What was this going to be?

II

At three in the afternoon the town-crier, a bell in hand, a green rosette in his hat, walked through the cattle-run, the sheep-compound and pig-market and called to the populace:

"Monster Meeting on Square opposite the Police Barracks. Hour, three-thirty. Address to be delivered by Lanty U. Hanlon, Esquire, G.H., Treasurer, B.D.S. Come in your thousands!"

The parish was there at the stated hour. Lanty Hanlon, on Garibaldi, addressed the audience. His words were few but to the point.

"Good people," he said, removing his silken castor and rubbing his massive forehead with his pocket-handkerchief, "many considered, when I first put the plans of the Ballykeeran

Development Society before you, that the project was a mere chimera evolved in a disordered imagination. (Vociferous cheers.) But you were wrong in that thought! Now at the present moment, despite hardship and handicap, I can say, and I do say, that the great idea is accomplished. (Voices: Ballykeeran for ever!) And as token of my word, follow me and see!"

That was his speech. To the shout of "Three cheers for Lanty Hanlon," he turned his horse, and in a great burst of acclamation he rode towards the railway station. The crowd followed, and at the rear of the crowd the Ballykeeran band (fife and drum) struck up *The Peeler and the Goat.* A day of great good-feeling, surely, for the twelve straight policemen of Ballykeeran stepped to the measure and whistled with the band.

We arrived at the railway station. The station-master stood at the entrance, saluted my master, and helped him to dismount.

"Where is it?" my master enquired.

"In the siding, sir."

We trooped to the siding, and lo! the surprise. On a long-bodied truck stood a wonderful machine, a strange contraption, with beams and bars and cranks and wheels—a power-loom!

The crowd stopped dead, their arms slack by their sides, their eyes open. They looked at one another, then at the loom, then at Lanty Hanlon. And Lanty Hanlon, in an indifferent voice as if nothing uncommon had taken place, turned to the station-master, and asked:

"Have you found out why this has been three days late?"

In reality the machine had come three days ahead of time, but that did not really matter. My master had to look business-like!

"Three cheers for Lanty Hanlon!" someone called from the rear of the crowd.

A few cheered—those farthest away from the machine. Those in front looked foolish. Cheer on such a sublime occasion? They might as well be asked to cheer in church! A murmur of awed whispering could be heard in the crowd; all were overwhelmed.

The lips of the Secretary curled in a cunning grin.

"Power-loom!" he said. "It will need a power of work to take it from here to wherever it's going to be put!"

Was not that a sly joke?

III

Night was falling. Homespun Hall was crowded. At the door the Ballykeeran band was playing and inside a fire blazed against the sooty chimney. The whisky jars were uncorked, porter black and creamy flowed from the barrels, tea bubbled in the boilers; on the tables butter was set forth in lordly dishes, cream-heavy milk was to be had for the asking, stirabout in tubs was within spoon-reach of all!

The full tables were piled to bursting point with turkeys and geese and sheep—sheep roasted whole, seven in all, from the mountains, and the best.

Crowding in were the people, the hale and hearty, aye and the halt. A free meal and open cellars had done in a night what medicine could not do in years. The bedridden had thrown aside their blankets and walked. Peter Ruddagh was there! Only a whisper, of course. Peter, a great glutton in his day, was under clay seven years. But the merry-making must have its joke!

Looking out from the door on the fields, I could see that the cattle and sheep of the fair were freed of all mastery. The young beasts were trying their horns in fight. The heavy udders of hefted cows trailed on the ground, dripping milk on the greensward. Stray cattle ate the rich grass. Whose cattle? Whose grass? What did it matter?

Strangers were there, people whom we had never seen before and whom we have never seen since. Dark men, not of Ireland, with noses twisted like parrots, sold queer fancy articles, brooches and pins. Men who must have been half devils; belched fire from their mouths, and swallowed swords as long as crow-bars. Ballad-singers sang at the top of their voices for hours on end, a hard job, surely, and the day such a hot one; others sold pipes, sticks, prayer-books, ginger-bread, apples and oranges. This and much more was to be seen; card-players, clothes-sellers, wheels of fortune, a cow scratching its rump against a tree, reflections of light in the dark water of the river, spluttering naphtha lamps in the booths, the heads of the people with rings of glory round them like that of angels over the sacristy door of Ballykeeran Church.

Homespun Hall was filled, another entry and the place would burst! But they were still coming in, sitting down, eating. How the food was consumed! The sheep were getting less, disappearing.

Oonah was there—and why not?—eating a little but gripping more. A goose tucked in the corner of her shawl, and maybe a bit in the pocket of her quilted petticoat. Who knows! And going out heavy, she came back light. No more than ten minutes absent! Where could she be hiding it and all?

Paddy Cosdhu (secretary) was there, looking quite important. He knew things. Round him there was a subdued murmur; people were afraid to speak openly. Paddy was not the great light, of course, but he was a light, the man in the know. He was not exactly doing anything, just looking round, touching a fowl with a careless finger and murmuring "Ah, ah!" Enough, everyone became silent and waited. But nothing further.

IV

"Mr. Cosdhu!"

Who was the bold person? Manus Glynn, the half-witted son of the Widow Glynn.

"Hold your tongue, Manus!" groaned the crowd.

"And what would I be holding my tongue

for ?" asked Manus. "Doesn't Paddy know me as well as his own mother, God rest her in hell to-night! And didn't Paddy and me fall together into the ditch, the night we were up at Ballyon, and Paddy after Ellen, his wife that is. And the dirt on his clothes when he pulled himself out! Oh, my a my!"

There was a quiet titter, not at Paddy's expense, of course. It was merely a dry titter of pity for the poor plaisham who could speak of ordinary ditches at that moment.

As for Paddy, he looked at the roof, a lip-droop of contempt on his face. In his position an idiot's remark did not matter. Then he fixed a look of pity on the man, pity that was half contempt. One word from the Secretary, and Manus would be flung out, not by Paddy, you may bet, for the idiot was a strong man, one of those capable of anything when roused. But a word to the stewards (the Freelys, no less) and Manus would be on his back outside! Paddy, however, was tolerant in his power.

"And Lanty Hanlon," Manus went on in the same silly voice. "Doesn't he know me, for wasn't it I that gave him a red petticoat when the cow ate his trousers, and him on the way from Ballyroon, two years back? And a good, red petticoat it was. And he had nothing under it at all—mother-naked, like a pig at the fair. And the cow that ate the trousers died two days after. 'Twas the dye that was in the trousers. There's poison in some dye, but not in others."

He looked round, taking stock of the clothing in the hall. His eye rested on Oonah Ruddagh's shawl.

"I'll bate that that shawl has no dye in it," he said, approaching the woman and fingering the shawl. "None," he went on with the air of a judge. "None," and he lifted up the corner of the garment and a duck dropped to the ground. (On this happening several women stepped back hastily towards the door, as if ashamed of seeing one of their kind in such a predicament.) "None," said Manus, the fool, lifting the corner of the shawl to his nose and sniffing it. "Never knew dye, and a cow might ate dozens of these and they would do the poor beast no harm."

Filled with his one thought, he had not seen the duck fall. Oonah, red with anger, turned on him, her bone-dry fingers working like the claws of a hawk.

"Ye plaisham, ye, Manus!" she roared. "It's at home ye should be, tied up with the cows. Sticking your nose in everybody's business!"

"Never heed him, Oonah Ruddagh!" counselled Paddy Cosdhu. "Just lift your duck and put it into your shawl again!"

There was a very sly look in the corner of the Secretary's eye. Oonah looked at the ground and saw the fowl. Mystification showed on her face. Her duck, indeed!

"That was your fault," she said, her eye on Manus. "Pulled it off the table with your gawky hands!"

"'Twas in your shawl," Manus explained.

"Taking it home with you, you were, just like the rest of them!"

He looked at the other women. Their shawls hung slackly. Nothing hidden there, of course! They had just been out and had returned.

"And that's the way you talk to a widow woman," moaned Oonah. "A lone widow woman that never did anybody any harm, never!"

"The true word," said Ellen Cosdhu, who stood at the doorway, her shawl about her ears. "And that fool"—her fingers straightened towards Manus—"coming in here when he should be under the blankets. Did ever such a silly thing walk God's earth on two feet?"

"I may be silly," said Manus, quite undisturbed, though the look on the women's faces was enough to damn a saint. "I may be silly, but if I am, it is the will of God, and who can go against that? Nobody in the world, nobody!"

"Now, what's wrong with you, Manus, my boy?"

It was my master speaking. He had just come in, his eyes bright with the glory that was his, his ears ringing with the applause of the people outside. He wore two green rosettes, one on his breast, one on his castor. These became him so well, that one would almost think that they had grown where they were placed. With his face beaming like a cherub, he looked at Manus Glynn.

"Now, what is wrong with you, Manus, boy?" he repeated.

"What's wrong with him!" shrieked Oonah

Ruddagh. "Well may you ask, Lanty Hanlon, what's wrong with him. Putting the black word on me, saying as much as that I was cheating and no less. And me a poor widow woman that never did anybody any harm. Cheating indeed, and the money that I have in the bank that could buy him body and soul any day of the week."

"Yes, my good woman," said my master, always polite, always a gentleman, even under the most trying circumstances! "You have money in the bank, money without stint, I may say, but Oonah Ruddagh, you know——" He did not say anything further, but tapped his head with a forefinger and inclined the head towards Manus Glynn.

Oonah sensed Lanty's meaning.

"A nod's as good as a wink to a blind horse," she remarked, lifting the duck from the floor and putting it on the table.

"And you, Manus," said my master affably. "Go to the door and tell the people to hurry in. And here's a few shillings for you!"

He put his hand in his pocket and handed Manus a fistful of silver pieces. A master of any situation, Lanty U. Hanlon, G.H.

"Ah! you're the decent man, Lanty," said Manus, as he put the money in his pocket. "A decent man and no mistake, and that's what I said, my own words, when the cow ate your trousers and I gave you the red petticoat, that hadn't the bad dye in it, not like the trousers that killed the cow, the poor beast. And the petticoat became you, Lanty——"

"Just go to the door, Manus, if you please," my master said hurriedly, for the house was listening. Though the company had a great pride in Lanty Hanlon that night, it still had ears for something of bad repute. That is the way of the world all over.

Manus went to the door and stood there, that side of his face on which the lamplight shone as rugged as a lichened boulder. Outside, the evening was calm and the naphtha lights stood in air without a flicker. An angry woman was chasing a cow away from her booth, her voice rising shrilly above the pandemonium.

"This way, ladies!" came the voice of Manus Glynn. "This way, or it will all be over. As much as you can eat and drink, and all for nothing! All for nothing! This way, Eamon Larrimore, this way!"

Eamon Larrimore entered, a frightened look on his face. All that long hot day he had been at work in his river holm, cutting the late corn, his thoughts more on the yield of the harvest than the success of the Society. Good, easy man, he was not at all suited for the intricacies of industrial life.

"Here's Mr. Larrimore," said the Secretary to the Treasurer.

"So it is, so it is!" Lanty Hanlon turned round, and went towards Larrimore with outstretched hand.

"Mr. Larrimore, we're getting on, getting on. The fortune of the place is made, made . . . as sure as you're here standing in front of me. Money!" My master raised his arms in ecstasy. "Bowls of it, creels of it! And you weren't here to-day when we inspected the power-loom. And we were wanting you, Mr. Larrimore."

Eamon started at his name. As yet he had not accustomed himself to being called "Mr." by those who had previously called him Eamon. The Secretary, however, was of a different brand. He took to his title as a midge takes to a naked leg.

"Well, it was like this," Eamon remarked in his slow, easy way. "The late corn was, as the saying is, dropping its head to the ground, praying to be out. And after all, when all's said and done, what is best for a hungry man, a bin of meal or a bin of money?"

"One of the old stock, Mr. Larrimore," my master said approvingly. "The peasant proprietor! The harvest of grain is more than the harvest of gold."

"There's nothing like gold," said the Secretary. "A gold coin is a friend in any market."

"I agree with that, of course," said the Chairman, who above anything else did not want to quarrel. "But for myself, myself, mind—I'm not meaning anybody else—for myself—I wouldn't like to see Hall'eve come round and find me without a good bin of corn, a fat haystack and three dry cuttings of turf. When a person has that, with the rent paid, and out of debt, he's all right night and noon through the Winter."

My master was on the point of replying, but hearing a commotion at the door, he swallowed his first word and looked in that direction, to see the quality of the place enter, Genevieve Flaherty leading, decked in proud array, a dress of soft satin that looked as if it were polished, gold spectacles, a hat with a feather, white shoes with silver buckles, and a green rosette.

And whom do you think came in after Genevieve? Could anybody guess in a hundred years? A lady, she was. But wait till I tell you how she came. I was one of the first to see her at the door. Manus Glynn, talking in his same foolish way, just like a baby, saw her and looked at her with his mouth hanging open as if the lower lip were suspended from a slack string.

"This way!" he said to the girl. "This way. I don't know who you are, lady, but you'll be well received. As much to eat as you want and more!"

She was a pale, winsome-looking lass, twenty-three or four as far as I could judge, but her face was pale, the cheeks a little hollow as if she had the decline. She came in noiselessly, like a cat, and looked round the room with the greatest unconcern, almost indeed as if she were looking on people who belonged to a lower station of life than herself.

But there was something very charming about the girl, in her dark brown hair, her soft cheeks and white hands. Others may have thought different, but even up to this day I can picture the girl as she came in that night to the Inaugural Dinner of the Ballykeeran Development Society, and the picture is still sweet to my mind.

Miss Flaherty sensed that something out of the ordinary was taking place, for the eyes of the assembly were not on her, as the eyes of an assembly generally were, perhaps in reproof and condemnation. But what does a woman care for that, when dressed in her best. As long as she is noticed, nothing else matters.

She turned and saw the strange girl who had followed her into the room. And in the look, the look of Genevieve, the look which she directed at the new-comer, there showed that sudden hate which rises like a night-light from a quiet pool, that green-eyed hate, which comes to the eyes of a woman who looks on a rival.

V

Oonah Ruddagh was as yet busy about the table, not wasting her time, of course. She never did. Suddenly she became conscious of the great hush, and looked round. Had the neighbours noticed anything ? No. Their eyes were not on Oonah, but on the strange lady who had just entered.

Oonah saw the girl, and rushing to her, caught her in her arms and kissed her.

"Mother of God, it's Maldy!" exclaimed the old woman, while tears fell from her eyes and fowls fell from her shawl. "Back you are to me again, back to your old mother who was so lonely without you, with nothing in the house to keep me company at all, at all. Not even a clock, Maldy, my heart's love. Here, Lanty, asthor!"—the old woman looked at my master, who was standing near—"here she is, back with me again! And it's years and years since she went away on the big ship from Ireland!"

"Welcome back, Miss Ruddagh!" My master gripped the girl's hand. "What a pleasure to find you here on this auspicious occasion. Just what we wanted to crown the gathering!"

"We all heard about the Ballykeeran Development Society in the States, Mr. Hanlon." Maldy's voice was rapturous, and there was great charm in her honeyed words. Happiness and childish simplicity showed in her eyes. "I was really dying to get back and see all that was happening."

"Come with me and sit down here, please." My master ushered the girl to a seat on the form, beside Miss Flaherty. "You remember Miss Ruddagh, Miss Flaherty," Lanty Hanlon went on, his voice filled with good feeling, and there was a look on his face such as I had never seen before.

"We know one another quite well, don't we, Miss Flaherty?" Maldy exclaimed with extraordinary warmth. "And it's so good to be back again."

"Oh, yes, we've met before." Genevieve

took Maldy's hand, but her voice was very cold. "And you must tell me how you liked America. I have never been there myself, you know. I've been to England and France" (Had she?), "but America—well, it never appealed to me. It has not the romance of the older countries."

My master poured out two bowls of tea and handed them to the ladies.

"Have a bowl each," he said in his great, hearty voice. "There are no cups and saucers —but a bowl holds more. I suppose, Miss Ruddagh, you are altogether tired of cups and saucers over there in America? For myself, I prefer tea in a bowl, any day."

"So do I, Mr. Hanlon," piped Genevieve. "It is so simple and so close to nature."

"I guess I prefer a cup and saucer," Maldy remarked. "But for all that, I think tea in the old bowl is hard to be beaten."

"Those who took tea in a bowl when they were young never like to come back to it," Genevieve lisped sweetly. "Now, Lord Kingarrow—and he was brought up on cups and saucers—likes tea in a bowl—and he told me so himself."

"The decaying Irish aristocrats will drink from anything," said my master.

"Do you mind the day you knocked Lord Kingarrow into the river?" asked Miss Ruddagh.

"I've forgotten," said my master.

"What do they think of this Society in the States?" Genevieve enquired, and fixed her eyes on Maldy.

"They think it's a grand thing," was Maldy's admission. "Is it just starting?"

"To-night," said Genevieve. "And it will be a splendid thing for the country, more particularly for those young girls who go away from their own homes and wear their lives in steaming underground kitchens in distant countries. You have seen the prospectus of the Society, Miss Ruddagh, I suppose?" Genevieve enquired sweetly.

"Well, I saw just what was in the papers," Maldy answered, with a careless air as if to show that the Ballykeeran Development Society was of little account in her scale of things. "A bully Society, I guess."

"I suppose you have seen how these poor girls work in these kitchens?" Genevieve enquired. Her air was very polite.

"I'm afraid I have not," was Maldy's answer. "I worked in an office, you see."

"How interesting," piped Genevieve, who if the truth were known was thrown a little off her balance. An office meant something great, surely. "And your other two sisters? How are they keeping?"

"They're very well, thank you."

"Of course they *are* in service?"

But before Maldy could answer this question, her mother, who had cut a leg of the best, and the very best, from a turkey (she had gone outside to do it), came with the leg on a plate and placed the plate on the table in front of her daughter.

"Now, Maldy, child of my own, you've

got to put something inside of you," said the old woman. Tears of happiness were streaming from her eyes. "After that long journey on deep water you must be weak with hunger. And it's not me to be the one to ask you all sorts of questions and you half dead with weariness."—Oonah looked at Miss Flaherty.—"Fill yourself up, Maldy, asthor. It won't cost you one penny piece—and then when the fun is over we'll go home and have a good night's sleep and a talk of them that you've left. And are they well on it, Maldy?"

"Oh! very well, thank you, mother," Maldy made answer, raising her voice a little. "Oonah is going to get married to a rich man, and Norah is engaged to a grand doctor."

Genevieve was listening.

"Engaged! What's that at all?" Oonah enquired.

"Engaged," said Denis Freely, who happened to be loitering near at hand—"that means that she is almost as good as buckled to him."

Here it may be necessary to mention that Maldy's entry into the hall produced an extraordinary effect. Everyone present came forward to greet her, pay compliments and enquire how America was getting on. But the younger men of the party did not retire when they did what duty demanded. In fact they occupied all the seats in her vicinity, and now refused to budge and allow those who had not as yet spoken to Maldy to come forward and do so.

In fact a certain underhand rivalry broke out amidst the young bloods. Sharp pokes of the elbows, angry digs in the ribs and vicious kicks on the ankles were exchanged. Little whispers went through the throng, whispers no louder than a genteel spit, but charged with venom and rancour. Through the murmuring I could hear a lot of spiteful words, threats that filled the smoky air; but prior to Maldy's entrance Homespun Hall was a residence of good feeling and fellowship.

"What the hell are you shoving for!" blurted one.

"Wait till I get you outside!" said Denis Freely, catching a young buck by the neck and endeavouring to drag him back from a point of vantage.

"I never saw a Freely that I couldn't lick!"

"Do you mean that?"

"I'll have a try!"

And all this was due to the fact that a well-dressed, comely slip of a woman had entered the hall. But it is the way of the world. I have seen more fire blaze from a wisp of hair than a mountain of dry heather.

My master had early wind of the blaze, and made haste to temper it. Getting up on the table, he stood amidst the bread, bottles, bowls of tea, glasses of egg-nog, egg-flip, punch, porter and cordials.

"Neddy MacMonagle!" he called.

"Here I am," said I, looking up at him.

"Get those," he ordered, pointing to the heap of bonbons and candy boxes which stood on the stillion. "Take them here and lay them on the table at my feet."

I did as he desired. The party was all attention now, the subdued rib digging and vicious ankle tapping ceased in the vicinity of Miss Ruddagh. Paddy Cosdhu, full but firm, who was explaining what the duties of a secretary really were, put a stop to his gab. Lanty Hanlon began:

VI

"Ladies and Gentlemen:—"

Cheers.

"For years it has been my dream and my ambition to raise the parish of Ballykeeran to the first position in the land. Not me, however, to say that the parish is not that already. It is and no one can deny it. Can they?—"

Applause. A voice: "Aye."

"Who denies it? A Ballyroon man?—"

Two Ballyroon men who had not spoken were ejected.

"Don't do that, my friends! If you are the strong men of Ballykeeran, you must be gracious in your power! If Ballyroon is not as well off as we are, why should we trample it into the dust?"

A voice: "Why shouldn't we?"

"Well, I'm not going to dispute the point. Instead I will take it on myself as Treasurer of the Society to speak a little about what we have done, what we are doing, and what we are going to do. And in doing this I would like the estimable Chairman and no less estimable Secretary, the good men who have borne the burden and heat of the day—of the morning, I might say, when the skies were dark and the face of the future was not as clear as it is now—I would like these two gentlemen to come forward and stand by my side while I speak to the shareholders!"

Mr. Cosdhu, Secretary, was standing by the door, steadying himself against the jamb. Quite civil he was and not drunk—but he wasn't used to so much porter all at once, you know. And wasn't it strong! And the way it had of going to the head!

"I will stay where I am if it's all the same to everybody else," he said. His voice was very thick. "I am the Secretary—nobody will deny that—the Secretary of the Ballykeeran Devilment Society—but on a point of order I will stay where I am! That's all right and above board, Mr. Hanlon, isn't it?"

Mr. Hanlon was quite willing that Mr. Cosdhu, Secretary, should stay where he was if he chose. It was quite sufficient if the shareholders knew that the estimable Secretary was in the hall.

"Hear! Hear!"

"Now, it is only necessary that the Chairman should come forward, Mr. Edward Larrimore, a modest man, a worthy man, and a man well suited for the position of honour which he holds. He has done his duties nobly, discharged them without fear or favour. Now he will probably come forward and allow the shareholders to show their appreciation of what he has done. Did I say 'probably come forward'? If I did it was a mistake. Mr. Larrimore must come forward. It is the desire of the Hall to give due honour to the great Chairman!"

"Good old Eamon! One of the best!"

"Three cheers for Eamon!"

"Hip-hip-hooray!"

Mr. Larrimore, rising, admitted that he had done what he could, but that wasn't much at all! He had of course a little learning, but not the great learning.

"Three cheers again for Eamon Larrimore!"

Confused, the Chairman sat down, but immediately got to his feet again, and his eyes were filled with the strong determination of a quiet man.

The truth was that when he came to the dinner to-night, he only intended to remain for a few minutes, he admitted. One of his cows, the brindled cow, you know—he had bought it three months ago—was near note and might calve any minute. A good milker, and stirabout with her milk was a feast and no lie! The cow might calve in his absence, and he had stayed too long already, far too long. Besides, he had to get up early to-morrow morning, to go to his work. And as far as he could tell by the way the sun set that day, and the way the sun got up that morning, with the wind coming from the west, off the shore of the sea, there was rain in the air. And looking at everything, it would be better if he went home.

Having had his say he went out from the hall, his head high. Were they looking at him! What did he care? He was as good as the best of them, but why the devil had he come, making a fool of himself? He didn't want a big name, and what was the good of the Society, anyway?

Outside he met Neal Hannigan: Norah was at the door.

"Going home, Eamon?" asked Neal.

"I'm going home!" said Eamon in an angry voice.

"Going home and missing all the fun," said Neal.

"This fun doesn't suit me," was Eamon's answer. "Cheering at me like they would be a tinker on the road, when he's drunk and them making fun of him."

"But they weren't making fun of you," said Neal Hannigan. "It's because you are a great man that they were cheering you, Eamon."

"Well, I'm not used to it, Neal," Eamon confessed in a whisper. Now that he was not the lion any longer, he regained his courage. "They'll maybe start their capers again if I go in, but if you, Neal, would just bring out a drop under the trees here——"

"I'll do that, Eamon," said the obliging Neal, and made haste to bring out a drop which would be consumed under a tree.

The first cow of Eamon's to calve, calved on the following May!

VII

Meanwhile Lanty Hanlon, inside and on the table, was giving tongue to his great speech. His strong voice rose high above the clatter of knives and spoons and plates, above the strident snore of Paddy Cosdhu who now lay by the door, mouth open and head pillowed on his bent elbow.

Those near the speaker were looking at him with rapt eyes, and were so excited that they could no longer listen calmly to his words. The excitement grew more and more intense, all faces were radiant with triumph, acclamation was loud, hands holding pannikins were outstretched towards my master, who stood calmly on the table, his golden tie-pin glittering like a star through the tobacco smoke.

"This, the aim and ambition of my life, has at last been realised," he was saying. "What were we, the people of Ballykeeran, yesterday? Nothing! But to-day we are the talk of the world! We are known in all places where the tongue of man is heard, and where a newspaper is read! And who is responsible for this?"

"Lanty Hanlon!"

"Not me," my master continued. "Not to me the honour, but to the good people who throng this hall to-night, those with the green rosettes on their breasts, the simple,

God-fearing people who came forward at the start and gave of their best, their hard-earned money, and helped to found the Society which is now the shining light of all Ireland. All honour to your own good selves, the simple workers of the fields, the makers of creels, the fishers of the sea and shepherds of the hills!"

Cheers!

"To-day at Ballykeeran station we have one power-loom; in a month we'll have a dozen, and in a year's time we'll have five score."

Vociferous acclaim.

"Hear! hear!"

"I look into the future and I see a vision," said my master. A great light showed in his eyes. "Too long have we of Ballykeeran been asleep, too long have we been huddled with our cattle in our cabins, too long have we carried manure on our backs to the potato fields, too long have our roofs been thatched with straw that will not keep out the very dew, too long have we remained in ignorance. But with the grace of God and our own strong hands all will change.

"We'll have bridges on the rivers where we now use stepping stones; we'll pull down the walls of mud and replace them with walls of stone, Irish granite; the thatched roof will be slated with Irish slates! Aye, and we'll have marble doorsteps, Irish marble!"

Cheers.

"Then we've got to see about the planting of trees on the upper moorlands. All that is needed is to dig a hole in the ground and put in a seed, and the tree will grow even while you're sleeping. God never forgets His handicraft. The moors must be drained, the moors that will mean subsistence for us all, the moors that will be white with wool and alive with sheep. Yes, my friends, we have to make drains and plant trees. The future of Ballykeeran depends on irrigation and afforestation!"

Vociferous cheers.

"Yes, my friends, all will soon be living and animated in Ballykeeran," continued my master. "I can hear the joyful chant of labour, the sound of the hammer and the swish of the shuttle, the new houses, clean and healthy, the wide fields of corn and rye, the hills planted with trees, and Ballykeeran a parish of sheep-folds and stables, byres and dairies and barns, all well tended and beautifully arranged, and in the days to come those who follow us will look back with tears in their eyes and bless the day that saw us start the Ballykeeran Development Society. Yes, you men of the parish who are here to-night, you men with the green rosettes in your button-holes, can scarcely realise the benefit which you are conferring upon the future, upon your sons and your sons' sons down even to the thirty-third generation."

Cheers, and a voice: "Good old generation!"

"But it would be amiss and lacking in Irish courtesy," said my master, "if I forget to mention the good work that the women of

Ballykeeran have done for the Society and refrain from thanking them, they who are the fairest blossoms that grow on our native soil. Neddy MacMonagle!"

I stood with Norah at the door. Outside, in the shade of a beech, Neal Hannigan and Eamon Larrimore were swilling heartily. I ran to my master.

"Where is that box?" he enquired, and I handed him up the great box which had the green ribbon round it and the picture of the grand lady on the lid.

"This is a present," said Lanty Hanlon, as he gripped the box, "which the Society has great pleasure in giving to Miss Genevieve Flaherty."

Cheers. A voice, Oonah Ruddagh's: "H'm! h'm!"

"Miss Flaherty has done a great deal in helping the Society. Almost at the beginning she came forward, her heart in the cause and her purse open. Then we were in monetary difficulties, but she was not slow in advancing us the wherewithal, which has helped in no mean measure to make the Society such a success. Therefore and now, on behalf of all, I have great pleasure, Miss Flaherty, in giving you this as a small token of our hearty esteem!"

VIII

All that day, and through the evening, prior to Miss Ruddagh's entrance, this box had been a famous subject of conversation. In fact the

Inaugural Dinner was second to this in the minds of all the women and a good percentage of the men. I even heard Kevin Roe say that morning, that as far as he could judge, it was not chocolates that were in the box but diamonds, real diamonds, worth hundreds and hundreds of pounds.

"You'll see to-night when she gets it," I heard him say. But, strange to say, Kevin Roe was not now in the Hall. No doubt he envied my master's glory, and for that reason he did not come.

Evidence of the curiosity which this box aroused was made manifest when my master bent and handed the box to Miss Genevieve. The people drew nearer and crowded around her, their eyes aglitter with envy and curiosity.

Ecstasy beamed from her face as she reached forward and caught the box. My master bowed gallantly, and she, clasping the present to her breast, performed a graceful curtsy, and so featly was it performed that it seemed as if she had trained herself for the occasion.

"And to-night, at this grand Inaugural Dinner," continued my master, "we find that an exile has returned to grace the feast, Miss Maldy Ruddagh.—"

Cheers.

"This, if I may say so, is an earnest of the success which is in front of us. And what makes me say that? This and this only!—"

"Hear! hear!"

"The exiles are returning already!"

Tremendous cheering.

"Now, ladies and gentlemen, I take it upon

myself as the Treasurer to give a little token of appreciation to the exile who has graced our board to-night. On behalf of the company and myself, and as a mark of gratitude, I have pleasure, Miss Ruddagh, in offering you this little gift!"

As he spoke the last word he took the gold pin from his tie, and bending from the table he fixed the pin in the bodice of the fair Maldy.

The Hall, with one exception, applauded the action. The one exception was Genevieve. She was opening her box, the beautiful box with the green bow and the picture of the grand lady. Presently it was opened (I watched from a distance) and Genevieve's dainty fingers pulled the paper shavings aside to see what they concealed.

Suddenly a queer look showed on her face, a look similar to that which might show on the face of a dignified bride at the marriage service if a pin pricked her in a tender place.

She raised the box to her nose, sniffed it, then pressed that which it contained with her fingers. At the same moment, Maldy, who had eyes for the box, uttered an expressive "Ah!" and gave vent to a chuckle. Genevieve looked at the Yankee, then closed the box again, tied the bow very nicely (how careful she was to tie it nicely!), and with the box in hand went to my master, who was now busy helping the children to conversation lozenges, rock and candy.

"Mr. Hanlon! This is yours, I believe!" She held the box towards him. Her voice was icy.

" My box ? But it was a present to you ! "

" Mr. Hanlon, what have I ever done to you that you should insult me with such a gift ? "

" But, Miss Flaherty, I don't understand. Have another cup of tea, another bowl. Maybe, maybe "—my master was mystified—" maybe they've put whisky in what you had ! "

" Mr. Hanlon, I never take whisky. Here is your present ! " She threw the box to the ground.

Having spoken thus, she gave a snort of disgust, turned and went towards the door, her head high amidst the tobacco smoke, that head with dignity its pose and propriety its perquisite.

" Neddy MacMonagle, what upset her ? " my master enquired, when she had made her departure.

" I don't know," was my answer. " Maybe it was the chocolate in the box ! "

" What the devil's wrong with the chocolate ? "

" She stuck her nose up when she touched it," I said.

" And went green when she smelt it," said Oonah Ruddagh. She, too, had been watching.

" Well, I must see what's in the damned box," said my master, whereupon he opened the box, touched that which it contained with his finger, then with his nose sniffed that which his fingers had touched.

" Throw it out, Neddy ! " he ordered. Then as if something had occurred to him, he asked : " Do you know where Kevin Roe is ? "

" I don't, indeed," I answered.

"Is it diamonds that is in it?" asked Oonah Ruddagh, her one open eye fixed on the box.

I threw the box and its contents outside. Coming back again I saw my master seated on the edge of the table, his legs hanging as if they were dead things, a look of disgust and chagrin on his face.

"And this is the diamonds!" came a voice from outside. Somebody was inspecting the box which I had thrown out.

"God! I wish I could get hold of him!" my master groaned, and his eyes rested on me. The look on his face was terrible. The same look had been his on the night he rode Garibaldi on the trail of Kevin Roe. I drew back a step.

"What is coming over poor Lanty at all, at all?" wailed Oonah. "Now above all times, and you back, Maldy, and the money that he has in hand. Oh! wirra, wirra! And what would be in the box that he gave to that woman? What was in the box, Neddy MacMonagle?"

Her arm stretched out, her lean fingers tightened on my shoulder and she shook me with great strength.

"What was in it, Neddy?"

"Sheep's insides," I told her. There was another word which I had often used of old, but now being a gentleman I could not lower myself to the level of the road. And my master had forbade me to use that other word.

At that moment there was a certain commotion at the doorway. Looking in that direction I saw the caps of several policemen, then the red face of the sergeant, he whose children were all born on the month of June.

"Mr. Hanlon!" he called.

"What is it, sergeant?" asked my master.

"Meenaroo is burned to the ground!"

"Eh!"

"Meenaroo is burned to the ground." The sergeant wiped the sweat from his forehead, coughed and spat on the floor. "We saw the sky red and we went there as hard as we could pelt. 'Twas all one flame when we arrived and the weather was so dry all summer that the house just went—went like the head of a match that you rub on the leg of your trousers!"

After these few simple words there was a strange silence, broken by nothing save the snore of Paddy Cosdhu, whose head was still pillowed on the bend of his arm. All eyes were fixed on Lanty Hanlon.

"Burnt to the ground?" he enquired.

"To the ground," said the sergeant.

"That means that the Society is burned out," said my master, and his voice was terribly calm.

"Aye! But the christening!" mumbled Oonah Ruddagh, and blessed herself. "What else could anyone expect!"

XI

My master stood upright and looked at the diners, then as if he were unable to keep facing them, he lifted his castor hat from the table, pulled it down over his eyes, and walked slowly towards the door. His step was not the step that took him in. He walked carefully, as if afraid of stumbling over something, his shoulders hunched, his head hanging, as though he were deep in thought.

"Where are you off to, Mr. Hanlon?" asked Denis Freely.

"Where!" said my master. "That's it. Where?"

He came to a dead stop.

"There's no Meenaroo to go home to, to-night," remarked the sergeant.

"I suppose my henchman and I will have to sleep in the barracks," said my master. His voice was very calm, and he even laughed when he spoke. "Or maybe we'll have to go to the workhouse," he put in as an afterthought.

"I never saw a place blaze like it!" said the sergeant.

"There was no fire in the place when we left," said my master.

"But with the hot weather, a place can go on fire, and no spark being applied," the sergeant explained. "Spontaneous combustion it's called."

"Spontaneous Roe-bustion is a better explanation." My master was still quiet. He was holding himself in.

"Combustion is the word," said the sergeant. "I saw it in the dictionary. Not 'robustion.'"

"It's no good trying to trace a criminal through a dictionary," said my master. "Listen to this story, sergeant. On one occasion I was interested in a certain local industry. The law did not altogether approve of my activities then, and, getting into motion, despatched a certain individual to serve a summons upon me. Under compulsion, that individual ate the summons. But at the same time he happened to observe where I kept my money. That showed a lack of wisdom on my part. And if I say that he waited an opportunity to get the better of me, I may not be very far wrong. But I would not say that he ransacked Meenaroo and took the funds of the Society which were hidden there, and, having taken them, set fire to the house. All that I will say, sergeant, is that that man, whose name I will not mention, did not show his face within Homespun Hall to-night. And it was not spontaneous combustion, but spontaneous Roe-bustion, that started the fire."

"Meaning?" queried the sergeant, taking a book and pencil from his pocket.

"Nothing," said my master.

"Well, if anyone wants to know where Kevin Roe is," said a man who had just come in, a dealer in cattle, "I can tell them!"

"Where?" asked the sergeant.

"He's away to Dublin on the cattle train!"

"Now, everybody come and make a night of it!" roared my master, jumping to his feet, taking off his castor, and reaching for a glass. "Here, Denis Freely, fill this up!"

Denis Freely, who was making for the door with a whisky jar under his arm, looked at the glass which Lanty Hanlon held. Where was Freely going with the jar? is a question that anybody might ask. And the true answer to that was that Freely, an astute man, seeing the hour of ruin had arrived, was making the most of the occasion.

"There's a jar over there on the stillion," said Freely. "And there's a sup in it yet!"

"Any in that jar?" asked Lanty Hanlon.

"What jar?"

"The one you're carrying!"

"It's empty, and I'm just going to throw it outside."

"Don't throw it out yet, Freely!" Lanty Hanlon's voice was polite and urbane. "Just place it here on the table."

"I'll bring over the one that is on the stillion," said Freely, who was looking rather uncomfortable. "There is some whisky in it!"

"Bring the one you have, please," said my master in a cold, slow voice, and Freely obeyed.

"Now, fill my glass!"

"From the jar on the stillion?"

"From this one!"

"Glory to God, but I thought it was empty," said Freely as he drew the cork and saw to his feigned surprise that the whisky was neck-high.

My master drank and filled himself out another glass. The hat which he had placed on the table dropped to the floor and Oonah Ruddagh picked it up. What use was it to her?

"Now, clear the Hall for a dance!" my master ordered. "Come and let us fiddle while Meenaroo burns! Come, sergeant, and drink! Spontaneous Roe-bustion, eh! Do you remember Hanlon's prime blend? Here's to the month of June, sergeant!" The whisky was in his head already.

But it is not me to describe how the Dinner

ended, that sad, terrible Dinner which marked the foundation and fall of the Society, that Dinner which left wrinkles on my beloved master's heart as well as forehead.

Prior to the sergeant's entry with the story of the burning of Meenaroo, the fun had been decent and respectable. Those who drank, drank with discretion, tempering their drink with common sense. If a few got over-excited, they were taken in hand by the stewards and gently persuaded to go.

But after Lanty Hanlon lost control of himself and sat to his beakers (he consumed five in as many minutes), the well-ordered assembly fell to pieces. There was no further stewardship; the Freelys, who had behaved themselves up till then, started drinking. All the pot-walloping scum of the market gurgled in: the sword-swallower gave token of his ability in swallowing much that was not steel; a ballad-singer danced a hornpipe on the table, tripped at the final step and dropped into a stirabout tub, where he fell asleep; quarrels started, and at two o'clock in the morning, when all the women had departed, there were more black eyes than green rosettes in the assembly.

It was at that moment that the band came again to the door. The players, very excited, struck up *The Night before Larry was Stretched.* The Hall sang to the measure, and used "Lanty" instead of "Larry."

And Lanty was stretched! In compliance with the ancient tenets of his long-dead father, he lay nude as a nymph, asleep under the table.

CHAPTER XIII

THE TOSS OF A CROWN

She would not yesterday! She will to-day!
Not strange, my son—'tis a woman's way.
As her fishing season has its rise and fall,
Better a sprat than no fish at all.
—*A Ballykeeran Proverb.*

I

FOR a day the power-loom lay at Ballykeeran station, for a day, two days, a week, a fortnight, and the best part of a month! Why had it come ? was the question asked many a time in the years that followed. Many answers were given, but there is only one true answer, and this is it. Fat in funds, my master had overstepped himself in the manner of the foolish husbandman, who buys a steed before he builds the stable. He had ordered the loom, trading on the boom which the Society had got in the papers of the world, and paid a certain sum in advance, promising to pay the remainder at some future date. "A business deal," he explained to me at the time.

But now, with Meenaroo burned to the land, the Society was at an end. Nothing beyond the broken jars in Homespun Hall, the new tables in the homes of the Freelys, the rain-beaten bills on the walls and bridges, the green rosettes which were saved from the Inaugural Dinner, and the power-loom at the Ballykeeran station, remained as testimony of the Society's existence.

Letters still came in, however, were opened by my master, and their contents used for his own special need—that need which enriched the licensed grocers of his native town. And Lanty Hanlon lived, as he had often lived before, heaving largely down the road of his days, asking nor sparings of death, nor ease of his sojourn, throwing the Society's means to the winds, asking no recompense, stuffing the Society's substance in his belly and asking no interest.

Now he had not a roof to his head. But not he to care! Primed against adversity, he slept at night in the open, a rock his pillow and the moon his lamp, or in a byre, the flank of a sleeping cow his sanctuary, and woke at dawn to lighten the mail bag of the merciful postman.

Meanwhile I, his henchman, turned my hand to other labour. Following the Inaugural Dinner came a critical period in my life. No home was mine when Meenaroo was ashes. Came also the news that the MacMonagles, tin, tacks and solder, were sighted at Ballyroon on their way to Ballykeeran.

"I'm going with them when they leave here," I told Norah.

"But you cannot," she said.

"But why can't I?" was my question.

"Because I won't let you," she told me, and it was not in me to go contrary to her wish.

So I stayed, servant in the house of Neal Hannigan, and from a safe distance watched the passing of the MacMonagles. Even from the security of a meal-chest in Hannigan's home, I heard the voice of my father. He came and wanted to know if Neal wanted a kettle mended, a pot legged or a pandy made, and if Neal (a decent man) knew if there was a young vagabond in the parish, a youngster called Neddy. Neddy was his son, and he wanted this son, wanted him badly, for he was going to skin him alive!

"And what was this boy like?" asked Neal, a civil and obliging man, who was willing to go out of his way to help anybody. If he knew what the boy was like he would do his best for my father.

The chief of the MacMonagle clan went to great pains with his description. And Neal listened, putting a meet question now and again. Had this boy dark hair? had he grey eyes? had he a limp?

"Limp!" said my father. "Not when he left me, but I'll give him one when I meet him!"

In the end he left with three spoons in his pocket (this was discovered afterwards, when we sat to supper), and I went out to my work in the fields.

II

It was six weeks following the day of the Inaugural Dinner. I was on my way back from

Ballykeeran, over my shoulder a spade which I had bought from Mick Flaherty.

Eamon Larrimore, ex-chairman of the B.D.S., was digging potatoes in a field near the high-road, his red flannel shirt unbuttoned at the neck, its sleeves thrust up as far as his shoulders. On each foot he wore two socks, but no boots. He had only one pair, and these were being repaired by the village cobbler. Across the march ditch Paddy Cosdhu, ex-secretary, was working his own plot of land, also digging potatoes.

Where the march ditch lipped the road I came to a stop, and—

"Eamon Larrimore!" I called.

"What's wrong?" asked Eamon. This was a usual question of the man since the Society went to smithereens.

"There's a gentleman coming from Ballykeeran on a car, and he's looking for the Chairman," I informed him.

"Me?" asked Eamon, and a frightened look showed in his eyes.

"You, and no other," said I. "Edward Larrimore, chairman."

"What kind of man is he?" asked Eamon, dropping his spade and looking towards the hills. Yes, the Chairman was ready to take to his heels!

"A big man with a collar on him and a gold chain to his watch," I told Eamon. "A gentleman and no less."

"Is Lanty Hanlon down the road at all?" asked Eamon.

" He is that," I answered. " Lying in ditch, with his heels up."

On hearing this Eamon Larrimore called to Paddy Cosdhu, who made his way across the dyke. The two men came together and entered into an earnest conversation. While they spoke a car swung round the bend of the road and came to a stop opposite. A well-dressed man, a stranger, sat on the car. For a moment he looked at the two ex-officials.

" Pardon me!" he called. " But can any of you gentlemen direct me to the residence of Mr. Edward Larrimore, the Chairman of the Ballykeeran Development Society?"

" That's you, Eamon," said Paddy Cosdhu in a whisper. " Tell him you're not here."

" But that can't be done," said Eamon under his breath. " He sees me."

The more astute Paddy saw a way out of the difficulty.

" The Chairman, Mr. Larrimore, your honour, is away buying sheep at the fair of Ballyroon. And he won't be back here for two or three days," said Paddy Cosdhu.

" Where is the Secretary?" enquired the stranger.

" He's away, too, to the same place," was Paddy's reply.

" I've come here to look up the Society that ordered a power-loom from my firm some months ago, and from which we cannot since get any reply to our various letters," said the stranger. " But I cannot find a single member of the Society. Do any of you happen to know where the treasurer, Mr. Hanlon, is ? "

" Oh, he's not far away," said Paddy Cosdhu. " Maybe you've passed him on the road from Ballykeeran."

" I've passed no one except a man lying drunk by the roadside," said the stranger.

" Then if that's anybody in the parish, it's Lanty Hanlon," said Paddy Cosdhu.

" Well, I've never seen such a damned queer thing in all my life," said the stranger, and he looked very angry and much upset. " We in England, in the firm to which I belong, got a letter written in a very intelligent and business-like manner, from a Society called the Ballykeeran Development Society. This letter, signed by the officials of the Society, made a certain proposal to which we lent a ready ear and, acting on the instructions of the Society, despatched a power-loom to a certain address. But I find on coming here that nobody has claimed the loom. The station-master says he does not know for whom it was intended. The police force has never heard of the Ballykeeran Development Society. I have been shown Meenaroo, the head office, but it is nothing more than a heap of ashes. The chairman and secretary are gone to the fair of Balloon——"

" Ballyroon," corrected Paddy Cosdhu.

" And the treasurer is lying drunk in a ditch! What in the name of goodness do you people want ? "

" To be left alone," said Eamon Larrimore.

" Yes," said the stranger angrily. " And as

far as I can see it will be for your own good, as well as the good of others, to leave you alone!"

Even to this day I cannot understand what the stranger meant when he said these words.

III

On the late afternoon of that very day, when light was fading into dusk, when the last potato of the day's digging was housed snugly against the winter's cold, when the last puff of the train that bore the power-loom away died in the distance, when Eamon Larrimore cleaned his spade and looked towards the little home where his supper was waiting, two figures came along the parish road.

One figure was in front, its movements very erratic. For every step it took forward it took three to the right and three to the left, elbowing the hedges on either side of the road. The figure that followed did the same, took a step forward, then three to the right and three to the left, but the movements of both figures were done with such unison, that from a distance, from the point where Eamon Larrimore watched, it looked as if only one person were coming towards him. But there were two, Lanty Hanlon, G.H., and Oonah Ruddagh.

Eamon, putting his spade in the black earth, came to the road. Paddy Cosdhu followed.

"Well, Lanty Hanlon," said Eamon, when the treasurer came abreast, "and how are you this night?"

“H’m!” grunted Lanty, coming to a stop. “H’m! In the toils of a woman!”

“Meaning me, Lanty Hanlon?” asked Oonah, coming to a stop at the rear of the treasurer. “Me, Lanty Hanlon, the widow woman that was your godmother when you were christened in whisky, and that you robbed of her white shilling.”

“H’m!” grunted Hanlon. He swayed unsteadily and gripped the air for purchase. “A white shilling! The widow’s mite! Are we alone?”

“No, I’m here, Lanty,” said Eamon Larrimore. This could not be contradicted.

“And me as well,” said Paddy Cosdhu.

“And us into the bargain,” came a number of voices. Their day’s labour at an end, the able men had come to the roadside to discuss the events of the day.

“Then all are here,” said Lanty Hanlon drunkenly. “McLoons, Muldoons, Larrimores, Cosdhus and Freelys, and Oonah Ruddagh as well!”

“I’m here,” said Oonah. “And now, what have you to say for yourself? Robbing up and down on the high roads and low roads and face of the world, and even a poor widow woman——”

“Whisht, Oonah Ruddagh, whisht!” Lanty Hanlon steadied himself on outspread legs. “All is over. The Ballykeeran Development Society is at an end!”

“And the grand loom is gone,” said Paddy Cosdhu. He spat sideways, rubbed his mouth with the back of his hand, and wiped his hand on the leg of his trousers. " And two steam-engines had to draw it ! "

This latter remark was pure imagination.

" And all of us robbed ! " groaned Oonah Ruddagh. " And him going about and his pockets filled with gold and white money ! "

" Is that the way indeed ? " asked Denis Freely. Hearing money mentioned he edged closer to Lanty Hanlon.

" Are all here who placed money in the funds of the Society ? " asked the Treasurer. He put his hands in his trousers pockets and rattled the coins which those pockets contained. " Are you all here ? "

" Every one of us," said Denis Freely, who, it will be remembered, had really paid nothing.

" Then, this is yours ! " With these words Lanty Hanlon threw a fistful of money to the crowd. There was a hurried scrambling and gathering of spoil. " And this ! " he roared. " And this ! "

Gold and silver rattled on the roadway.

It was at this moment that Maldy Ruddagh appeared. Where she had come from it was impossible to say. I was the first to notice her. The others had no time, for a matter of greater urgency engaged their attention. Oonah Ruddagh, flat on the camber, was covering with her body what her hands could not grip. Two of the Freelys were fighting.

Maldy saw her mother, and, bending down, she caught her by the scruff of her neck and lifted the old woman to her knees.

"What are you doing, Maldy, dear, asthor?" asked the mother, looking at her daughter. "There's a white shilling, two white shillings, a crown, all gone and because of you. Am I going to be robbed again?"

"Get up!" ordered Maldy. "Get up at once!"

"I'll not, then!" said the mother, stretching forward and gripping a florin.

"Very well, then!" said the girl. Her words had the snap of breaking ice. "If you don't get up, now and at once, I'll go back to America to-morrow morning."

Cowed and sullen, the old woman got to her feet. She shoved the money which she had gathered into the pocket of her quilted petticoat.

"Give that back to Mr. Hanlon!" Maldy ordered.

"I won't, then. The way that he has robbed me, and me a widow woman," said Oonah.

"If you want money, I'll give it to you," said the girl, bringing a purse from her pocket. "As much as you want, and more. Now, give the money to Mr. Hanlon."

The mother took the money from her pocket. She was now highly pleased, not because she had to return the money to Lanty Hanlon, but because Maldy made manifest that she, daughter of her own, had money and to spare.

The silver was held towards Lanty Hanlon, but at the last moment the old woman was overcome with a pang of remorse. It was a great heap of money, surely! More than a guinea! If things had gone right, she could have it all, all for nothing! And she had picked up more than anyone else!

"Gather up your dirty money yourself, Lanty Hanlon!" she screeched, and threw the silver pieces to the ground.

Immediately Denis Freely was on the spread, like a hawk on sparrows round a winnowing sheet.

"Indeed, Denis Freely!" said Maldy Ruddagh, and the bite in her voice would have snapped a scratching-stone. "And it's on the road you should be, begging your keep from door to door like the beggarmen of Ireland!"

And that finished it. Denis Freely had more than a passing notion of Maldy Ruddagh at the time, and if talk were to be believed he was making more than a little progress with the suit. Now to cut him in this cruel way!

But it was in keeping with the effect which the downfall of the Society had on all concerned. It was sad to think how the parish and the people of the parish fared now. Kevin Roe was abroad, on his own keeping a wanted man; Genevieve, who had forsaken one lover for another, had lost both; Denis Freely was made the laughing-stock of the country by the hard word of a woman; I was almost a beggar again, having nothing between me and the road but the grace of a girl and the charity of a man; and he who was greatest of us all wandered roofless on the highways of the world.

The great man had fallen, but, like Samson at Gaza, he did not fall alone.

"And now, Lanty Hanlon, do whatever you like," Oonah croaked, putting one eye on Lanty Hanlon and one foot on the silver which littered the road. She might have it yet! "Whatever you like, Lanty Hanlon!"

A smile, half of forbearance and half of mockery, showed in his face. He grunted as if he were going to say something, but stopped short on the point of utterance, then looked at Maldy, the smile, half of forbearance and half of mockery, still on his face. Eamon Larrimore's stockinged foot stole quietly out and as quietly rested on a silver piece.

"A shilling, Eamon, a shilling!" Lanty Hanlon remarked, and the smile on his face was still the same as he turned round and strode loftily away.

The evening had turned cold and there was a frosty nip in the air.

IV

The cold that fell on the world that night was past all understanding.

A strong raking party had gathered in the house of Neal Hannigan, and the men and women of this party sat round a full open fire with their feet to the flames. But even there in that snug house, with a flannel blind on the window and crack and keyhole stuffed with mountain wool, the visitors felt the cold, felt it, for while the heat blistered their toes, their backs were as cold as a stepmother's breath.

"And the cold snap came all at once!"

said Nelly Cosdhu. She was very much offended by this act of God. "If it only came slow, the way it always does!"

"It never was like this in my memory," Eamon Larrimore remarked. "But they say that the cold of the old ancient times was worse than it ever is now. They say that Hudy Flaherty (dead long since), of Ballyroon, and sib to him of the same name in Ballykeeran this day, had once two-score sheep on the hills of Ballyroon in a frost, and their horns were froze off, all but one, and that horn was made of iron."

"And on that same night the feathers were froze off an eagle," said Paddy Cosdhu. "And that was the last eagle ever seen in Ireland—a great eagle, too, and it used to carry the children away."

"And it was then that the blind salmon of Kingarrow lost its eyes," said Neal Hannigan. He ran a spale through the shank of his pipe and cleaned out the bowl with a rusty nail.

"Indeed, and was it?" asked the listeners.

"Indeed, and it was," Neal made answer. "The frost came all of a sudden, and it a fine evening, with the sun setting, and the flies on the water. The salmon rose to get the flies, and as soon as it left the water the frost came. By the time it got back, there was a sheet of ice on the water. The salmon couldn't get through, and it was then that the last eagle of Ireland came and picked its eyes out. And that salmon is in the River Garrow yet, for it was seen two years ago, when they were building the Ballykeeran bridge."

"Well, it must be a great age, surely," said Eamon Larrimore.

"The oldest living thing in the seven corners of Ireland," said Paddy Cosdhu. "And they say that even himself saw it one night, and him sleeping by the river."

"And did you hear him saying that with his own tongue?" asked Eamon Larrimore.

"With his own tongue, and him sober," Paddy admitted.

"Well, I wonder where he sleeps this night?" This was Neal Hannigan speaking. His pipe was now in full smoke.

"The devil out of hell wouldn't kill the man, but this night will be hard on him," said Eamon Larrimore. "And maybe it's a cold he'll get and die. A man that's a hard liver is always an easy dier. There was old Peter Ruddagh, healthy to the last breath, and in the end he went like a snuffed candle."

"It's a poor way of dying, to go off without knowing it," said Paddy Cosdhu. He sighed heavily, as if he were afraid that his death would not be a lingering one.

"And it would be a great pity if Lanty died now, and him scattering his money on the roads of the world." Nelly Cosdhu spoke. She had missed the "scatter" that day. But wait till to-morrow!

"You have just come in, Neddy MacMonagle!" Neal Hannigan was speaking to me. "Have you seen where he is at all?"

"I have," I said. "He's in Oonah Ruddagh's byre, sleeping with the cows."

"Like a rowan tree at Candlemas?"

"Aye! Without a stitch on!"

"There's an old blanket at the bottom of the bed," said Neal. "If you just run over to Oonah Ruddagh's byre and throw it round the man, it will keep him from getting his death of cold!"

"And if he wakens up, when you're there, tell him that it was Neal that sent the blanket," Mary Hannigan ordered me. Mary Hannigan, God be her comforting this day! was a woman of great understanding.

"I'll tell him that," I said, as I lifted the blanket from the foot of the bed.

V

The night was one of stars, the wind north-east and the far hills looked near to hand. A hard night for the road, surely, and as I went on my errand I thanked God that I was on my own keeping far from the MacMonagle clan.

I arrived at the house of Oonah Ruddagh. The door was open, and inside, on the lip of the dresser, was to be seen a paraffin lamp with a draggle-tailed wick and a soot-blackened globe. The old woman was on her knees, telling her beads.

Six good paces from the gable-end of the house stood the byre where the live stock of the farm, three in all, chewed the cud. But louder than the noise made by the cattle came the sound, half hiccough and half whistle, which told of the sleep of one who was once my master. I went to the door of the byre.

Standing by the door was Maldy Ruddagh. A blanket hung from the crook of her arm, and comely the maiden looked in the dark.

"Who's that now?" she asked when I came close to her.

"Me," I told her. "Neddy MacMonagle!"

"You are the very person I was waiting for, Neddy," said the girl. "And what is it that you're carrying with you?"

"It's a blanket," I said.

"Indeed," said Maldy. "And for him?"

"It is indeed," I told her.

"And why have you brought it?"

"Sure, he is a great friend of mine," I said. "Nobody was ever as good to me as he was!"

"But what about Norah?" Maldy asked, with a quiet laugh. Even *she* knew!

"Well, it isn't the same, you know," I said.

"You love her?"

"I don't know!"

"Now, Neddy MacMonagle, answer me this question." Maldy came very close and looked into my eyes. "If Lanty Hanlon went away from Ballykeeran, what would you do?"

"I'd wait till he came back, but I'd be very sorry."

"If Lanty Hanlon died, Neddy MacMonagle?"

"I'd pray for him ever and ever!"

"But if Norah Hannigan went away, what would you do, Neddy MacMonagle?" asked the girl.

"I'd go with her."

" And if she died ? "

" I would die too."

" Love is a great thing, and the strongest thing in all the seven corners of the world," said the girl. By her talk now, one would not believe that she had ever left Ballykeeran to become a lady. " No hill is as high as love, no sea as wide and no water as deep. Stronger it is than ties of blood, than the honour of a name, than broad acres. It is the laughing glory of God, Neddy MacMonagle ! "

That was a great speech surely, with poetry in it, and for Maldy it was a wonderful thing to speak so eloquently. For all her wanderings her learning was little and her spelling was poor. This I came to know in after years.

" Now take this blanket and put it round him, as well as the one you have yourself," Maldy said, and handed me her blanket. " And maybe he'll be throwing them off him and lying bare to the night, so here's a pin and tie the two blankets together. And pin them well, Neddy MacMonagle ! "

I went into the byre and put the blankets round my master. The pin which pinned them was that which my master had given Maldy Ruddagh on the night of the Inaugural Dinner.

She was waiting me coming out.

" Neddy MacMonagle, is he snug and warm ? " she asked.

" He is."

" I'll walk a wee bit along the road with you." She got hold of my arm as she spoke.

"Do," I said, and hoped at the same time that Norah would not meet us.

"When I was away abroad, did he ever talk much to you?" she enquired, keeping step with me.

"More to me than to anybody else," I replied.

"Indeed! And it would be all about the Society?"

"Not all," I told her.

"Not all, but maybe about them that helped a lot in the Society?" She squeezed my arm when she said this.

"He talked a lot about them, about the Chairman and the Secretary."

"But more, maybe, about them that gave a lot of money to the Society?" asked Maldy. "Who gave the most money, now?"

"Miss Flaherty," I told her.

"Then he would speak a lot about Miss Flaherty?"

"Not so much," I said. "He didn't like her."

"Is that truth, Neddy MacMonagle?"

"Cross on my neck!" With my free hand I made the cross.

"And maybe he talked about some who were not in Ballykeeran?" she enquired.

"Maybe he did," I said, and put great meaning into my words.

"Who, now?"

"Well, who do you think?"

"About me, maybe?"

"Aye, he was always talking about you. 'I'd rather have Miss Ruddagh with a hen than Miss Flaherty with a horse,' he said."

"He said that?" asked the girl.

"He did, and more than once," I told her. It was not the exact truth, but the happiness that lit her eyes repaid me for the sin. However, it is never a great sin, the lie that gives pleasure to a woman.

"I think we'll be great friends, Neddy MacMonagle, you and I," she said in a strange calling voice. Her face came very close to mine, and mine, God pardon me that moment! came very close to hers. Whether her lips were to blame for coming so close, or mine to blame for going to meet them, I do not know, but anyway I am willing to bear the blame if there is any.

But it was a sweet moment surely, so sweet that I only realised the wrong of it when Maldy Ruddagh said: "Now, Neddy MacMonagle, get home to bed. Seven you've had and that's enough!"

She had counted them.

"Don't tell Norah," I implored.

"If you don't tell, Neddy MacMonagle, I'll not tell."

And that was the only time I was ever false to my little girl. But why is it that from amidst a thousand kisses those seven stand out the most vivid in my mind?

VI

Morning of the next day! From the sea that claimed it to the well that gave it first water the River Garrow was a straggly ribbon of ice. Three salmon broke through at dawn, looking for air, it was said, and slithered about on the ice until they were caught, two by Neal Hannigan and one by Paddy Cosdhu.

"Two are big feeding," said Neal to me. "Take one of them to Oonah Ruddagh. She was always the one for a toothsome bit of salmon. And have your eye open for the blanket that you gave Lanty and take it back here with you."

"And don't forget it was Neal that sent it and tell Lanty that same when he's opening the letters," Mary Hannigan advised.

"I'll do that," I answered, sticking my fingers in the salmon's gills and going off on my errand.

"And here you are at this hour in the morning," said Maldy, when I came to the door of her mother's house. "And what is that you have with you?"

"A salmon," I told her, going in and leaving the trout on the table.

"Mother of God! a salmon," croaked Oonah. A big fire was ablaze on the hearth, a teapot stood on the hob and three cups and saucers were arranged on the table. Cups and saucers were never the property of the house before Maldy came home. But why three this morning?

"It's nice to see a fresh salmon," said the old woman. She took a pinch of snuff and wiped her nose with the corner of her apron. "But it's not blind, is it?"

"It is now," I told her.

"But it wasn't caught blind, was it?"

"No."

"There was a blind salmon long ago in the River Garrow," the old woman said. "It was there years and years ago and it is there to this day. A blind salmon, and it would give the evil eye to anybody that ate it!"

"This is a good salmon, mother," the daughter told her. "We'll put it on the pan and fry it for breakfast."

"Is he up yet?" I asked.

Maldy looked at me, and a funny smile showed at the corner of her eye. Was she thinking of last night?

"He is just dressing himself. Will you run out and tell him to come in to breakfast when he is ready?"

Lanty Hanlon was buttoning his waistcoat when I entered. Although his clothes were rather the worse of wear, he in himself was as fresh as a daisy. Proof against adversity was his iron constitution.

The two blankets were hung over a beam and in the fringe of one was the gold tie-pin.

"What is the news of the parish?" he enquired.

"There is a heavy frost on the Garrow," I informed him.

"Any salmon caught?" he asked.

"Three," I said. "Maldy Ruddagh is frying one for your breakfast."

He looked at the blankets, at the pin, then at me.

"Explain," he ordered, and I explained.

"As man to man, what do you think of

Maldy Ruddagh ?" he enquired when I had finished my explanation. He caught me by both shoulders and looked into my face.

"I think she's a fine lady——"

"Aye, Neddy ?" He wanted me to continue.

"A very fine lady!"

"Aye ?"

"There's not one like her in the whole of Ballykeeran!"

"Aye, Neddy, Neddy, I know!" He was very impatient. "She's the finest lady in the world, so that settles that! She came out last night with the blanket, because she thought I would be cold. She met you here and told you to put the blanket on me because it was a cold night. And then she was happy when you did what she told you. And what have you to say now ?"

Thank God he didn't know everything!

"Well, you should marry her," I said.

"Then I'll toss for it," said he, and took a crown piece from his pocket.

He placed the crown on the tip of his thumb and birled it in the air. "Heads I do, and tails I don't," he shouted while the coin journeyed from thumb-nail to floor.

Heads it was when it fell.

"And will you ?" I asked.

"I never go back on my word," said Lanty U. Hanlon, G.H.

THE END

HALLOWMAS, 1921.